Night Intruder

☆

Nan threw back the bedclothes and sat on the edge of the bed, listening all the while. The sounds came again—a long faint whine and a distant padding step. The two things together said Bran; but instead of reassurance, a wave of fear rushed in. The dog padding up and down and whining....It frightened her beyond her own power of knowing why.

Then she saw Bran reared up on his hind legs at the window with the curtain blowing round him. The moonlight threw a monstrous shadow almost to her feet. His nails scraped on the sill.

She ran to him and pulled away the curtain.

"What is it? What's the matter, Bran?"

He shook himself free and leaned forward. She could hear him growling now. A pale violet flare of lightning changed the sky and was gone again. A second flare lit everything with a sudden brilliance. Nan saw the man on the edge of the ravine—a black shape. And that shape was the shape of her enemy...

Published by
WARNER BOOKS

PATRICIA WENTWORTH

NOTHING VENTURE

WARNER BOOKS

A Warner Communications Company

WARNER BOOKS EDITION

This Warner Books Edition is published by arrangement with
Harper & Row Publishers, Inc., 10 East 53rd Street, New York,
N.Y. 10022

Cover design by Anne Twomey
Cover illustration by Bob Scott

Warner Books, Inc.
666 Fifth Avenue
New York, N.Y. 10103

 A Warner Communications Company

Printed in the United States of America

First Warner Books Printing: September, 1990

10 9 8 7 6 5 4 3 2 1

I

"YOU WERE SAYING?" SAID MR PAGE.

At the moment, Mr Ambrose Weare was not saying anything at all. He had been speaking, but had fallen silent. His bed had been pushed close to the big jutting window, and his eyes had gone from his solicitor to the green lawn and the lilacs, white and mauve and purple, and beyond the lilacs to the bright, glittering blue of the sea. It was a May day. There was a wind blowing, and small white clouds raced before it across a rain-washed sky. Ambrose Weare sat propped up in his bed. He was dying, for no very discernible reason except that, having lived eighty-seven years with energy and a masterful disregard of everything except the whim of the moment, he had now taken it into his head to die.

Mr Page tapped upon his writing-pad.

"You were saying?" he repeated.

Ambrose Weare turned his head. The eyes, under shaggy grey eyebrows, still held a spark of malicious fire.

"I wasn't saying anything. What you mean is that you want me to get on with it."

"Well—" said Mr Page.

Ambrose Weare laughed. It was not a very pleasant sound.

"*Lord*, Page! What a bedside manner you've got! You're thrown away on the law! Why can't you say straight out that I've no time to waste, and that even if I had, it's the deuce of a fine afternoon and a pity to spend it in a sick-room, when you might be a great deal more pleasantly occupied in having tea over there by the lilacs with the young people?''

Mr Page experienced a faint resentment. He had managed Ambrose Weare's affairs for some thirty-five years without ever becoming accustomed to his habit of tearing away those decent veils by which we hide from one another such feelings as distaste, boredom, and ennui. It was true that he had been thinking that it would be pleasant in the garden when he had got through the business which had brought him down to Weare; but, put as Mr Weare had just put it—well, what was one to say? His bedside manner became a little accentuated. He smiled and said nothing.

''Well, let's come to the point,'' said Ambrose Weare. ''The legacies stand as they were, but Rosamund only gets five hundred. She can buy her trousseau with it. If she weren't going to marry Jervis, she'd have had three hundred a year, but since they're engaged, that comes out. It keeps a girl steady having to come to her husband for money.'' He drew in his thin lips and chuckled. ''Jervis shall have the purse-strings—but she'll get round him and help herself to as much as she wants! Hey, Page?''

''Miss Carew is very charming.''

''So was her grandmother,'' said Ambrose Weare—''prettiest girl in the county, if she *was* my sister. And what good did it do her? She might have had Croyston, or Ledingham, or half a dozen others—and she chucked her cap over the windmills and bolted with a penniless artist like Carew!''

''Mr Jervis is to be congratulated,'' said Mr Page.

''Well, well,'' said Ambrose Weare. ''Who's getting off the point now? Restrain your enthusiasm for Rosamund and let's get back to my will. After the legacies—you've got 'em down?—everything to Jervis, lock, stock and barrel. Securities, house, property, and family temper to my grandson, Jervis Weare, *on condition*—''

Mr Page lifted his fountain pen from the writing-pad. His look of serious inquiry was met by a keenly mocking one.

''You're thinking now what the deuce has the old devil got up his sleeve? Hey, Page?''

Mr Page reddened. He was comfortably stout and comfortably ruddy, with a fringe of thick grey hair about a round bald patch. The ruddy colour deepened quite perceptibly. One didn't say things like that—one really didn't.

"What is the condition, Mr Weare?"

Ambrose Weare looked out upon the lawn. Two figures were crossing it as he looked—Jervis checking that impatient stride of his to keep pace with his companion. Rosamund never hurried. She wore a lilac dress. The sun touched her corn-coloured hair, and the light wind ruffled it. Anyone might have thought that they made a handsome couple. What Ambrose Weare thought, no one could tell but Ambrose Weare. He watched for a moment, saw Jervis lift that black head of his and throw out his arm with a vigorous sweep, saw Rosamund look up at him smiling, and then he turned again to Mr Page.

"Well, Page? You're on hot coals? Well, here's the condition—provided he marries within three months of my death. Put that into your infernal legal jargon, and don't leave any loopholes."

Mr Page was looking relieved. He did not know quite what he had expected, but with Ambrose Weare it might have been anything. He was certainly relieved. He said with a smile,

"Almost a superfluous condition, Mr Weare, since he is engaged."

The hawk nose above the thin mouth twitched a little.

"Engaged isn't married," said Ambrose Weare. "He's been engaged for six months, and when I talk to him about getting married, he doesn't want to hurry her. And when I talk to her, she thinks being engaged is so delightful that she'd like it to go on for ever. Damned nonsense! Not want to hurry her? I'll see to it that he hurries her! He'll have to if he doesn't want to go to her for pocket money!" Mr Weare chuckled. "If he don't marry before the three months is up, she gets the lot."

Mr Page was plainly startled.

"Miss Carew?" he exclaimed.

"My great-niece, Rosamund Veronica Leonard Carew. What any man or woman wants with more than one name, is beyond me. Pack of nonsense! But take 'em down—

Rosamund—Veronica—Leonard. If Jervis isn't married in three months and a day—we'll throw in the day for luck—she comes in instead of him and gets the lot."

"But, Mr Weare—"

"Get along and write it down!"

"Mr Weare—I must point out very seriously—"

A look of fury passed over the face against the high white pillow. The right hand lying on the crimson eiderdown clenched and lifted.

"Write what I tell you! It's my will isn't it?"

"Mr Weare, I must point out—"

The clenched hand fell, the head tilted a little. Mr Page, alarmed, broke off.

Ambrose Weare shut his eyes.

"Write-what-I-told-you," he said in a changed, fluttering voice.

Mr Page wrote with a reluctant and disapproving pen.

II

NAN FORSYTH LOOKED UP FROM HER TYPEWRITER AND dropped her hands from the keys. He was coming out. Half an hour—twenty minutes—ten..... She really did not know how long it was since he had come in with his frown and the jerk of the shoulders which said, as plainly as any words, "For heaven's sake let's get this over!"

He always came in like that; and then, after ten—twenty—thirty minutes, out again, with his black head up and the frown gone, as if he had got rid of something, for the moment at any rate. He never spoke to her except to ask for Mr Page, and then he might as well have been speaking into a telephone. Even on the day when Mr Page had been kept by old Sir Elphinstone Brady, who never stayed less than an hour, Jervis Weare had merely stood by the window drumming on the sill with a lean brown hand and frowning, as Nan put it, like a complex depression likely to break at any moment into local thunder.

It was a false alarm. He wasn't coming after all, though she had certainly heard him push back his chair a minute ago. This was his last visit. She and Miss Villiers had been called in to witness his signature to the deed of settlement. Miss Villiers, who had typed the deed, had been loud in praise of its generosity—"*My*, dear! She's a lucky girl! Five hundred a year just to spend on herself! And just as likely as not she'll have no idea of how to do it justice. Why, some of these high-up people are right down dowdy, and not half the looks of others that's got to dress themselves and pay their board and maybe help to support a poor invalid mother on three pound ten a week and no pickings." After which Miss Villiers surveyed herself in a pocket mirror and began absently to touch her lips with a Coraline caress-proof lipstick.

"If Mr Page catches you using lipstick in the office—" said Nan warningly.

Miss Villiers sighed.

"Sorry dear, I forgot. A perfect beast—isn't he?" She wiped off the Coraline, took a last lingering look at her pretty peaked features and rolling blue eyes, and slipped the glass back into her hand-bag. "Well, she's a lucky girl, money or no money. I'm crazy about him myself. Aren't you, dear? I do like a man that looks as if he could just strike you down with one blow of his fist and scarcely know he'd done it, so to speak. Don't you?"

Nan burst out laughing.

"What an ass you are, Villiers!" she said. "Look here, have you found that mortgage Mr Page was asking for?"

"*My!* No! I clean forgot."

"Then you'd better go and look for it."

Villiers went reluctantly.

"And as likely as not I'll miss him when he goes, and next time—if there is a next time—he'll be a married man." She paused with her hand on the door which led into the room sacred to deed-boxes and office files. "Are you going to the wedding?"

Nan shook her head. The keys clicked under her fingers.

"I'm going," said Miss Villiers. "I shall wear my new hat—you know, the one I got for two and eleven pence halfpenny in the Sales, and I'm sure it looks like a three guinea model. P'raps I'll get taken for a bridesmaid—I shouldn't wonder if I did. Yes, I'm going. I say, dear, if there's one thing I envy that girl besides the money and the man, it's her name. Rosamund—Veronica—Leonard—Carew. Fancy being able to stand up in church in a gold tissue that cost goodness knows what, and a *point d'Alençon* train, and a halo of orange-blossom, and say, "I, Rosamund Veronica Leonard, take thee, Jervis! Funny, his only having one name—isn't it?"

Nan went on typing.

"Ass!" she said. "Sorry to repeat myself, but you are— and if Mr Page asks for that mortgage again and you haven't found it, I should say the odds were that you'd be an ass out of a job."

Miss Villiers giggled tolerantly and shut the door. Desperately Nan hoped that she would not find the mortgage until Jervis Weare had come striding through the room. She wanted just that one moment—to see the inner door open, to see him come out, to see him pass, to see him go, to know him gone. It was going to hurt horribly. She wanted it even if it hurt her beyond everything she knew or could guess about pain. But you mustn't be watched when things are hurting you like that—you mustn't have people looking on and chattering—it wasn't decent.

Nan waited for her moment. Would he look very happy and relieved now that all the tiresome business connected with his marriage was done? Would he look very happy on his wedding day? By an hour or two after this time to-morrow he would be married to Rosamund Veronica Leonard Carew.

Nan tried to picture him looking happy, and failed. She had seen him frowning, she had seen him bored, she had seen him angry; and once, for a moment, she had seen him with a lost, hungry look that caught her heart and turned it in her breast. That was when he had stood at the window looking out and drumming on the sill. There was just that one moment when the drumming fingers stayed, the impatient frown smoothed out, and a lost child, hungry, bewildered and astray, looked out of the dark eyes. Nan's heart ached still when she thought about that look. It was one of the things that could not be borne, and yet had to be borne.

She took up one of the sheets that she had been typing and began to correct it. And then quite suddenly the inner door was opened and Jervis Weare came out. Mr Page was behind him, ruddy, smiling, and bland; his horn-rimmed spectacles pushed up; his head slightly thrown back as he talked to the tall young man who preceded him in what the late Mr Ambrose Weare would have described as his best bedside manner.

"Not at all—not at all. You've been most patient. A very troublesome business getting married." Mr Page laughed his mellow laugh.

Jervis Weare did not laugh, but neither did he frown. He turned with a trace of effort and said, speaking quickly and boyishly.

"It's you who have been patient, Mr Page. I—I'm afraid I'm not a very patient person. I—I'd like to say thank you for all the trouble you've taken." And with that he shook hands impetuously and was gone. The door slammed.

Mr Page put up his hand to his glasses.

"Dear me!" he said. "Very like his grandfather—but I think more heart. Well, well, he is marrying a very charming girl—quite beautiful in fact. A most satisfactory affair in every way. Yes—yes. Ah, Miss Forsyth! Do you know whether Miss Villiers has found that mortgage I was asking for? The Heaston estate. Gross carelessness if it has been mislaid—very gross carelessness indeed. What is the matter, Miss Forsyth? You look extremely pale. Are you ill?"

"Oh no, sir."

"You look extremely pale. It would be most inconvenient if you were to be ill at this juncture, but I do not want you to work if you are not feeling fit."

"I am quite well."

The outer door had shut with a clang. It was this clang

that had shaken her, and shaken the room so that everything in it was trembling just a little. The door-frames, and the window-sill, and the table at which she was sitting were all moving, shaking, trembling, as if she was seeing them through a shimmering haze. She bit hard into her lip and bent forward over the table. The room cleared; the furniture and the door-frames became solid and distinct.

Jervis Weare had gone out of her life.

III

"I HAVEN'T FOUND IT," SAID MISS VILLIERS. "WHAT TIME did you say it was? One o'clock? My! Well, that means I'll have to give up lunch and go on looking for it. Regular old Bluebeard, I call him, to keep me starving, while as likely as not he's drinking port and champagne and eating the best of everything. I know what I'd have if I was him—chicken and mushrooms, and one of those ice puddings like they gave the recipe for in last week's *Ladies' Friend*—pine-apple and cream inside, and a hot chocolate sauce all over." She sighed voluptuously. "One thing, going without lunch is good for the figure. I say, dear, you wouldn't like to stay and help me, I suppose?"

Nan shook her head. She was pulling on a small black hat. She picked up her hand-bag and made for the door.

"I've got to get home," she said.

Miss Villiers stared.

"What do you want to do that for? If you bus it, it costs you as much as the difference between feeding at home and feeding out, and if you walk, why it's as much as you'd do to get there and back in the time."

Nan nodded absently.

"Right as usual, Villiers," she said.

As a rule she brought sandwiches to the office, or had a cup of tea, and an egg if funds were high, or a bun if they were low, at a tea-shop round the corner. She only went home when it seemed impossible to leave Cynthia for the whole day. Today was one of the days when it did not seem possible. She committed the extravagance of taking a bus, because this would give her forty minutes with Cynthia. She had ten minutes to put Jervis Weare out of her thoughts, and get the colour back into her cheeks. She rubbed them vigorously as she climbed Mrs Warren's stair, which smelt of lodgers' dinners, to the room at the top of the house which had been home for the last two years.

She opened the door, and if she had had a thought to spare for herself, she would have known at once that, like Miss Villiers, she would probably have to go lunchless today. She had told Cynthia that she was coming back. They would have scrambled eggs and mashed potatoes, cooked on their gas ring. Cynthia was to buy the eggs, but it was quite obvious that Cynthia had not done so, since she was still in her dressing-gown.

Nan took a breath, and shut the door behind her.

"Well, Cynthy?" she said.

Three months ago Cynthia Forsyth had possessed the frail, translucent beauty which compels a startled admiration and an almost terrified sense of its evanescence. The bloom on a wild flower, the iridescence of flung spray, the passing colours of sunrise and sunset, have this same power to astonish and to charm. Now she was just a too thin, too pallid girl with fair hair, a smooth skin, and rather appealing dark eyes reddened by hours of weeping. She sat on the floor, leaning sideways with one arm on the rickety double bed which the sisters shared at night, her faded blue dressing-gown falling away and showing a torn night-dress that had once been pink. On the honeycombed coverlet lay a pile of letters.

"Now, Cynthy!" said Nan.

Cynthia looked up.

"I'm sorry, Nan—I didn't mean to."

"You promised you wouldn't," said Nan gravely. She

came across to the bed and began to pick up the letters. "You'd much better burn them and have done with it."

Cynthia's hand tightened on the soaked handkerchief which she held squeezed up.

"Nan, you won't!"

"No, of course I won't—but I wish *you* would." She sat down on the bed and pulled Cynthia's head against her knee. "What's the good of keeping them, my child? You lock them up, and you promise me you won't look at them, and when my back's turned you get them out and cry yourself to a jelly."

Cynthia turned and clutched at her with a wild sob.

"It's so *hard*—when we love each other—when it's just money! If he didn't love me, I'd—I'd try—to get over it—I would—I really would! But when we love each other—" Her voice was choked, her hot thin hand was clenched on Nan's knee.

Nan stroked the damp fair hair.

"It would be better to try, Cynthy," she said.

Cynthia shivered.

"I don't want to. If I can't marry Frank, I want to die—only it takes such a long time. In books people die quite quickly when their hearts are broken, and I'm sure my heart's quite as broken as anybody's in a book—and yet I'm quite strong. I've lost my colour, and I've lost my looks, and my hair won't curl any more—but I'm not dying."

Nan's heart gave a foolish little jump. It was silly to mind Cynthy talking like that. She said,

"You'd feel better if you washed your face, ducky."

Cynthia sniffed and dabbed her eyes.

"Yes, you would. And did you get the eggs?"

Cynthia dabbed again and shook her head.

"Then I must fly, or we shan't have anything to eat. We'll have to have them boiled. Now, up you get and put on the saucepan! I won't be a minute. Perhaps the old rabbit will oblige."

Mrs Warren having duly obliged, Nan returned with a couple of eggs, only to find that Cynthia had neither washed her face nor put on the saucepan. She had got up from the floor and was gazing tearfully out of the window.

Nan pressed her lips together and said nothing.

Whilst she put on the eggs, Cynthia walked up and down talking in a soft exhausted voice.

"You can have both eggs—I don't want anything. It's all very well to say pull yourself together, but Frank's just as miserable as I am, and I'm not only thinking about myself, I'm thinking about him. And in ten days he'll be gone to Australia, and I shall never see him again. And to think that it's just money that's keeping us apart! If his uncle hadn't changed his will at the last minute, he'd have had two thousand pounds and been able to buy that partnership."

"Your egg's done," said Nan. "I don't know why you like them nearly raw." Frank Walsh's nonexistent two thousand pounds was a subject to be escaped from with all possible despatch.

"If I only had two thousand pounds!" said Cynthia. She stood still in the middle of the floor and flung out her hands. "Isn't there *anything* one can do to make money quickly?"

"I don't think there's anything *you* can do, ducky," said Nan.

Cynthia turned away with a sob. She went back to the window and stood there twisting her fingers and crying. Through the faded dressing-gown Nan could see her shoulder-blades moving as she drew quick sobbing breaths. She went on speaking in a matter of fact sort of way.

"Cynthy, you really would feel much better if you would dress and have something to eat. Sitting and thinking about things makes them a hundred times worse."

"It's all very well for you," said Cynthia in a hopeless voice. "You don't know what it is to want someone all the time, and to know that he's going right away and that you'll never see him again. You've never been in love, so you don't *know*."

"No," said Nan. "Cynthy, do come and eat your egg or it will be cold, and a cold egg is simply unutterable."

IV

NAN WAS VERY TIRED WHEN SHE GOT BACK TO THE OFFICE. She had got Cynthia to eat something, to dress, and to promise that she would go out. She felt as if she had been moving a lot of very heavy furniture. Cynthia was loving and sweet and gentle, but she was a dead weight, and there were times when it took the very last of Nan's strength to carry it.

She found Miss Villiers on her knees in the deed room sorting papers after her own peculiarly languid and dilatory fashion.

"No, dear, I haven't found it. But I've had a perfectly lovely idea for making up that length of georgette I got—you know, the pale blue with the faded patches. Well, if I have it scalloped just where the fade comes—Oh, I say, dear, you're not going! I made sure you'd give me a hand when you got back."

"I've got the Harrington deeds to type," said Nan.

She took off her hat, sat down to the typewriter, and passed with relief into a formal world of set, correct phrases and stilted repetitions.

Mr Page came in presently with a pleasant word.

"Feeling all right again, Miss Forsyth?"

Then click, click, click, the swish of the moving key-board, and such words as, *hereditaments, messuages, hereinbefore,* and *party of the first part.*

Nan began to feel less tired. It wasn't work that tired you; it was fighting with yourself and trying to carry someone else all the time. If Cynthia would only get a job. But standing in a shop tired her feet, and typing made her back ache, and she didn't seem to be able to manage children. Besides, her looks had always been against her; she was too pretty and too fragile, and too gentle.

Nan forced her attention back to that comfortable formal world in which there were no emotions.

And then suddenly the outer door was flung open and Jervis Weare strode through the room, wrenched at the handle of Mr Page's sanctum, and disappeared, slamming the door behind him. It was the most sudden thing that had ever happened. Between the bang of the first door and the slam of the second there was just a momentary impression of Jervis with his face set in a black rage. Nan had hardly time to catch her breath. He plunged past. The second door banged. She had the feeling that he had taken the room in his stride without seeing it, or anything in it. And then his voice struck harshly on her ears in a violent oath.

She stood up, shaking a little, and came out from behind her table. He had slammed the door so violently that it had latched and then unlatched itself. It stood now an inch ajar, and she could hear Mr Page's startled exclamation.

"Mr Jervis! What has happened? I beg of you!"

Nan stood still in the middle of the floor. It was most clearly her duty to close the door. She stood quite still, and heard Jervis Weare go tramping through the room beyond; and as he tramped he swore in a steady bitter flow; not speaking loudly, but with a deadly effect of weighing every word.

"Mr Jervis! Mr Jervis! I beg of you! Something has happened—I beg that you will tell me what has happened. I—I—*Mr Jervis!*"

There was a silence. Mr Page's voice left off, and nothing else began. There was a dead silence.

Always after that moment Nan knew what was meant by a silence being dead. Something was dead in there. She knew what Mr Page must be looking like. In her own mind she could see his face, surprised, shocked, distressed, the ruddy colour a little sunk. She thought that he had risen, or half risen, from his chair. But she couldn't see Jervis in her mind—only the back of that black head of his, the furious tilt of it, the forward thrust of his shoulders, all frozen in the silence—the dead silence. It seemed to go on for a most intolerable time.

Then Jervis said in quite a quiet, low voice,

"She's thrown me over."

Mr Page exclaimed. Nan did not know what he said. It was just a sound to her; it left no mark.

Jervis Weare spoke again.

"She's thrown me over."

He said it twice. And then he laughed, still on that low, quiet tone; only just at the end it broke sharply, harshly, and so ceased.

Mr Page's voice sounded nearer. He said at once in a distressed tone,

"Miss Carew? Dear, dear—how's this? Mr Jervis, I—I—" he stopped, commanded himself, and took up the last word again, but in an altered manner. "I am very much distressed at this. Won't you tell me what it is? Is it—is it irremediable?"

"Oh, quite," said Jervis Weare.

Nan could imagine a quick gesture to point the words. Voice and gesture thrust Rosamund Carew into the limbo of things out of the question.

The sound of Mr Page's feet came after that. If there had been any other sound, Nan would not have heard them. They went across the room to the window, halted, and came back again. Then Mr Page's professional voice, grave and concerned:

"Sit down, won't you? Yes—it will be better. This is a very serious matter. I don't mean only personally—though, as I am sure you know, you have my deep sympathy. But there is another aspect—" He stopped as if he balked at this aspect to which he alluded. "This—this unfortunate breach has a consequence which may not have occurred to you, and cannot have occurred to Miss Carew."

Every time Mr Page stopped speaking, that dead silence closed upon the room.

Nan's whole being so strained towards what was happening in the silence that she seemed to see Jervis still standing with the office table between him and Mr Page. She could see him standing there, but not his face. She wanted to see his face.

Half a minute went by. Then he said harshly, answering Mr Page,

"You think not?"

Mr Page coughed.

"Mr Weare, I am obliged to point out that the terms of your grandfather's will make this breach a most serious matter. I am bound to tell you this, and to ask whether there is not any chance of—in short, a reconciliation."

Another measure of silence, and then Mr Page breaking it.

"Mr Weare—will you tell me what has happened? I am in ignorance. How can I advise you? Since you have come to me, I must suppose that you want my advice."

"No," said Jervis Weare—"not your advice, Mr Page."

"Then what do you want?"

"I will tell you." He spoke now in a cold, composed tone.

There would be no gesture with a tone like that. He would be standing at the table, just touching it perhaps with a steadying hand as he bent to speak to Mr Page.

He dropped his voice a little and went on:

"You say that I'm probably not aware of my position. That's a mistake. If I'm not married within three months of my grandfather's death, Miss Carew—" the name halted him—"Miss Carew steps into my shoes. How very charitable to suppose that she doesn't know it! No, one minute—you wanted me to speak, and you'd better let me get on with it. You talk about a quarrel, and you ask whether it can't be made up. There hasn't been any quarrel. There has been nothing but a polite note to say she's very sorry but she finds she can't marry me after all."

"My dear fellow—my dear boy—" The professional manner had given way. Mr Page was being personally shocked and aware that, after all, he had known this large furious young man in sailor suits.

Jervis went on speaking.

"My grandfather died on the fifteenth of May. This is the thirteenth of August. I suppose she had this in her mind all along. She wouldn't hear of being married before the fourteenth. She said it would give us both a pleasant thrill to feel we were running it so fine."

"No, no," said Mr Page. "No, no—don't tell me the thing was planned!"

Jervis Weare laughed.

"And you've been a lawyer for forty years! Planned? Of course it was planned! My grandfather—you—me—I daresay we've all had quite a good opinion of ourselves. And we've just been puppets—damned cardboard dolls—whilst Rosamund has pulled the strings and laughed at us. Why did he put that clause into his will? You don't know, and I don't know—but Rosamund knows, and now that she's played the dirty trick, she thinks she can get away with it and scoop the lot. Well, I'm damned if she will!"

Nan heard him strike the table. Something fell—a book— no, the almanac—there was the tinkle of breaking glass; and then that frozen control quite gone as he raged up and down the room.

"My position—oh yes, she knows it, and I know it, and you know it. If I'm not married by the fifteenth—that's what she's reckoning on. I told you I'd let you know why I'd come in a minute. I've come to find out how I can do her in. She thinks she's got me in a cleft stick, but there's nothing in my grandfather's will about marrying *her*. I've got to get married by the fifteenth—but I've not got to marry Rosamund Carew. There are about two million more women than men in England, aren't there—and any one of the odd two million will do. Find me a girl who'll marry me at twenty-four hours' notice!"

"Mr Jervis—Mr Jervis! It can't be done."

"There are such things as special licences, aren't there?"

"Yes—yes—it takes three days except in extraordinary circumstances."

"Aren't these extraordinary enough? I should have thought—"

"A moment, a moment, please. You have the three days—your grandfather's will specifies three months and a day as the period. We have always spoken of the period as three months, and possibly Miss Carew—" He broke off with a cough. "No, no, one shouldn't impute such motives— not without absolute proof."

Jervis Weare had stopped pacing the room.

"I've three clear days? Good! You have only to find me a wife."

Mr Page had got his professional voice back.

"Mr Jervis, you must give me time for consideration. There are other courses open to you. In the circumstances I have no doubt that the Courts would extend the time. It could be argued that you had done your best to carry out the provisions of the will. I should like to take counsel's opinion. The question of conspiracy might arise. In my opinion Miss Carew would be very ill advised if she made any claim. There is also breach of promise. You would without doubt be awarded very heavy damages."

"And make myself the laughing-stock of the whole country? I'd rather let her get away with it—and I'll see her damned before I do that! I tell you I'll see her damned!" His fist struck the table again.

"Mr Jervis!"

"She's played her ace, and she thinks the trick's hers, but if I can trump the ace—" He broke off to laugh again and went on with a rush. "What's the good of counsel's opinion and a decision of the Courts? I want to beat her at her own game. She's made a fool of me, and I'll make a fool of her. She's left me standing, and I'm hanged if I'll be left. Who'll be the fool when she picks up *The Times* on, let us say the seventeenth, and sees that I'm married—'On the 16th instant, at St. George's, Hanover Square, Mr Jervis Weare to Miss Blank Dash.' And that, you see, is where you come in. You've got to fill in the blank and the dash—you've got to find me a wife."

At this point Nan became aware of the slow, heavy beating of her heart. It seemed to be knocking against her side. The beats did not quicken, but they grew heavier, and with each thud there came a drumming in her ears, so that she could not listen—and she must, must listen. She took a step forward, her hand at her throat. She heard Mr Page protest. And then, so loud that it came through the loud beating of her heart, Jervis Weare's voice:

"If you won't help me, I'll help myself, if I have to pick her up off the streets!"

And right on that the door of the deed room must have opened, because Miss Villiers was saying,

"I can't find it, dear, and if I've been through one file, I've been through a dozen."

At the sound of Miss Villiers' voice something happened to Nan. She stepped forward and closed the door of Mr Page's room with so steady and gentle a touch that neither Mr Page nor Mr Jervis Weare were aware that it had been ajar and was now latched. Then she turned round and spoke in a matter-of-fact voice,

"You'd better go on looking."

"Cool as a cucumber she was. 'And you'd better go on looking for it,' she said." Miss Villiers was afterwards in considerable request as an authority on what had taken place on that August afternoon—" 'You'd better go on looking for it.' Well I must say I thought she might have given me a hand, but she just picked up her hat and out she went and down the stairs, and I heard the door shut, and that's the last I saw of her. And a minute later if Mr Weare didn't come bursting through the office as if he'd been fired out of a gun. Well, that's just my way of putting it—but you know what I mean, dear. And Mr Page so put about he never so much as thought of asking for the paper I'd been looking for—which was just as well, for I didn't find it till next day."

V

WHEN NAN FORSYTH HAD SHUT THE STREET DOOR BEHIND her, she crossed the road. She wasn't tired any more. Her feet carried her lightly. She felt as if she was being swept along by a strong current. The current carried her and she went with it. Her heart had stopped knocking against her side, and this was a great relief.

She walked a little way, and then back. As she turned

again, Jervis Weare was striding down the street, and, still
without any sense of effort, she quickened her pace so as not
to be left too far behind. When he turned the corner, she
crossed to the same side of the street and ran. She had to
keep him in view and to find out where he was going. She
had no thought that it would be difficult to come to speech
with him. She hoped that he was going home to the big
Georgian house in Carrington Square, which was one of the
things that would pass from him to Rosamund Carew if he
did not marry within the time set by his grandfather's will.

Nan lifted her head. Neither the house nor anything else
that was his should pass to Rosamund Carew. The current
that was carrying her along was a current of protective love.
Ten years ago she had saved his life, and he had never
known it. Now she was going to save him again. Rosamund
shouldn't rob him; neither should he rob himself.

She looked back across the ten years to the little girl of
twelve, with her passionate adoration for the dark boy of
twenty who did not so much as know of her existence. He
had never noticed her, never spoken to her. But when the
great adventure came, she had flung down her life with both
hands to save his. He had never known, and he would never
know, but it was her most secret happiness. She dreamed
sometimes of the rocky pool with the salt, cold water
coming in on a flood tide. She felt his weight on her
straining childish shoulders, and the sea flinging her against
jagged rock. Then she would wake and touch the white scar
on her arm and go over the whole adventure in her mind.
Sometimes she wondered whether she would ever come
across the little man with the queer name who had come to
their rescue—Ferdinand Fazackerley. Such an extraordinary
name. It would be odd if they met again—but odd things
happen, for she had met Jervis Weare.

Jervis Weare walked straight on, giving her enough to do
to keep up with him. Nan became more and more certain
that he was going home. She came up with him just as he
was crossing into Carrington Square.

The sun struck hot on the dark rusty green of the trees.
The little square was empty. She crossed the road half a pace
behind him and spoke his name as her foot touched the kerb:

"Mr Weare—"

He must have been very deep in his own bitter thoughts, for she had to speak again, and louder:

"Mr Weare—"

He flung round then, and she saw his face cut with deep lines of pain and rage, his black brows meeting over hot dark eyes.

"What is it?"

The hot dark eyes held not the slightest recognition.

She said, "Mr Weare—I'm from Mr Page's office." That was quite an easy thing to say, and she said it easily, the current still taking her on.

Jervis Weare stared.

"Well?" he said.

"I want to speak to you."

"Why?"

"I am from Mr Page's office. It's a business matter."

He paused, detached, not really aware of her.

"Mr Page sent you?"

Nan shook her head.

"It's a business matter."

Her repetition of the phrase caught his attention. He had not noticed her shake of the head. If Page had sent this girl—well—

"Where can we talk?" said Nan Forsyth.

"I don't know."

"You are going home—to your house."

"Is it mine?"

For a moment his look disturbed her strange calm.

"Will you let me speak to you there? I have something that I want to say."

He stared for a moment longer. Then he said,

"Oh, certainly."

They went on together. The house rose up before Nan, heavy and square and grey. Jervis used a latchkey, and they went through the hall into a room at the back of the house—a man's room, littered with a man's belongings, littered also with what were obviously wedding presents—a handsome standard lamp; a cigar-box with the signatures of several donors sprawling across the crude new silver; half a dozen boxes half unpacked, with glass, china or silver showing here and there. Two windows framed in dark velvet curtains looked out upon a fair-sized garden bordered with trees.

Nan passed into this room, and felt its atmosphere close about her. When Jervis Weare had followed her and shut the door, she was standing against one of the heavy curtains. The current had brought her here. Now it ebbed away from her. She was Nan Forsyth facing something that was going to decide all the rest of her life, and all the rest of Jervis Weare's life. For a moment she felt fear as she had never felt it before. And then courage rose in her like a flood.

He turned from the door and said,

"You wanted to speak to me?"

"Yes."

"Do you mind saying what you want? I'm rather busy."

"Yes," said Nan. She put her left hand behind her and found the window-sill; she felt the need of something hard and firm to hold on to. Then she lifted her eyes to his frowning face and said, "I'm in Mr Page's office."

"Yes—you said so." There was just the least impatient twitch of the lip as he spoke.

"I'm in Mr Page's office. When you came in this afternoon you slammed the door. It didn't latch. I was in the office. I heard what you said to Mr Page."

She had been prepared for anger, but not for quite so bleak a look as this.

"You listened. Well?"

The look hurt her beyond bearing. She winced away from it, then gripped the window-sill and kept herself steady.

Jervis Weare did not see her wince. He was not really seeing her at all. His anger turned a cold edge upon this confessed eavesdropper.

"Well?" he repeated.

Nan kept her eyes on him. She didn't mind his being angry; she only minded his being hurt. He was angry because he was hurt—and in his hurt, what further hurt might come to him? He was like a wounded man staggering blindly toward a precipice. If someone you cared for was doing that, you couldn't stand aside and let them go on— you had to stop them even if they hated you for doing it.

A third impatient "Well?" brought stumbling words to her lips:

"I heard what you said to Mr Page."

Jervis walked to the table and stood there. He touched it with one hand and leaned forward a little. It was the picture of him which had formed in her mind when she stood listening and heard him say in his bitter voice, "You have only to find me a wife." He must have been recalling his own words, for he was looking at her, really looking, for the first time.

He saw a girl in a neat grey dress and a close black hat, a girl who held herself very straight and looked at him with steady grey eyes. Her face was pale, her lips pressed firmly together. He looked at her and said,

"Did Mr Page send you?"

"No," said Nan.

"Then—will you explain?"

"I heard what you said to Mr Page."

"So you said. And what did I say?"

Nan held her head a little higher.

"You said that you must be married by the sixteenth. You asked him to find a girl who would marry you at twenty-four hours' notice."

The hand behind her drove the edge of the window-sill deep into her palm. She saw the cold anger of his face break suddenly. Something broke it—a different anger, a flash of humour, a something else which she could not define.

"So that's it? You've got a nerve—haven't you?"

Nan said, "Yes," quite soberly.

He burst out laughing.

"Well, why not? I haven't time to pick and choose. Since you overheard what we were saying, you know that. To be married on the sixteenth, I must put in for a licence today—but it is unfortunately necessary to give the lady's name, so if you're really offering to step into the breach, perhaps you'll begin by giving me your name."

"Nan Forsyth," said Nan.

He took his hand off the table and swung a chair round.

"You'd better sit down."

He came round, took the writing-chair, picked up a pen, and filled it.

"Did you say Anne Forsyth?"

Nan came forward. It was very difficult to let go of the window-sill. Her legs felt as if they belonged to someone else. She sat down a little stiffly. It was like being interviewed for a situation. She was being interviewed for the situation of Jervis Weare's wife. It was like something in a dream. But there was Jervis, looking at her and repeating.

"Anne Forsyth?"

"No—just Nan. I was christened Nan."

"Nothing else?"

"No, nothing else."

He wrote "Nan Forsyth," and without looking up asked her age.

"Twenty-two."

"Parents?"

"Dead."

"Any near relations?"

"A sister." She thought suddenly and warmly of Cynthia, and the dream shook a little.

"Older, or younger?"

"Younger—" She paused, then added, "Nineteen."

Jervis had stopped writing. His pen dug holes in the paper. He didn't want to know the answers to any of these questions. She had a well-bred voice. If she was in Page's office, she was likely to be a respectable girl. . . . What did it matter to him what she was? She was the stone he was going to send smashing through Rosamund's plan. What did it matter where the stone came from? He looked up, and met her steady eyes. He asked abruptly,

"Why are you doing this? For money?"

There was only a moment's hesitation before she said,

"Of course. It's a business arrangement."

"Oh, entirely. That ought to be quite clear."

"Yes," said Nan. The hand that had held the window-sill went down and gripped the edge of her chair. She repeated her "Yes." Then she said, "If it's a business matter, do you mind discussing the details?"

She got a curious look, and he laughed again.

"Mind? Why should I mind? And what details do you want to discuss?"

Nan's hand tightened on the chair.

"I'm earning my living," she said. "I'm doing it because I have to."

"Yes?" said Jervis.

"If I do this, I shall lose my job."

"You mean you'll lose your job if you marry me."

"I don't think Mr Page would keep me on."

Jervis laughed with a certain hard amusement.

"I don't suppose he would. But the law obliges me to support you, you know."

She never took her eyes from his face—serious, steady eyes.

"That's not what I mean."

"What do you mean?"

"If it's business, it ought to be done in a business way."

"I see—you want a settlement."

For the first time her colour rose. It flushed her pale cheeks and ebbed rapidly.

"No, I didn't mean that."

"Will you say what you do mean?"

Nan gripped the chair and thought hard about Cynthia. Impossible to leave Cynthia unprovided for.

"I want something now."

He did not laugh this time, only looked at her with the hard amusement in his eyes.

"What—cash on delivery? Is that it?"

Nan didn't speak.

He thought suddenly that she had courage at any rate.

"Well?" he said. "How much? Five hundred pounds?"

Nan shook her head.

"What—not enough?"

She shook her head again, then spoke.

"It isn't enough. I shall lose my job, and I've got someone depending on me."

She felt better when she had said that. But Jervis was staring at her.

"Depending?"

"Yes—my sister. I couldn't just take this on and leave her."

He threw himself back in his chair.

"Well, how much?"

"Two thousand pounds," said Nan, and set her teeth.

Jervis Weare regarded her with frank admiration.

"You certainly have a nerve!" he said.

It was heartening to be told so. At the moment Nan felt exactly like a sawdust doll from which the last grain of sawdust has leaked away, leaving it quite flat, quite empty. She said, in what she was surprised to find was a steady voice,

"It's because of Cynthia. I can always get a job."

"And she can't?"

Nan shook her head. She looked young, mournful, and serious. The contrast between her appearance and what Jervis Weare had just described as her nerve was so extreme as to be ludicrous.

Jervis pushed back his chair and got up.

"So you propose to turn two thousand pounds over to Cynthia? And how much do you want for yourself?"

"I don't want anything—I can get a job."

"And why should I give Cynthia two thousand pounds?"

Nan looked up at him with a perfectly steady gaze.

"You won't give it to Cynthia—you'll give it to me. Mr. Weare left you a hundred thousand pounds. I'm helping you to keep it. The two thousand pounds will be my commission."

"What a business head!"

"I've had a business training."

She looked away at last, not in embarrassment, but because she had said what she had come to say. She relaxed a little, let go of the chair, folded her hands in her lap, and waited.

Jervis Weare walked across the room and back again.

"All right," he said, "you can have your commission."

VI

At nine o'clock on the morning of August 16th Jervis Weare was married to Nan Forsyth in the church of St. Justus, Carrington Square. It is a peculiarly ugly church. The heavy old-fashioned gallery which runs round three sides of it induces a perpetual dusk. Nan came out of the bright morning sunshine into the dusk, which smelt of pews and varnish and old age. It was a very depressing smell.

Mr Page gave her away disapprovingly, and he and the verger were the only witnesses. She looked once at Jervis, and saw him as a tall, aloof shadow. She could guess at the frown she could not see. When he took her hand and put the ring on it, his was hot and dry. He rammed the ring down, and there it was.

They got up from their knees and went into the vestry. She wrote herself for the last time Nan Forsyth.

"And now your father's name here, Mrs Weare."

It was the two things coming together that took her off her balance. Mrs Weare—and her father dead in a far country, not knowing. There wasn't anyone to know or care. She had not told Cynthia, because there would have been too much to tell. Tears stung in her eyes; the register disappeared in a mist.

"Your father's name—just here, please. Full Christian names."

She closed her eyes for a moment hard, then, opening them, bent and wrote, "Nigel Forsyth," and stood aside whilst Mr Page and the verger signed.

They came out into the sunlight again. Mr Page shook hands with them both and walked away. They watched him go. Then, as he turned the corner, Jervis Weare became aware that his wife was addressing him. Her voice had reached him, not her words. He saw her standing there in her grey dress and black hat, and said,

"I beg your pardon—I didn't hear what you said."

"I said good-bye," said Nan.

He looked a little startled. Since their first interview they had not met till now. He said,

"Where are you going?"

"Back to Cynthia," said Nan. "I haven't told her yet."

Jervis was not interested in Cynthia. He frowned and said, "I think we must talk first."

"Nan said, "Why?" and got a hard look.

"One talks because one has things to say. I've got things to say, and I don't propose to say them here. If you'll come over to the house—"

They crossed the square in silence. Nan wondered what he was going to say to her. She had got hold of herself again. There was a blue sky overhead and a light fresh wind; the sun shone. She wished that they could have talked to one another under this clear sky.

Jervis's room was not dark like the church, and the two windows were open to the garden. The air that flowed in had been warmed by the sun. She went and stood by the window so as to get as near to the garden as possible. Nan was always friends with a garden.

"What did you want to talk to me about?" she said, looking across to where he stood on the hearth, one foot on the fender and an arm lying along the mantelshelf.

"I wanted to tell you that Mr Page is seeing about that two thousand pounds. Have you a banking account?"

He saw her smile for the first time.

"Oh no," she said.

"You will have to have one. You'd better see Mr Page about it, and when you have opened the account he will pay the money in. Then, as regards yourself, I have signed a settlement which gives you five hundred a year."

The colour flamed into Nan's face.

"Oh, you mustn't!"

"Did you imagine that I shouldn't make you an allowance?"

"I don't want you to. I can get a job."

Mr Jervis Weare assumed a lordly tone.

"As to that, you can please yourself. A hundred and twenty-five pounds a quarter will be paid into your account."

The colour flamed higher. Women are strange creatures. She would take two thousand pounds for Cynthia without a qualm—it seemed a very right and just arrangement—but to take an allowance for herself was a thing that shamed her through and through.

"I can't take it," she said in a voice whose distress pierced Jervis Weare's self-absorption.

He reacted with a feeling of acute annoyance.

"Do you mind considering my position for a moment? Do you really expect me to marry a girl and leave her penniless? For heaven's sake be rational! Why should you have married me if you were going to take up a position like this?"

Why! Nan could have laughed and wept at the question. If they had been in the Palace of Truth, she would have said, "Oh, my dear! Why? To save you from being robbed. To save you from the sort of girl you might have married. To save you from picking someone up off the streets." But since these were things to be hidden at any cost, she frowned, looked at him gravely, and said,

"I hadn't thought of it like that."

He jerked an impatient shoulder.

Nan looked away. Such a large creature. And how many years older than herself? Eight at least. But that jerk had put him back into the nursery before her eyes—a hurt, angry child; hurt and angry past his power of concealment. Her heart went out to him with a rush, and she looked away for fear he would see what was in her eyes. Her heart said, "Oh, my *dear!*" Her lips spoke quickly,

"I quite see your point of view; but it is too much—*really.*"

The hurt, angry child disappeared. A rather lofty stranger said in tones of icy politeness,

"The deed is already signed. I would prefer not to discuss the matter any more."

Nan looked up with a sparkle in her eyes. And then the sparkle died, because she saw him suddenly so tired, so done. She could guess that he had not slept for nights, and, because she loved him very much, she could guess how his anger had ridden him at this fence of marriage and now had left him bogged upon its farther side. He had had one aim—to defeat Rosamund; to score in the game of wits; to keep what she had planned to take from him—and in order to win he had mortgaged all his future. Now that the game was won, he had no pleasure in it. He did not care whether he was a beggar or not. He saw himself tied to a stranger, and all that he wanted was to be rid of her as quickly as possible.

Nan gave a little nod.

"Very well," she said.

Then she came up to him with her hand out.

"Good-bye."

For the second time that morning their hands touched. He said "Good-bye" with an air of relief. Then, with her hand still in his, she looked past him and saw the photograph. It hung with other groups above the mantelshelf. Nan did not see the other groups at all. She saw a lawn set about with trees; an old man in a chair—Mr Ambrose Weare, whom she had seen once; a woman standing beside him—Rosamund Carew, whom she had never seen at all; and a third figure—a man walking across the lawn, his back to the camera.

It was at the third figure that Nan stared. Her hand tightened unconsciously on Jervis Weare's hand.

"Who's that?" she said.

He turned. Their hands dropped apart.

Nan stood on tiptoe, pointing.

"Who is that?"

He threw her an astonished look. She had a bright colour in her cheeks; her lips were parted. Before he could look away she flashed round upon him.

"Who is that man?"

Jervis became, if possible, a shade more distant.

"His name is Leonard—Robert Leonard—a connection of—my grandfather's. I don't think you are very likely to have met him."

"Is he a friend of yours?"

His voice stiffened.

"A family connection."

Nan's right hand took hold of her left.

"You are thinking it's very strange that I should ask questions about Mr Leonard, but I've got a reason. Will you please tell me where he has been for the last ten years?"

He took a little more serious notice of what she was saying. Ten years ago she would have been a child; her interest in Robert Leonard could not possibly be a personal one.

"Why do you want to know?"

"Because I think I saw him once ten years ago."

"Once! Ten years ago! Good Lord! What sort of memory are you giving yourself?"

"Don't you remember anything that happened ten years ago? I do—little things—all sorts of things—like little sharp pictures in my mind. When I saw that, I remembered him. Won't you tell me what I asked?"

He laughed outright.

"Why, the photograph doesn't even show his face!"

Nan wasn't remembering a face; she was remembering just that square thickset figure, and just that turn of the head.

"Tell me," she said.

"What do you want to know? Ten years ago—ten years ago . . . . well, exactly ten years ago he was over on a visit from South America staying with my grandfather. I remember that because I know he was staying in the house when I nearly drowned myself out on Croyston rocks."

"Yes?" said Nan in a little half voice. "How—how did you do that?"

"Oh, slipped up on the rocks and banged a hole in the back of my head. The tide was coming in, and they only found me just in time."

Nan had turned very pale.

"Mr Leonard found you?"

"Oh no—he wasn't anywhere about. It was an American fellow who was taking photographs."

Mr Ferdinand Fazackerley rushed into Nan's mind—important, efficient, and immensely talkative. And then he was gone again, and she saw the beach, the jagged rocks which hid the pool, and the thickset figure of a man coming from behind the rocks and walking away towards the headland. He was walking away from her, and he was walking away from Jervis, who lay half in and half out of the pool with a hole in the back of his head and the tide coming up. She said breathlessly,

"I want to know about Mr Leonard. What happened to him after that?"

"He went back to South America."

"At once?"

He stared at her.

"I don't know—I was ill."

"And when you got well—was he there then?"

"No, he'd gone."

"Where is he now?"

"Down at Croyston. He's got a chicken farm."

"Is that—near your house?" It was a child's question asked in a child's troubled voice.

"Three and a half miles," said Jervis Weare.

"Thank you," said Nan.

She put out her hand again.

"Good-bye," she said.

Then just by the door she turned. He had crossed to open it with mechanical politeness. Her movement brought her round facing him as he stood with his hand on the door. Her lips were parted, and that direct gaze of hers puzzled him. It was evident that she wanted to say something. But what did she want to say, and would she say it, or would that astonishing nerve of hers fail to bring her up to the scratch? If he had known that what Nan wanted to say was, "Won't you stop bothering about this wretched business and go off and play golf or something, and—and—go off to bed early and have a drink of hot milk the last thing?" would he have been moved to laughter, or to furious anger, or just possibly to something else? Nan wanted most earnestly to say these things, but her nerve failed before the bored politeness with which he was waiting for her to go.

This time she went without saying good-bye.

VII

CYNTHIA WAS MARRIED ON THE TWENTIETH OF AUGUST, and on the twenty-second she sailed with Frank Walsh for Australia. He was to be there for six months and then return to take up the junior partnership which his own small capital and Cynthia's two thousand pounds had made possible.

Nan looked at Cynthia as she came down the aisle on Frank's arm, and wondered at the miracle which happiness had worked. Once again Cynthia bloomed in fragile beauty. She walked as if she trod on air. Her blue eyes were as full of light as the sky on a sunny morning. It seemed odd that good, plain, commonplace Frank Walsh should have the power to charm this beauty into being. Frank would never set the Thames on fire, but he would make Cynthia a kind and faithful husband.

Nan went to the station to see them off. She was dutifully kissed by Frank, and rather perfunctorily by Cynthia. She walked back to a room strewn with all the odds and ends which had not been worth taking to Australia, with the feeling that she had come to a dead end. She was married, and Cynthia was married. She had lost her job. Cynthia didn't want her any more. Jervis Weare certainly didn't want her.

She tidied the room, and then sat down to face the future. She had been married six days, but it was the first time she had really had time to think. To get Cynthia married, to buy Cynthia's outfit, and to get her off by the same boat as Frank, had taken every bit of her thought and time and energy. It was characteristic of Cynthia that she had not even asked what Nan was going to do. For the moment her consciousness was so saturated with Frank as to be unable to take in anything else. She had gone as completely, if not as irrevocably, into another world as if she had died. Some day she would come back. Some day she would probably want Nan again. But Nan was not able to derive a great deal of comfort from this thought. She had mothered Cynthia ever since Cynthia was born and she, a baby of three, had cuddled the new baby in her small strong arms.

When she had sat on the edge of the bed for about half an hour she got up, put on her hat, and went out. It was perfectly clear to her that she must have a job—and jobs do not just drop into your lap; you have to go out and wrestle for them.

When she had been to three agencies, she felt better. None of the agencies had anything to offer her, but one of them had asked whether she would care to make a voyage to South America in charge of children. She toyed with the idea over a cup of tea. It was not without its charm. Very, very badly she felt the need of someone to look after. What she really wanted to do was to look after Jervis Weare. She wondered if he was sleeping better. She wondered if he had left town. She wondered who darned his socks. She wondered if he was very much in love with Rosamund Carew.

Rosamund's name brought up Rosamund's picture as she had seen it in the group hanging over the mantel-piece in Jervis' room. Rosamund was tall, fair, and very good looking. The photograph showed her bare-headed. She had lovely hair and an oval face. She began to wonder about Rosamund Carew—what sort of woman she was; and why, when she might have married Jervis, she had let him go. She wondered where Rosamund was now. Would she have stayed in town, or would she have gone away? It would be quite easy to find out. Mr Page would know. She couldn't ask Mr Page; there was no need to ask Mr Page. She knew Rosamund's address well enough, since she had often taken letters for her from Mr Page's dictation—29 Leaham Road.

She paid her bill at the tea-shop and walked slowly along. It would be quite easy for her to walk down Leaham Road. It was, of course, very improbable that she would learn anything by doing so. It was irrational to expect to learn anything. It was irrational to want to see Rosamund.

"But I *do* want to," said Nan to herself. "And why shouldn't I walk down Leaham Road if I want to?"

She walked down Leaham Road. The door of No. 29 was shut, and the blinds were down. The house had every appearance of being shut up. When Nan had walked to the end of the street, she turned and walked back. This made it necessary for her to pass No. 29 a third time. She had passed it twice on the opposite side of the road, but now she crossed over and walked slowly down the near pavement.

No. 29 stood at the corner of a small side street, with its entrance on Leaham Road. Nan stood still and looked at the house. The front door was painted a bright dark blue. There were blue window-boxes full of white and yellow daisies. Behind the flowers the blinded windows faced the street. Something came to Nan from the house. She didn't quite know what it was, but she didn't like it. She obeyed an impulse that she did not understand and turned into the side street.

The house had no windows on this side. It stood up over her like a grey wall. And as this thought went through her mind, she saw a taxi coming up the street towards her. As it passed her, it slowed down. She heard it turn the corner behind her, and then she couldn't hear it at all. The taxi had stopped, and Nan felt as sure as she had ever felt of anything in all her life that it had stopped in front of No. 29.

She whisked round and ran back to the corner, keeping close in to the blank wall of the house. She was in time to see Rosamund Carew emerge from the taxi and mount the steps which led up to No. 29. Nan received an impression of height, grace, and brilliance. Rosamund Carew was a beautiful woman, and she held herself as if she was very well aware of the fact. She went up the steps, and a man got out of the car and followed her.

Nan leaned sideways against the wall of the house, and felt it shift and rock. She tried to step back, and the pavement lifted under her foot. The man was Robert Leonard. After ten years, she was just as sure of that as she was that when she had seen him last he had just struck down Jervis Weare and left him to drown—and she was just as sure of that as she was of being Nan Forsyth. She took a grip of herself and looked again. He had gone up the steps after

Rosamund Carew. She could not see either of them now. The taxi stood by the kerb with its back to her. The driver was looking straight in front of him.

Nan walked out of the side street and stood behind the car, looking towards the door of No. 29. It was open. Miss Carew had disappeared, but before Nan had done more than reach the car Robert Leonard ran down the steps. Nan saw him for a moment in profile, and then the car was between them. He wore a light felt hat and a grey suit. His face was florid and tanned. He had a small fair clipped moustache and a straight line of light eyebrow. The eyelids beneath it had a crumpled look.

Nan pressed close up against the car. She did not want Robert Leonard to see her. He must be a cousin of Miss Carew's—she remembered that Rosamund was Rosamund Veronica Leonard—there was nothing odd that he should be with her. These thoughts just flickered in her mind. And then Robert Leonard's voice disturbed them.

"It's the four-fifteen all right. You'll have to hurry. Let him come out of the station and get well away. He's sure to walk—he has a craze for exercise." A sneer just touched his voice. Nan thought involuntarily of scum on dirty water.

"And supposin' he takes a taxi—what abaht it then?" This was the driver, in a hoarse, throaty voice.

"You must do the best you can," said Leonard impatiently. "And you'd better be getting going—you haven't too much time."

He turned away. The driver's voice followed him.

"Look 'ere, guvnor, I'm not so keen on this job as I was."

Leonard turned round again.

"Take it or leave it!" he said.

"Five 'undred pound's five 'undred pound," said the hoarse, complaining voice.

"Exactly."

"And jug's jug."

Leonard laughed.

"A couple of months for dangerous driving! What's that?"

"Well, you've not got to do it," said the driver. "And it might be a blank sight more than two months."

"Well," said Leonard carelessly, "you needn't touch it if

you don't want to. I promise you the money won't go begging."

"Oh, I'll do it," said the driver. "I'm a man of my word I am. Four-fifteen it is, and I'll be getting along."

Nan heard the whirr of the starter. Her knees were shaking. The taxi began to move. It slipped away, leaving her shelterless.

Robert Leonard, with his back to her, was mounting the steps of No. 29.

VIII

NAN DID NOT KNOW THAT SHE WAS GOING TO RUN, BUT she found herself running back down the side street, past the blank wall of No. 29, and breathlessly, blindly on. When at last she stopped running, she had no breath in her and she was shaking from head to foot. She had turned the corner and was in a street she did not know.

She stood still—not thinking—getting back her breath. Then she began to walk again mechanically, her mind pulled this way and that by her clamouring thoughts. They all seemed to be shouting at once, and the one word which stood out above all the rest was "danger."

She set to work to quiet these clamouring thoughts, to make them speak reasonably, and to weigh what they said. It was very, very difficult, because, instead of being calm and judicial, she was quivering with shock and fear. The fear was not for herself, but for Jervis.

Robert Leonard had come out of the house. He had spoken to the driver of the taxi. She tried to put together what he had said.

Someone was arriving by the four-fifteen. The driver was

to hurry up or he would be late. He was to earn five hundred pounds by doing something for which he might be sent to prison. There was something about getting two months for dangerous driving.

The more Nan thought, the more an anguished fear took hold of her. For ten years she had believed that Robert Leonard had struck down Jervis Weare and left him to drown on Croyston rocks. Now she believed that there was to be another attempt upon his life. Robert Leonard had said, "He is sure to walk—he is crazy for exercise." She was quite sure that the "he" was Jervis. The driver was to "drive dangerously." If "he" took a taxi, he was to do the best he could. He was to risk prison, and he was to earn five hundred pounds.

An *accident*. The word sprang into her mind. It seemed to make a loud noise there. Nan felt as if someone had let off a gun close to her ear. The word deafened her. An *accident*—to Jervis. That was what they had been planning.

As the noise of the word died down, everything else died down too—fear, shock, and the clamour of her thoughts. She found herself walking quickly and thinking clearly. The train got in at four-fifteen. She must go and meet Jervis and tell him what she had heard. She looked at her watch. It was five minutes to four. No station had been mentioned, but trains from Croyston ran to Victoria. If Jervis was coming up from King's Weare, he would drive into Croyston and get a train there. Of course he *might* be coming from anywhere else.

Nan pushed that away with both hands. If he wasn't coming up from King's Weare, there was nothing that she could do. But if she had overheard this wicked plan, it must be because she was meant to warn Jervis. She felt quite sure that he was coming up from King's Weare, and that she would be in time to meet him and tell him what she had heard.

She took a bus, came into the station with two minutes to spare, and reached the barrier as the train drew up beyond it. She wasn't frightened any more. She was going to see Jervis, and everything was going to be all right.

She watched him come down the platform carrying a

suit-case, and laughed in her heart for pure joy. He had come, and he had lost the haggard, sleepless look which had pulled at her heart. He looked brown and well, and profoundly bored. Whatever it was that had brought him up to town, it was not anything which roused feelings of pleasure.

He came striding up to the barrier, thrust a ticket at the collector, and wènt striding on. Nan ran after him, let him get clear of the crowd, and touched his arm. He turned, stared, took off his hat.

Victoria Station became a place where anything might happen. It had the true atmosphere of romantic adventure. Nan was so inspired by it that a dimple came out on either side of her smile as she said,

"You didn't expect to see me."

"Did you expect to see me?" he asked.

Nan nodded.

"I came to meet you."

"Did Page tell you I was coming up?"

She shook her head.

"Nobody told me."

"Then how did you know?" said Jervis Weare.

He had come up in response to an urgent telephone call from Mr Page. An hour after the call had come through he had been stepping into the train. How could anyone else have known that he was coming up? How could Nan Forsyth know? Just then and there it took him between the eyes that she was Nan Weare.

Nan saw the dark colour rise in his face, and wondered what had brought it there. Her dimples trembled away. She said quickly,

"I'll tell you how I know. I've got things to tell you—important things."

They were standing still, with a stream of people flowing past them. A fat man swung a bag of golf-clubs within half an inch of Nan's ear, and as she ducked and stepped aside, she heard an exclamation, and out of the stream there burst a small thin man with ginger hair and bright twinkling brown eyes. He had a Gladstone bag in one hand, a tin hat-box in the other, a camera slung from his shoulder, and an extremely ancient rucksack bound like a hump upon his back. He burst from the stream, cast the hat-box clanking upon the pavement, bumped down the Gladstone bag, and caught Jervis by one hand and the wrist of the other—the second hand being occupied with his suit-case. He pumped both arms up and down with enthusiasm.

"Well, if this isn't the best thing that ever happened? I'll tell London it is!"

Nan looked on breathlessly, and saw Jervis break into a smile.

"Fazackerley!" he cried.

The little man puffed harder.

"I'll tell the world! This is the best thing I've struck since—well, there isn't any since about it. I'd liefer have run up against you than have gotten an invitation to tea with Mussolini with *carte blanche* to print every word he said and film him whilst he said it—and I can't say more than that. So far he's eluded me. I've interviewed President Hoover, and Ramsay Macdonald, and Clemenceau, and Trotzky, and the unfortunate late Czar, and Gene Tunney, and Dean Inge, and Don Bradman, and Al Capone; but so far Mussolini has eluded me. I'm not making him my life-work, but I'd like to get him; so when I say I'd rather have run up against you—well, there it is—right from the heart—straight from the pulsating fount of the emotions!"

Jervis continued to smile.

"You'll collect a crowd, F.F."

"What else do I live for?" said Mr Fazackerley. He turned, holding Jervis by the arm. "I've got to apologize for butting in—" His bright brown eyes darted a question at Nan; his manner intimated plainly that he awaited an introduction.

Nan wanted to run away. She wondered what Jervis would say if she did. Then she wondered what he was going to say if she didn't. There was, actually, only one bewildered moment before he said,

"Let me introduce, Mr Ferdinand Fazackerley."

The next moment Nan's hand was being shaken by one that felt very thin and very strong, and Mr Fazackerley's high-pitched voice was saying earnestly,

"I'm very pleased to meet you—but he hasn't told me who I'm being very pleased to meet."

Before Jervis could speak, Nan said,

"Mrs Weare."

She said it on the impulse that would have prompted her to do anything disagreeable herself rather than leave Jervis to do it. To feel like that about it, and to proclaim herself his wife, thrust at her with such a sharply pointed pain that it was all that she could do not to cry out. The effort she made brought a flush to her cheeks.

The darting brown eyes went from her to Jervis, and back again to her flushed face. Mr Fazackerley still had his left hand on Jervis' sleeve; with his right he continued to shake Nan's hand.

"If that isn't great!" he said. "Mrs Weare, I've just got to say all over again how pleased I am. If this isn't just the greatest thing that ever happened! Where can we go and talk?"

"I've got an appointment with my solicitor," said Jervis. "But after that—"

"You'll both dine with me. If you're engaged, just telephone them and say you're dead. What's the good of a beneficent invention like the telephone if it can't get you out of an engagement? We'll dine at the Luxe in our gladdest rags. I've a tuxedo in my trunk—I've a claw-hammer somewhere—I'll go the whole hog and buy a white tie. We've just got to celebrate!" He beamed brightly upon Nan. "If you knew what a lot I've heard about Rosamund, and how badly I've wanted to meet you—"

Mr Fazackerley stopped there, because his left hand felt the sudden jerk with which Jervis drew back, whilst to his right was communicated a tremor. Nan's hand quivered for a moment in his and then stiffened.

Mr Fazackerley released it, stepped back a pace, darted a searching glance from a pale girl to a horrified young man, and exclaimed,

"Great Wall Street! Have I dropped a brick?"

He looked so alarmed and disconcerted that Nan stopped being embarrassed.

"I'm not Rosamund," she said quite simply. "My name's Nan. Please don't mind—it wasn't your fault a bit."

Mr Fazackerley recovered himself. It took a good deal to disconcert him, and he possessed recuperative powers of the first order. He congratulated Jervis in a manner quite untinged with self-consciousness. He congratulated Nan on having married one of the best fellows in a tight place that he ever wanted to see.

"*He* won't tell you how we fought twenty brigands in Anatolia, or the story of the one-eyed commissar—but I will some day. I've no false modesty—it don't pay in my profession."

Nan smiled at him, the smile that brought the dimples.

"What is it?" she said. "Your profession, I mean. What are you?"

"A Rolling Stone," said Ferdinand Fazackerley with a flourish.

He picked up the tin hat-box and the Gladstone bag.

"*Lord*, F.F.!" said Jervis. "Where did you get that relic? I thought the last Gladstone bag faded out before the war."

"It's a good little grip," said Ferdinand, "and a real antique into the bargain. If I was to tell you that I got this grip from a man that got it from Enrico Caruso with a dossier showing it had belonged way back in Victoria's day to the late William Ewart Gladstone himself—what would you say?"

Nan saw Jervis laugh, and felt the thrill of a young mother whose child does something new. She hadn't seen him laugh before. It changed his face; it softened it. It made Nan's heart dance.

"What would you say?" said Mr Fazackerley.

"I should say you were a first-class liar, F.F.," said Jervis.

IX

Mr Fazackerley left Nan and Jervis standing where he had found them. He shook them both warmly by the hand, adjured them to remember that they were dining with him at the Luxe at a quarter to eight, and left them, to be instantly engulfed by a stream of outgoing passengers exactly like the one from which he had been, as it were, thrown up. An eddy caught him, and he and his rucksack, his Gladstone bag, his camera, and his bright yellow boots were absorbed.

Nan and Jervis looked at each other, and for a moment a shared glint of humour gave to each of them a sense of intimacy. To be able to laugh at the same things is one of the three indissoluble bonds. If only for a moment, it linked them.

Nan said, "What a *lamb*!"

And Jervis said, "Good old F.F.!"

And then the moment passed. The laughter went out of Nan's eyes.

"You'll explain about my not being able to dine with him—won't you?" she said.

Jervis put his head back a little; it made his chin jut out. It was an obstinate chin.

"Why can't you dine with him?"

If Nan had assumed that she *was* going dine with them, Jervis would probably have felt annoyed. Since she assumed that she was not going to make an unwanted third, he at once discovered a number of good reasons why she should do so.

"You'll have heaps to say to each other. I should be in the way."

"Well, if you don't come, he'll think you're offended."

Nan considered this for a moment.

"Do you want me to come?" she said when the moment was over.

Jervis relaxed, smiled quite unexpectedly, and answered,

"Well, I do—if it wouldn't bore you too much."

"Oh, it wouldn't bore me."

"You see," he said, "if you don't come, he'll think it odd, or he'll think you're angry. I'm very fond of F.F. and I'd hate to have his feelings hurt that way, and—" He hesitated, then flashed her a look of something like appeal. "I—it struck me there isn't really any reason why he should think there's anything unusual about—us."

"I'll come if you want me to," said Nan.

Their eyes met, and Jervis felt something that he had not felt before. He could not have said quite what it was. It came, and was gone again. It was as if something had touched, very lightly touched, some sensitive spot so deep down in his consciousness that he could not tell what it was that was stirred.

Both of them came out of that moment with a faint sense of shock. Jervis caught sight of the station clock and exclaimed.

"Poor old Page will be cursing me!"

With a queer leap of the pulses Nan realized that she had forgotten, actually forgotten, why she had come to meet Jervis.

He was crossing the platform.

"I'll call for you if you will tell me your address. I don't know why I didn't ask you for it. I ought to have it."

She said, *"Please"*; and then, "I haven't told you why I came to meet you. It's very important."

He turned half round, frowning.

"Can't you tell me at dinner?"

"No, I can't. It's urgent."

He stopped, faced her, and said,

"What is it? Page *will* curse me"

The colour burned in Nan's cheeks. How can you tell an impatient, champing man that you believe someone is going to try and kill him in the open street in broad daylight?

She said with a gasp, "It's no good—you won't believe

me''; and could have said nothing that would so instantly have caught his attention.

"Why—what's up?"

"Will you believe me?" said Nan.

"Well, you might give me a chance one way or the other."

They were within a few feet of an empty bench. Nan put her hand on his arm and pointed to it. They went over to the bench and sat down.

"I don't see how you're going to believe me," said Nan desperately.

Jervis stared at her. What on earth was she going to say? He decided that it wouldn't hurt old Page to wait.

"Go on!" he said.

"People do get run over," said Nan breathlessly.

"Oh, constantly."

"Someone's going to try and run you over."

"What for?"

"Five hundred pounds," said Nan in a shred of a voice.

Jervis stared harder. She was awfully pale. Her eyes were wide, and solemn, and frightened.

"My dear girl, what are you talking about?"

Nan began to tell him as well as she could. Now that she had to put the thing into words, it set not only her voice but the whole of her shaking.

"I don't understand," said Jervis. "You heard these two men talking?"

Nan nodded.

"How could you? Why didn't they see you?"

She showed him with a finger set at right angles to another finger.

"It was a c-corner. I came up behind the t-taxi. The driver had his b-back to me."

"Tell me exactly what you heard."

She said it all over again.

"He said, 'It's the four-fifteen all right. You'll have to hurry.' He said, 'Let him come out of the station and get well away.' He said you were sure to walk because you had a craze for exercise."

Jervis was bending forward looking at her intently.

"You heard my name?"

"No—not your name."

"Then what does all this amount to?"

"Please, *please* listen."

He moved impatiently.

Nan went on.

"The driver said, suppose you took a taxi; and *he* said, 'Then you must do the best you can.' And the driver said he wasn't keen; and *he* said, 'Take it or leave it!' And the driver said that five hundred pounds was five hundred pounds, and that 'jug' was 'jug'—that's prison, isn't it? And then they talked about his getting two months for dangerous driving; and the driver was afraid it might be a lot more, but in the end he said, 'All right, I'll do it,' " She stopped and clenched one hand upon the other.

"And what's all this got to do with me?" said Jervis.

"I knew they were talking about you."

"But why? What made you think of it? Who were these people? Did you know them? What made you listen to what they were saying?"

"I knew them," said Nan in a small steadfast voice.

"Who were they?"

It was like being pushed when he spoke in that quick, impatient way.

"She got out of the taxi. I knew her at once." Nan didn't look at him; she looked down at her clenched hands.

"She? This is the first time you've mentioned a woman."

Nan nodded.

"She got out of the taxi and went into the house."

"But who?"

"Rosamund Carew," said Nan.

Jervis sprang to his feet, then, as suddenly, sat down again.

"What d'you mean by saying a thing like that?"

Nan lifted her chin a little. She wasn't a bit afraid of him when he was angry.

"I'm telling you what happened."

He threw back his head and laughed incredulously.

"Go on with the fairy tale!"

A fire of pure rage burned in Nan's cheeks and brightened her eyes. She stopped looking at her hands and let Jervis have the full benefit of the blaze.

"Mr Leonard got out after her and went into the house. That was when I got behind the taxi. I wasn't going to listen—I wasn't thinking about listening—I just didn't want him to see me. Then he came out of the house and talked to the driver. I told you what they said—and I told you before I began that you wouldn't believe me."

Stinging tears rushed to her eyes. Jervis saw the blaze go out, saw the grey darken, soften, deepen. He said in an angry voice,

"What have you got against Leonard? Good Lord—the thing's absurd! Why, you admit that I wasn't even mentioned."

"They were talking about you," said Nan. "They *were*."

He burst out laughing.

"My dear girl—what a mare's nest! What conceivable motive could there be?"

Nan looked up at him, white and steady.

"Who would come in for your property if you were killed in an accident today?" she said.

Jervis did not start, he stiffened. There was a tingling pause. Nan felt as if she had hit a lump of dynamite. She waited for the explosion, but it did not come. The silence went on. She could not take her breath while it went on like that; and just as she was feeling as if something must give way, he said in a low, concentrated tone,

"What a perfectly foul thing to say!"

This time Nan felt as if it was she who had been hit. She said,

"Yes, it's foul—" She paused. "But not because I said it."

He became vividly aware of her. There was a bright stain of colour high up in her cheeks—a round bright stain. Her eyes were bright and wide. There was something in them that winced and yet held firm. In his own consciousness an impulse flared—the impulse to beat down that wincing, resisting something. It flared, and went out.

He rose abruptly to his feet.

"I expect there's some explanation. Bits of a conversation are very misleading. Thank you for taking so much trouble about it."

Nan got up too. His being polite was worse than anything. It made her feel giddy with pain. The colour went quite out of her face. She said,

"Good-bye—I'd better not come tonight."

It was a relief to see him frown.

"Of course you'll come! We settled that. Give me your address, and I'll call for you."

He wrote it down on the back of an envelope with a scrap of pencil which he fished out of a trouser pocket.

"Old Page *will* be cursing me!" he said, and turned to go.

When he had gone a couple of yards he became aware of Nan running to keep up with him.

"I'm sorry—but what's a tuxedo?"

He looked over his shoulder at her and said,

"Dinner-jacket."

"Oh—but he said something about a clawhammer. What's that?"

"American for tail-coat. I must be getting along."

She was still running.

"Yes, I know—but—oh, you *will* be careful, won't you?"

This time she got a black frown. And then suddenly he laughed.

"I'll take a policeman along to pick up the bits!" he said, and was gone.

X

NAN HAD HAD NO ANSWER TO HER QUESTION. SHE DID not need one. She knew very well what would happen to Jervis Weare's property if he died without children. Everything would go to Rosamund Carew—Rosamund Veronica Leonard Carew. She had typed old Ambrose Weare's will, and she remembered its provisions. If Jervis wasn't married within three months and a day of his grandfather's death, everything went to Rosamund. And if Jervis died without leaving a child, everything went to Rosamund.

Rosamund Veronica *Leonard* Carew. . . . . Nan was unshaken in her conviction that she had heard Robert Leonard arranging for an accident to happen to Jervis. Perhaps Rosamund didn't know. She had gone on into the house, and Robert Leonard had come back to speak to the driver. A faint cold shudder ran over Nan. Rosamund Carew *couldn't* know. Only a week ago she and Jervis were engaged—they were going to be married. They must have planned their life together—they must have kissed. The shudder came again. She saw Jervis stooping his dark head to kiss beautiful Rosamund Carew. Rosamund could not know.

She began to walk, and came out of the station. What was she going to do next?

There wasn't anything for her to do. The affair had passed out of her hands. She had warned Jervis, and he didn't believe her. She wondered if he truly didn't believe her, or if he just wouldn't believe her. Whether he believed her or not, he couldn't un-know what she had told him. A man who has been warned can never go back to where he was before the warning. The weight that had been upon her lifted. A little of Jervis' own scepticism touched her. After all, she might have made a mistake. *No, she hadn't.* Then again, chill and reasonable, that "Suppose it was a mistake."

She had a vehement revulsion. She had been a fool to be frightened. There was nothing to be frightened of. She began to think about the evening. If she hadn't got to be frightened about Jervis, how frightfully exciting it would be to look forward to dining at the Luxe with Ferdinand Fazackerley. How extraordinary to meet him after all these years! She had always wondered whether she would know him again.

She got into a bus and sat there thinking how strange life was, and how interesting. Ten years ago Ferdinand Fazackerley, walking on Croyston rocks, had chanced on an unconscious young man and a frantic child of twelve. She shut her eyes and saw the rocks, the low grey sky, and the sea coming up, coming nearer, with its frightful irresistible force. It was a picture that had never faded. Like the scar on her arm, it no longer hurt. If she looked at the scar, she could see its triangular shape and the white crinkling of the skin; and if she looked into her mind, she could see the flooding pool, Jervis ghastly white, the stain of his blood on her shoulder, and her straining agonized efforts to keep his head above water. Then F.F.—Ferdinand Fazackerley—and the high, kind voice with its unfamiliar accent going right on through her half-consciousness . . . She was most terribly pleased to have met him again. But not for the world was he ever to guess that they were meeting *again.* a grown-up Mrs Weare couldn't possibly evoke any memory of the half-drowned child of ten years ago.

Having settled this to her satisfaction, Nan got out of the bus. If she was going to dine at the Luxe with Mr Ferdinand Fazackerley in a clawhammer, it was quite certain that she must buy herself a dress for the occasion, and she knew just what dress she was going to buy. Cynthia had not been married without a modest trousseau. To buy pretty frocks for Cynthia had been balm to Nan's own heartache. She had bought for Cynthia, and had resisted the temptation to buy for herself; but there had been one temptation which it had been very difficult to resist. She had got as far as trying the pretty filmy thing on. It had given her a delicious sense of being somebody else, someone who hadn't a care in the world.

She opened the door of the shop. Suppose it was gone. . . . . . The pleasant dark girl who had been so interested in Cynthia came forward.

Nan had a sudden brilliant idea.

"May I telephone?"

"Oh, certainly."

She gave Mr Page's number, and then had a nervous reaction. Suppose Villiers didn't answer the telephone. Mr Watson must be back from his holiday. Suppose it was he who answered. It was so difficult to realize that Mr Watson no longer mattered. She heard the click of the receiver, and the voice of Miss Villiers.

"Hello!"

Nan felt a difficulty about giving her name. She said quickly,

"Oh, Villiers—don't tell anyone I rang up. I only wanted to know if Mr Weare had arrived."

"Just come, dear. . . . . Yes, that's all right."

"Oh, thank you!" said Nan. A feeling of happy relief bubbled up in her. Even to her own ears her voice sounded warm and soft. She hoped it didn't sound like that to Villiers.

She rang off and turned to the now all-absorbing question of the grey dress.

Grey—any dull thing can be grey—hodden grey, field grey—grey sky, grey water, grey cloud. There ought to be a different word to give to beautiful things. Nan's dress was beautiful, and it had that last subtlest quality of beauty—it made her feel beautiful too.

She put it on and looked, half frightened, at her own reflection.

"I'm going to rather a special party tonight," she said to the nice dark girl.

The nice dark girl smiled.

"Well, you couldn't have anything that suited you better," she said.

Nan looked at herself rather solemnly. The dress gave her a slim elegance. There was just a hint of silver about it. She must have silver shoes to go with it, and she must have her hair cut and waved.

She bought the dress, and the coat that went with it, heard the amount of the bill without a tremor, and wrote her first cheque on the account which Mr Page had opened in her name. It was not only the first cheque on the new account, it was also the first cheque she had ever written. The dress wasn't a dress at all; it was a symbol. It meant that she was Nan Weare, and not Nan Forsyth any more. It stood for a plunge into the unknown.

This was all rather solemn; but under the solemnity there were little warm currents of excitement and anticipation. Would Jervis like the dress? Would he like *her*?

At half past seven she was ready and waiting. Her hair had been cut and done in loose waves. It was so becoming that she had arranged then and there to have it permanently waved next day. She had silver shoes. Her dress was like a silver mist. It darkened her eyes and hair, and brought out the fine quality of her skin. The excitement put a rose in each cheek. She knelt in front of the low dressing-table to see her head in the very small mirror, and then mounted insecurely upon the bed to catch a glimpse of her silver feet. She practised a dance-step, and then stopped for fear of getting hot. It would be dreadful if the wave didn't last through the evening. She wondered if they would dance. No, of course they wouldn't. It would be marvellous to dance with Jervis.

She looked at her watch. Twenty to eight. She made up her mind to sit quite still and peaceful. Jervis would probably allow a quarter of an hour to get to the Luxe. He ought really to allow a little longer—you simply couldn't count on not getting into a traffic block.

The church of St Tryphenius round the corner in Lasham Street chimed three times for a quarter to eight. Nan jumped up and went to the window. The entrance to the house was in Lasham Street, but her window looked into a narrow alley called Cutting's Way. Taxis sometimes used it to avoid the corner where Lasham Street ran into the main road.

A boy went past on a bicycle. Three or four foot-passengers followed him. A cart went slowly and noisily by.

It was ten minutes to eight.

Nan ran down into the hall. It was narrow and dark, and it smelt strongly of the kippers which the Warren family had been having for tea. She opened the door, went out on to the step, and stood looking up and down the street. Something was beginning to say horrible things to her in a whisper. The whisper came from deep down in her own consciousness. She couldn't really hear what it was saying; she only knew that it was something horrible. She stood on the step in her grey coat and her grey dress; and suddenly they were grey, not silver any more, and a shadow which she could not see came over the face of the sky and darkened her heart. She couldn't see it, but she could feel it. Everything in her darkened and shrank.

She watched a dozen cars go by. Not one of them stopped. A girl and a man came out of No. 31 and walked away arm in arm. The thing that was whispering to Nan came nearer and spoke louder, "Jervis—they've got him. He wouldn't take your warning. He wouldn't believe you— they've got him." It got louder and louder. The words rang in her ears, clanging and echoing back upon themselves. The clock of St. Tryphenius whirred, groaned, chimed four times for the hour, and began to strike eight.

XI

THE LAST STROKE OF EIGHT DIED AWAY AND LEFT NAN shivering. She couldn't go on standing here on the doorstep. She must do something, but she didn't know what.

She moved, and just as if her movement had broken into a set pause, a car turned out of Cutting's Way and drew up at the kerb. Jervis jumped out, and at the sight of him Nan knew how frightened she had been.

"I'm so sorry to have kept you waiting. I'm frightfully late, but I had to go back—"

She said something—she had no idea of what it was—and then they were in the taxi, and she was staring out of the window and trying to quiet the beating of her heart. Just for an instant she caught sight of the edge of a bandage where his left cuff slipped back. She was ready to swear that it had not been there this afternoon.

She got herself quiet, and turned round on him.

"What made you so late? I thought something had happened."

"Well, something did happen." She took a breath. "My tie wouldn't tie."

Nan looked at the tie. It had a very ordinary appearance. Her eyes, suddenly bright, gave him the lie.

"What has been happening?"

"Happening?" His eyes met hers with a hint of distance and a hint of mockery.

"Yes."

The distance went; the mockery remained.

"First new bulletin, copyright reserved?"

"Yes."

"Barometric pressure—" said Jervis.

"Is your wrist broken?"

"Certainly not. Why should it be?"

"Barometric pressure," suggested Nan.

"Nothing so original."

"Please tell me."

"There's nothing to tell."

"How did you hurt your wrist?"

Jervis leaned back into his corner of the taxi.

"You might say I had bumped it up against a coincidence."

"What sort of coincidence?" said Nan in a whisper.

She too leaned back. If she were too near him now, he might see or feel what she was feeling. She leaned back, but she could not take her eyes from his.

"A very neat one," said Jervis—"very neat and pat. You warn me against a villain in a taxi. I proceed to old Page's by tube—not, I'm afraid, on account of the warning, but because our agreeable conversation didn't leave me time to walk. I see Page. I walk uneventfully to Carrington Square and put on my best clawhammer. I then stroll across the square to the cab-rack, and just as I'm turning the corner a car swerves to avoid a dog and sends me spinning. If I hadn't seen him out of the tail of my eye and jumped for it, I'm afraid you'd have had to dine *tête-à-tête* with F.F."

"Are you hurt?" said Nan quickly and irrepressibly.

"The clawhammer is a wreck. That's what made me late. I had to fall back on my reserve, which won't really stand daylight."

"Your arm—" said Nan.

"A messy cut, efficiently bandaged by Jenks, who would be perfectly happy if I would arrange to have a minor accident once or twice a week to keep his hand in. He was a great performer with a first field dressing during the war, and complains that he's getting rusty. He buttles rather under protest."

Nan swept Jenks away with an impulsive movement.

"Did you see the driver of the car that knocked you over?"

"I did not," said Jervis. "I saw nothing except a lot of very fine coloured stars, and when I stopped seeing them, there was no driver to see."

"He didn't wait?"

"He did not."

"And you call that a coincidence!" There was a fine scorn in her voice.

"I think we will both call it a coincidence," said Jervis. His tone was light, cool, and even.

Nan took a breath and sat back. She felt easily, coolly, airily put in her place. Her place was a long way off. It certainly didn't entitle her to make suggestions about Miss Carew and Mr Leonard.

By the time they reached the Luxe she had herself in hand. Jervis talked pleasantly and lightly all the way; she had only to sit in her corner and listen.

Mr Ferdinand Fazackerley was waiting for them in the lounge. He looked very odd in evening dress. The clawhammer was not only an archaic model, but it looked as if he had made a habit of sleeping in it for years. His white tie was an obvious jemima. Beneath the electric light his hair was like a newly scraped carrot. His bright darting eyes welcomed Nan, and dwelt affectionately on Jervis. A prolonged hand-shaking attested his enthusiasm.

"This is great!" he said, and went on saying it at intervals whist he piloted them to a reserved table in the famous Gold Room.

He had an eager, affectionate manner that was pure balm to Nan. For the first time, she could see herself as Jervis' wife. F.F.'s admiring gaze approved her. It darted from her to Jervis, and told Jervis that he was a lucky man. It came back to Nan with a twinkling appreciation of just how delightful a thing it must be to be Jervis' wife.

"If you folks aren't hungry, you can go home. My last meal is way back so far that I've lost touch with it so to speak. I'm going right through this menu—and I won't say that I mightn't have a second helping here and there, just to fill up the corners. I've felt hungrier, but I've never felt greedier. It's a good menu.'' He skidded off into the story of how he once walked from Vienna to Berlin without a cent.

Nan enjoyed her dinner very much. With her first mouthful of food she realized that, like Ferdinand, she had rather lost touch with her last meal—it had not been much of a meal either. When you are tired and unhappy, you are apt not to notice how little you are eating—and Mrs Warren's cooking was not calculated to tempt a halting appetite. It was rather like a dream to be wearing a pretty frock and dining at the Luxe. In a dream there is no past and no future. She gave herself up to the dream, and a reviving tide of happiness rose in her and blotted out everything except the present.

She watched a new Jervis. She had never seen just that amused sparkle in his eyes or heard that warm, bantering note in his voice. She listened in a smiling silence whilst they capped stories and reminded one another of ridiculous or strenuous adventures shared. She learned by piecing scraps of their talk together that they had knocked about Europe and the Near East for the best part of a year in one another's company.

''I was doing hot articles on *Great Men's Hats*, and *Politicians' Pyjamas*, and *Brigands' Boots*—that's where we bumped up against it in Anatolia—and *What Criminals Like for Breakfast*. Now what do you suppose the biggest rip of the lot began the day on? You don't know—you can't guess? No—I'll bet my life you can't! Bread and milk—in a bowl with pink rosebuds round the edge. I tell you, I sat there and saw him putting it away—but you needn't believe me if you don't want to.''

''You were writing articles. And what was Jervis doing?'' said Nan. In this pleasant dream it was quite easy to say Jervis. It warmed and comforted her to say his name like that, as if it were her daily, familiar use.

''What was Jervis doing?'' Her colour rose and her eyes shone as she said it.

"Jervis was mending a hole in his head," said Ferdinand Fazackerley.

Was it fancy, or did he hold her eyes with his for a moment? She repeated his words mechanically.

"A hole in his head?"

With a wrenching sensation she looked away and saw Jervis frowning.

"I'd had a fall," he said. "I came down on some slippery rocks and broke my head. I was just down from Oxford, so I got a year's holiday and went racketing round with F.F. He picked me up just as the tide was going to finish me off, and has stuck to me like a burr ever since."

"Do burrs pick people up?" said Nan. "I thought it was the other way around." She laughed to cover the faint tremor in her voice, and was aware of Ferdinand Fazackerley's eyes upon her.

"Mrs Weare, don't you take any notice of him. He's no hand at telling a yarn, and I'm a whale at it. Besides, he was dead to the world, and if the tide had drowned him, he wouldn't have known a thing about it. No—if you want the goods, I'm your man." His restless, curious eyes thrust questions at her: "Am I going to tell this story? Do you want me to tell it? If not—why not? Yes—why, why, *why*?" The high light in the brown eyes was like a bright elusive question mark.

Jervis' voice broke in on them.

"There's nothing to tell. F.F.'s a professional yarn-spinner."

"Don't you want the story, Mrs Weare—exclusive tale of eye-witness? Or—do you know it already?"

Panic knocked at Nan's heart.

She said, "Please tell me," and heard her voice hurry and stumble. He couldn't know—he couldn't know anything. And if he did—no, he couldn't—she couldn't face it—not here, not now, with Jervis looking at her. No, he wasn't looking at her, he was looking with a half-frowning tolerance at F.F.; and F.F. was saying,

"Don't look so scared—he got out of it all right, thanks to the pluckiest kid I've ever run across." He flung round on Jervis. "Did you ever find out who she was?"

Jervis said, "No."

Nan leaned forward with her elbows on the table and her chin in her cupped hands. The movement was purely instinctive. Her heart was beating and her lips trembling. She pressed hard with one of her fingers against the corner of her mouth.

"Well then, Mrs Weare, you shall hear the story."

"It won't interest her," said Jervis.

"Mrs Weare—you hear him. What do you say to that?" Nan lifted her chin for a moment.

"Oh, please tell me," she said quite steadily. Her grey eyes were dark. They met F.F.'s dancing question marks with a certain soft dignity.

He knew—he knew her—and he knew that Jervis didn't know.

She dropped her chin on her hand again, and waited for what he was going to do with his knowledge.

"You shall have the exclusive story. If Jervis don't want to listen to it, he can light out and leave us to it. Now, let me see . . . . . nine—ten—it'll be ten years ago. Yes, exactly ten, because it was August and I'd gone down to Croyston— well, I can't remember just why I had gone down, but there I was, and being there, I went for a hike along the beach and as near as possible got cut off by the tide round Croyde Head."

"How many thousand words does this run to, F.F.?" said Jervis.

Mr Fazackerley took no notice.

"I was scrambling along pretty high up, when I saw something that gave me a jolt. You don't expect to see heads lying about on a British beach—and there, about a hundred yards away on the edge of a pool, was a gruesome looking head with a grey face and black hair and bloodstains all complete. Well, it gave me a jolt, and by the time my brain got to work on the probability that the head had got a body attached to it, and that the body wanted yanking out of that pool p.d.q., there wasn't much time to waste. The tide had fairly got going, and was coming in with nasty greenish rollers one on top of the other. I did a record over that hundred yards of beach, and I didn't get there any too soon. And when I did get there, I got another jolt and a much bigger one. The head was lying clear of the water, but only just, and the reason that it was clear was because there was a girl crouched down in the pool propping it up. She'd got her shoulders under his shoulders. The water helped with the weight, or she couldn't have done it, but every time a wave flooded the pool it came over her, and every time it ebbed she had to brace herself against the cutting edge of the rock to save him from being sucked down into the pool. The last wave broke clean over her head, and the return of it cut her arm to the bone against the rock. I should say she'd a scar there she'd never lose. And all she said when I pulled her out was, 'Is he alive?' Well—can you beat it?''

The scar was on Nan's left arm, three inches below the elbow. She moved naturally as F.F.'s bright eyes swept her face. The movement took her back, turned her towards Jervis, dropped her hands into her lap, and hid the small white scar against the cloudy grey of her frock. She caught a queer remembering look on Jervis' face.

F.F. was speaking to him.

"Pity you never found out who she was."

The queer look deepened.

"Is it a pity? I—don't—know," he said slowly.

Nan heard her own voice with surprise. She had not meant to speak, but she heard herself say,

"You would rather not know her, really?"

As before, something passed between them—a curious flash of understanding. Then he said with a short laugh,

"Well, it would be rather difficult to live up to that sort of beginning—wouldn't it?"

She nodded slowly and gravely.

"Now, that's just your crazy British fear of giving away the fact that you're chock full of romance and ideals. You're afraid of meeting that plucky kid, not because you wouldn't know what to say to her or how to say it, but because you'd know very well, and you'd be real scared of your romantic nature getting out of hand—slipping the collar, so to speak—and rushing into words which you'd never be able to think of again without blushing scarlet." He turned to Nan, his ginger head on one side, his eyes snapping. "Englishmen are very romantic—but it's a secret vice—they consider it indelicate. And that's why Jervis wouldn't meet that girl for the world and a little bit over—she might make him realize what romantic feelings he's got about her, and then of course he'd never be able to look her in the face again."

XII

IT WAS PERHAPS A MINUTE LATER THAT MR FAZACKERLEY, looking round to catch the waiter's eye, saw something which distracted his attention. He gazed with frank interest at a table set against the wall on the far side of the room. Two people had just risen from it, a man and a woman. Mr Fazackerley gave his wholehearted attention to the woman.

"Now that's what I call a looker!" he said.

The woman stood against the golden wall. She wore a dull gold dress that matched her hair. It clung as closely as a dress can cling to a singularly perfect figure. It was so plain and so heavy as to give her the appearance of a statue—a golden statue set against a golden wall. Then, as she moved, the statue came alive. The glowing white of her neck and arms, the brilliance of her eyes, took the light and enchanted it.

Mr Fazackerley's admiration rose to enthusiasm.

"Great Tammany! That's a looker!" he repeated. "Do you see her—over there against the wall?"

Jervis Weare had seen her twenty minutes ago. It was like Rosamund to be facing the music—he could still admire that in her. She was with Robert Leonard. Was she facing the music? Or had she perhaps counted on meeting nobody who would know her? A bit of folly, that; for nowadays even August is not to be counted upon, since anyone may turn up from anywhere at any moment.

He smiled slightly as he glanced about the room. Already, as they came in, he had returned an interested bow from Mrs Manning Temple. The three people with her were strangers, and it had instantly occurred to him that it would not be Mrs Manning Temple's fault if they remained strangers to his affairs. From where he was sitting he could without turning his head see at least half a dozen people whom he knew—old James Mulroy, a very competent and industrious gossip; Lady Tetterley, his nearest neighbour and a far-away cousin on his mother's side; the Carters—Nonie Carter pop-eyed with interest; and Mrs Melliter, with Enid who was to have been one of Rosamund's bridesmaids.

With a faintly sardonic gleam in his eye he turned from Enid to watch Rosamund. She spoke smilingly over her shoulder to Leonard and moved clear of the table. He looked away from her to Nan. She was sitting back in her chair, and she too was watching Rosamund Carew. Jervis looked at her, and, for the first time, really saw her. It was as if Rosamund had flung him a challenge, and he must look to his weapons. From the first, Nan had been a weapon against Rosamund. Now, in this public place, there came the first encounter.

He looked to see how his weapon would serve him, and was faintly startled. She was sitting back in her chair. A pretty turn of the neck and a graceful pose—that was what he saw first. And, directly upon that, he received the strongest impression of youth. Rosamund and he were nearly of an age, Rosamund a few months the elder. Nan, sitting there, with her eyes wide, her lips a little apart, and a flush on her cheeks, had the air of a child. Rosamund was a beautiful woman. Nan had freshness and grace, a direct gaze, a young round chin, and on occasion a dimple. Her hands lay in her lap. The direct gaze was fixed with interest and admiration on Rosamund, but the interest and admiration were alike tinged with something else. Jervis did not know what the something was. It drew her brows together and put a faintly distressed curve upon her mouth.

He looked where she was looking, and saw Rosamund and Robert Leonard coming towards them. Something inside him laughed—a hard, angry laugh. The challenge was to be pressed. This was throwing down the glove with a vengeance. And how damnably clever! If he could be pricked into rudeness, Rosamund would most undoubtedly score. He had not troubled himself as to what people were saying; but if he were rude to Rosamund in public, it would undoubtedly play into her hand—and if anyone in the world knew how quick and sudden a temper he had, it was Rosamund. Even with his brain laying down the law to it, he could feel the hot violent leap of the rage which he could only just control.

Rosamund Carew came on with Robert Leonard at her shoulder. Nan's lips parted wistfully, her heart sank. She was so very beautiful. Her hair was back in a smooth gold wave from her brow to the nape of her neck, where it broke into tiny curls that were caught in a dull gold slide. She moved as if she knew how beautiful she was; her eyes held the certainty of it.

She stopped at the empty side of the table, touched it with a hand that wore one big sapphire, and sent a faintly smiling look across it.

"Well, Jervis?" she said.

Jervis smiled too, a sudden brilliant smile which changed his face. It frightened Nan a good deal more than any frown of his had ever done. As he smiled, he rose.

Ferdinand Fazackerley was already on his feet.

Nan looked up at all these standing people. Her wide eyes and tilted chin gave her for an instant a look of piteous inquiry. Then she got up too.

"I haven't congratulated you," said Rosamund.

"No," said Jervis pleasantly. Then, "I hope you're going to."

"When you have introduced me to your wife." She turned her eyes on Nan. They were just like the sapphire of her ring—as darkly blue, as cold beneath the brilliance and the colour. She smiled with her lips, but the smile rose no higher.

Nan heard Jervis say her name. It was the first time since he had said, "I, Jervis, take thee, Nan." He said,

"Nan, let me introduce my cousin, Rosamund Carew." She was aware of his smile. "You have heard of her."

"And I have never heard of you," said Rosamund very sweetly. "That doesn't seem fair—does it?"

Jervis watched them with interest. To Rosamund's perfect social technique Nan had only youth and inexperience to offer; yet, to his surprise, she suffered less than he could have supposed possible from the contact. She had the air of a well-bred child a little unsure of what it must do next. But the breeding was there; it kept her head up and her eyes steady and clear. Jervis wondered how old Page's typist came by it.

He thrust F.F. into the breach.

"You've heard enough of Ferdinand Fazackerley."

"Are you F.F.?" said Rosamund. Her voice, like all her movements, had a slow grace. It was rather a deep voice.

"I am," said Ferdinand—"and I can't begin to say how pleased I am to meet you. I don't know why it's never happened before. As sure as ever I've been in this country, you've been somewhere else."

Rosamund smiled upon him and introduced Robert Leonard— to him first, and then to Nan.

Mr Fazackerley shook hands with enthusiasm. Nan acknowledged the privilege of Mr Leonard's acquaintance with the slightest, gravest inclination of the head. No one could have told how terribly her heart was beating: To be so close to the man who had tried to kill Jervis, not once but twice! With all her heart she believed that he had struck down Jervis ten years ago and left him to drown on Croyston rocks. With all her heart she believed that he had offered five hundred pounds to the driver who had run Jervis down an hour ago. It was horrible to be so near him. She forced herself to look him in the face. She had seen him twice before, but it was by his walk, the carriage of his powerful high-shouldered body, the forward set of the rather large head, that she had recognized him. She saw him face to face for the first time. He had a jutting brow with sparse fair eyebrows; the eyes were deeply and rather closely set, the nose insignificant, the chin jutting again and oddly cleft; a small colourless mustache clipped away from the corners of the mouth showed thin, pale lips; his hair was smooth and mouse-coloured.

Nan felt a stab of fear. The man frightened her. He looked at her over Rosamund's shoulder, and she breathed more freely when he looked away.

Rosamund turned from F.F. and spoke.

"Are you up for long? How can you tear yourself from King's Weare in this weather?"

"I've been seeing my sister married," said Nan. "She sailed for Australia today."

"Then you'll be going down tomorrow, I suppose."

Jervis said, "Yes, tomorrow." He added, quite lightly and smoothly, "So I'm afraid we shan't meet again."

Rosamund took her hand from the table. The sapphire in her ring caught the light. It was darkly blue. Her eyes resembled it as she said,

"We're dancing. Shall we see you—or are you running away?"

"No, we're not running away," said Jervis. That brilliant smile came and went.

Nan had a feeling that he would smile like that if he were fighting for his life. She thought he was fighting for something now. There had been the visible flash of meeting blades when his eyes met Rosamund's.

Rosamund Carew smiled and passed on down the room, spoke for a moment to Lady Tetterley, smiled at Nonie Carter, touched Enid Melliter on the shoulder, and after a word or two passed on and out of sight behind a golden pillar.

"*Well!*" said Mr Fazackerley. He put a wealth of expression into the word; his eyes darted questions from which his tongue refrained. Like King David, he held his tongue, but it was pain and grief to him.

Jervis looked at him rather maliciously.

"Whilst we eat our ices, you shall tell us what you've been doing for the last six months, and then—" He turned on Nan. "Do you like dancing? Would you care to dance?"

They were seated again. A faint sparkle came into Nan's grey eyes. Her mouth did not smile, but a dimple appeared quite close to it, quivered a moment, and was gone.

"I don't think we'll run away," he said. "I think we'll dance. If F.F. makes a clean breast of all his villainies, he shall dance with Rosamund—and I'm sure you'd love a turn with Leonard.''

Her face went blank; her colour was gone.

She said, ''Oh no—I'd rather not.'' Then, with a pathetic earnestness, ''Oh, please don't make me.''

''Then you'll have to put up with me—and I'm nothing like the performer that he is.''

XIII

THE LUXE HAS THE BEST DANCING-FLOOR IN LONDON. Ferdinand found Miss Carew graciously willing to accord him a dance. If Robert Leonard resented having to give way to him, he showed no sign of it, but stood in the mirror-lined archway and watched the curiously matched couple go by.

F.F. was at least an accomplished dancer. As he danced, he talked with considerable verve, whilst Rosamund smiled and listened.

A moment later Jervis and Nan went by. If Ferdinand was an accomplished dancer, the new Mrs Jervis Weare was an exquisite one. Jervis experienced an elusive feeling of being for once at the top of a form to which he had never previously aspired. He looked down at Nan's brown head. He could just see one of her ears. It was little and delicately shaped; the lobe showed pink between short waves of hair.

''I suppose you know how beautifully you dance. I wouldn't have dared ask you if I had known.''

She looked up for a moment—one of those direct looks of hers.

''I was a dancing partner at Solano's for six months before I went to Mr Page,'' she said.

"Did you like it?"

She could hear the frown in his voice.

"No." It was a very sober monosyllable to cover a good deal of shrinking distaste. After a very little pause she added, "I did like the dancing."

"Why did you do it?"

"I couldn't get anything else to do."

"Haven't you any people?"

"Only Cynthia—really."

He was down on that like a flash.

"Who isn't real?"

"An aunt. I couldn't possibly ask her for anything."

"Why?"

She looked up again.

"She's that sort. She finished our education."

"And then?"

"She washed her hands of us. She washed them *very* thoroughly."

He was silent after that. They moved in the rhythm of the music. Nan didn't want him to speak; for when he spoke they were two people with a gulf between them, but in the rhythm of the music they were near, like the blended notes of a chord moving from modulation to modulation, always together, part of a perfect harmony. He held her lightly and firmly. It was like a dream. And then like a dream it changed and broke. The music stopped.

There were seats between the half pillars on two sides of the ballroom. They moved to the nearest and sat down. Now they would have to talk. A little wondering thought as to what they would say to one another came up in Nan's mind like a bubble rising through dark water.

They were hardly seated before Jervis spoke.

"I want to talk to you."

Nan said, "Well?"

He was frowning. By now she knew what that meant. Not anger. When he was angry the frown was different; and when he was very angry he didn't frown at all, he smiled. This sort of frown meant impatience, shyness, perplexity. He said, as if with an effort,

"I want to ask you something."

"Yes?"

"I've been thinking things over. Would you object to coming down to King's Weare for a bit?"

Nan's colour played her a trick. It came into her cheeks with the sting of fire. She looked up startled, and found that he was not looking at her at all; his eyes were on the arched doorway through which Rosamund Carew was passing with Ferdinand Fazackerley. She said,

"Why?"

The last gleam of Rosamund's gold dress disappeared. He jerked his eyes away from the doorway.

"That is what I've been thinking about. Do we want to give people something to talk about, or don't we? It's for you to say of course. Personally—" he met her eyes with a kind of gloomy sparkle in his own—"well, personally, I'm for scoring them off."

"He'd like to score off Rosamund," said a quick insistent thought; and then, "Well, why not? Why shouldn't I help him score?"

"We took this on as a business arrangement, so—just as a matter of business—will you come down to King's Weare?"

Nan very nearly hated him then. She didn't exist for him except as a retort to Rosamund.

"What is the good?" she said, and got a frown that was all impatience.

"How do you mean, what's the good?"

Her courage failed her. Her thoughts said passionately, "We're not husband and wife—we're not going to live together—so what's the good of pretending?"

She managed to say the last words:

"What is the good of pretending? That's what I mean."

"I'm not asking you to pretend anything—I'm asking you to come down to King's Weare."

"Why?"

"Why? Well, do you like London in August? Personally I think it's foul. There's a goodish garden. You'll get tennis—I don't know if you play—and there's quite decent bathing."

"But that's not why," said Nan. Her lips smiled because she told them to smile. Her eyes stung.

Jervis' face changed suddenly; the angry gloom went out of it. With the look of a teasing schoolboy he said,

"You could see I didn't get run over again."

Nan felt a ridiculous warmth and softness flow over her. What was the good of pretending to put up a fight when she knew very well that she couldn't say no to him?—"If he wanted your head on a charger, you'd just tumble over yourself to let him have it."

She did not know how fast her hands held one another. Jervis, looking down, saw the fingers strain and the knuckles whiten—little hands, and rather brown, so that the knuckles showed bone-white. He looked up, pricked to a sudden wonder. He wanted her to come—she'd got to come.

"Well?" he said.

"I'll come," said Nan, and relaxed with a sigh.

When the music began again they crossed the floor. Jervis had fallen silent. He stopped when they reached the arch, and watched one couple after another leave the side and glide into the rhythm of the dance. Something in Nan said, "He's waiting for Rosamund."

He had not very long to wait. Nan knew by the change in his face that he had seen her before she heard Fazackerley's voice and saw the gold dress and the heavy dull gold hair. They came up to the arch, passed through it, and stopped. Rosamund passed Nan as if she were not there, stood all but touching her, and spoke to Jervis.

"Are we going to dance?"

Jervis said, "I don't think so." His face had no expression at all.

Rosamund's faint, smooth laugh sounded.

"It's much too hot really—we'll sit out instead."

Something hung in the balance. Then Jervis laughed too. It was not quite such a pleasant sound.

"Come along," he said, and they went back across the room, her hand on his arm—the handsomest couple there.

An extraordinary flatness descended upon Nan.

"Well, that's a motion I'd like to second!" said Mr Fazackerley with some fervour. "If anyone can think up a hotter wear than a clawhammer and a boiled shirt, I'll hand it to him—and, to come down to real steady bedrock truth,

I'd appreciate the opportunity of a conversation with you, Mrs Weare.''

Nan felt a little alarmed. What did he want to talk about? She walked beside him through the archway with the feeling that she was walking into unknown country.

XIV

ROSAMUND CAREW SETTLED HERSELF INTO THE CORNER OF a gold sofa and lit a cigarette. The smoke hung about her like a bluish mist. Jervis had not spoken a single word. His lips were smiling, his eyes aloof and dark. For a minute or two Rosamund smoked in silence. Then she said lazily,

"Nonie Carter and Enid Melliter have just come in. I hope we look companionable.''

"I hope so.''

She withdrew her cigarette for a moment.

"Hadn't we better talk?''

"Oh, certainly. What shall we talk about—the weather? They say it will be hotter tomorrow.''

She held her cigarette in the hand which rested upon her knee. The smoke went up in a delicate spiral; a fitful spark as fine as a needle-point fretted the edge of the paper.

"I want to talk to you about my money,'' she said.

Jervis continued to smile.

"Your money?''

"Yes.''

"What money?''

She put the cigarette to her lips, drew lightly at it, and laid her hand again upon her knee.

"You know as well as I do that Uncle Ambrose would have left me five hundred a year if he had not thought we were going to be married. He had his own ideas about the man having the purse-strings.''

''Yes—very sensible ideas.''

Rosamund's lashes came down upon her cheek. She conveyed without further effort a complete indifference to Jervis' approval.

''Hadn't we better keep to the facts?'' she said. ''He left me five hundred pounds. That's nothing—I can't live on nothing—and you have married someone else. Those I think are the facts.''

''Undoubtedly.''

''Well?''

The smoke went up between them.

''My dear Rosamund, as you say—those are the facts.''

She turned her head for a moment, sent a smile across the room to Lady Tetterley, and, still smiling, returned to Jervis.

''I'm afraid I wasn't listening. Mabel Tetterley caught my eye. Now—about this money. You will of course carry out Uncle Ambrose's wishes.''

''As?'' said Jervis.

''Well, I can't *live* on five hundred a year,'' said Rosamund.

''I'm afraid you've—miscalculated. There was never any question of five hundred. The original figure was three. Page will tell you that.''

Rosamund's eyebrows rose slightly.

''That is merely ridiculous,'' she said.

''I'm afraid I don't follow you.''

''I can't live on three hundred.''

Jervis' eyes hardened.

''I'm afraid we're talking at cross purposes. My grandfather didn't leave you anything at all except a sum down for your trousseau, so neither five hundred nor three hundred a year are in question.''

She lifted her cigarette again. The ash broke and fell, powdering the gold of her dress. She was silent for a moment, inhaling the smoke. In the silence thoughts moved between them—violent, resentful, dominant, resisting. With half closed eyes Rosamund continued to smoke. Whatever happened, he should speak next. If it was a battle between them, she knew where her advantage lay. She sat entrenched in silence. In the end it was he who broke it.

"I don't think there's anything to be gained by this discussion. You played me the dirtiest trick I've ever heard of—and now you want your legacy."

"And a bit over," said Miss Carew, her blue eyes veiled.

"I'm afraid you won't get it. You can have the three hundred a year, but I won't discuss the matter with you. You must see Page."

She held the cigarette a little away and opened her eyes upon him.

"My dear Jervis, what do you expect me to do? One doesn't *live* on three hundred a year!"

"One might work," he suggested.

Rosamund's riposte was swift.

"I believe Mr Page has a vacancy for a typist. Shall I apply for it?" She smiled her exquisite smile, then leaned towards him. "I'm not clever enough, I'm afraid. What's the good of quarrelling? Make it five hundred, and let's be friends. Family quarrels are so exhausting, and there's a heat-wave coming." She paused for an answer, and got none. "Come—five hundred—and I'll owe my dressmaker the rest."

Jervis rose to his feet and offered her his arm.

"Nothing doing, I'm afraid. Shall we dance?"

Ferdinand Fazackerley had taken Nan by way of a long corridor into one of those immense rooms with gilt mirrors and brocaded furniture which are, mercifully, only to be met with in hotels of the more expensive sort. They sat down in a window-seat framed with rose-coloured satin curtains looped with gold. Their feet rested upon a carpet an inch thick, also rose-coloured.

"Well!" said Mr Fazackerley, "If we aren't grand! Now last time I had the pleasure of a conversation with you—"

Nan coloured a little, but her dimple showed.

"Is that my cue? What do I say?"

"You say, '*Last* time?' "

"Do I?"

"I should say you do. And I—"

"Yes, you?"

"I come in with, 'Last time we weren't as grand as this.'"

Nan caught the corner of her lip between her teeth.

"Have we met before, Mr Fazackerley?"

"Oh yes, Mrs Weare."

"Have we? Are you sure?"

"Oh, quite sure. I've been quite sure since twenty minutes past four this afternoon."

Nan caught her eyes away from his. They were twinkling, but under the twinkle he was dead serious. She looked down into her lap, and then of her own free will she tilted her head and looked back at him.

"Well?" she said. Her lips just parted on the word, and then closed in a firm, sweet curve that was not quite a smile.

"If you'll go back in your mind," said Mr Fazackerley, "maybe you'll remember that after I'd picked Jervis out of that pool on Croyston rocks, I came back for the plucky kid who'd saved his life by holding him up in the water. She'd got herself out without my help, and she was standing there wringing out her skirt and dripping as if she's just come out of the Flood. Perhaps you can remember what I said."

"Me?" said Nan. "No."

"Well," said Ferdinand, "I put my arm around her and I said, 'You're the durned pluckiest kid I've ever struck—and that's the truth, the whole truth, and nothing but the truth.' And she said—you know what she said."

Nan shook her head.

"Supposed to be suffering from loss of memory," murmured Mr Fazackerley. "She grabbed me with both hands and said, 'Is he dead?' And I said, 'Not within eighty years of it, thanks to you.' Come—you remember that."

"I?" said Nan.

"Yes, you. I said, 'I'd like to know your name,' and she said, 'Nan.' And when you said 'I'm Nan,' this afternoon at twenty past four at Victoria Station—well, I knew you at once—so what's the good of all this in and out fighting? I'm not an inquisitive man, but I'd like to know what's behind all this, and why Jervis don't know you saved his life."

"Well, I think *you* saved it," said Nan.

Ferdinand shook his head.

"He'd have been gone long before I got him out of the water if it hadn't been for you." The bright darting eyes went through her armour. "You were clever at dinner, but I saw the scar before you moved your arm—just where I knew it was bound to be. Well, now I'm being impertinent— but *why* doesn't Jervis know?"

Nan was silent for a moment. He was certainly impertinent, but she wasn't angry. He cared about Jervis, and that was all that mattered. She said quite simply,

"I don't want him to know." Then, as if putting all that on one side, "Mr Fazackerley, I want to talk to you. I—I must talk to someone, and—perhaps Jervis will listen to you."

"Won't he listen to you? I should have thought—"

"No. Please don't talk to me like that. It's serious—it's very serious."

"What is it, Mrs Weare?"

Nan clasped her hands in her lap.

"I'm very frightened about Jervis," she said. "He's in danger, but he won't believe it."

"Danger?" said Ferdinand. "That has a very intriguing sound."

"You're laughing at me," said Nan in a despairing voice.

"How can I, when I don't know the first thing about the situation? What's the matter with it anyway?"

"You don't believe me," said Nan. "But it's true. He tried to kill Jervis ten years ago, and he tried to kill him again today."

"Great Wall Street!" said Mr Fazackerley; and then, "Who did?"

"Robert Leonard did."

Mr Fazackerley beat with the flat of his hand upon his knee.

"Is that so?" he said. "The guy with the bulging brain-box and the jaw-bone of an ass?"

"Yes, he did," said Nan.

"Great Bronx!" said Mr Fazackerley with simple fervour. "He *did*, did he? Why?"

"Rosamund would get all the money," said Nan.

Mr Fazackerley sat back.

"Mrs Weare, you're not handing it to me that that beautiful lady is out gunning for Jervis!"

"I don't think she knows." She threw out her hands in a passionate gesture. "Oh, she *can't* know!"

They were alone in the huge formal room. Nan's little voice quivered in it, and was smothered by the silence and the emptiness. To say the word murder in this gilded, rose-coloured room, with its soft carpet, its glittering chandeliers, its painted ceiling, was like firing a revolver shot in a puppet show. Mr Fazackerley looked at her. He was in the grip of the most profound curiosity.

"I'm not an inquisitive man," he said, "but if you'd begin at the beginning and give me an idea of what this is all about, I'd appreciate it very much."

Nan leaned back too.

"It's all so tangled up—but I'm frightened—I'll tell it as well as I can—it goes a long way back."

"Take your own time," said Ferdinand. "Nobody's thought of taxing that yet, so you can have as much as you like."

"It goes right back," said Nan. "I don't know how you recognized me—it was very clever of you. I want to tell you how I came to find Jervis."

"I'm listening."

The colour stood high in Nan's cheeks. She didn't care whether he was listening or not. She wasn't going to tell Ferdinand Fazackerley that ten years ago she had had a child's adoration for Jervis which had made her follow him like an unseen shadow. She cast about for an opening. It would be quite easy if she could only get started. She began without any proper beginning at all.

"I saw Jervis come across the rocks. He was going down to bathe—he had a towel over his shoulder. He went behind those rocks where the pool was."

"What were you doing?" said Mr. Fazackerley.

"I was sitting on the beach," said Nan with her chin in the air. "There was a way down the cliffs just beyond me. A man came down it and went across to the rocks where Jervis was. I didn't see his face. I think he was walking on the cliff and saw Jervis and came down. He went behind the rocks, and in about five minutes I saw him again. He wasn't coming back, he was going straight on. There's another path up the cliff before you come to Croyde Head. He went up that. I saw him half way up it. I never saw his face at all.''

Mr Fazackerley's eyes were brightly attentive.

''Go right on,'' he said.

''I waited a long time. The tide began to come up. I wondered where Jervis was. I climbed up on to the path and looked out to sea, but I couldn't find him. The rocks hid the pool—I want you to remember that—I don't think anyone on the cliff could have seen it.''

Mr Fazackerley nodded.

''That's so.''

''I got frightened about Jervis. I went down to the pool, and he was lying half in and half out of it with his head bleeding and the tide coming in. The water was up to his shoulders. If I hadn't come then, he would have been drowned. If you hadn't come later, we should both have been drowned.''

''What are you meaning?'' said Mr Fazackerley.

''That man went behind the rocks and came out again,'' said Nan rather breathlessly.

''Now what do you mean by that?''

''You know what I mean—but I don't mind saying it. I mean that the man went behind those rocks because he knew that Jervis was there and that they couldn't be seen from the cliff. I mean that he picked up a bit of rock and struck Jervis with it, and went away and left him there with the tide coming in.''

Fazackerley's eyes went to the painted ceiling and down again. He did not shrug his shoulders, but the right one twitched.

''You can't prove that, you know.''

''Of course I can't,'' said Nan. ''But you can be sure of lots of things you can't prove.''

''That's so. But you didn't see him strike Jervis—you didn't even see his face; and now you say he's Mr Robert Leonard—and I take it you mean the Mr Robert Leonard who is with Miss Carew tonight.''

Nan nodded.

"Let me go on. After you'd got us out of the pool you went to get help, and I stayed with Jervis. As soon as I heard you coming back, I got away up the cliff path. You see, Cynthia and I were down at Croyston with an aunt, and we were going back to town by the afternoon train. I got into a most frightful row when I turned up at our rooms dripping wet with my dress spoilt and my arm cut. I was bundled into dry things, and we just caught the train. And afterwards I was ill—I believe I was very ill—and all the time I kept seeing that man, and Jervis in the pool. I want you to understand how it was that I could recognize him ten years afterwards. He was *printed* into my mind. All these years I've only had to shut my eyes and think about it to see him walking away, and Jervis in the water."

Ferdinand saw her eyes darken in a face that had lost all its colour.

"You say you recognized him," he said.

She gave another of those quick nods.

"Yes—at once. There was a photograph in Jervis' study—a picture of the garden at King's Weare, with old Mr Weare and Rosamund on the lawn and Robert Leonard walking towards them. It didn't show his face; it showed him walking away from me, just as I'd seen him in my mind all those years. I recognized him at once, and Jervis told me his name."

"Ten years is a long time," said Ferdinand, "and—there's a good proverb about letting sleeping dogs lie."

"They're not sleeping," said Nan. "He tried to kill Jervis ten years ago, and he tried to kill him again today."

Mr. Fazackerley leaned forward, resting his weight on his right hand.

"That's a whole heap more interesting!" he said. "I'm listening."

Again Nan found it difficult to begin. She couldn't tell Ferdinand Fazackerley what had made her walk up and down in front of Rosamund's house in Leaham Road. As before, she plunged.

"I saw Robert Leonard get out of a taxi. He was with Rosamund Carew. She went into the house."

"What house?"

"Her house. She went in; but he came back and spoke to the driver. I was on the other side of the taxi. I wasn't trying to listen, but I didn't want them to see me. Robert Leonard said, 'It's the four-fifteen. You'll have to hurry. He's sure to walk, because he's got a craze for exercise. Let him come out of the station and get well away.' "

"No names?"

She shook her head.

"No."

"What made you think—"

"I didn't at first. Let me tell you. The driver said, 'Suppose he takes a taxi.' And Robert Leonard said, 'You must just do the best you can.' Then he turned as if he was going away, but the driver stopped him. He said he wasn't as keen on the job as he had been. And then he said five hundred pounds was five hundred pounds, but jug was jug—that's prison, you know. And Robert Leonard said, 'What's a couple of months for dangerous driving?' And the driver said it might be a lot more than that, but he'd do it because he was a man of his word." Her voice stopped. It had shaken a little.

"Is that all?" said Mr Fazackerley.

"No," said Nan. She held her voice steady with all her might. "I met Jervis at Victoria—he came by the four-fifteen from King's Weare. I told him, and he wouldn't believe me; but because he was late for his appointment with Mr Page he went by tube instead of walking. He *would* have walked. And when he came out of his house on his way here, a taxi knocked him down. He saw it coming and jumped, or he wouldn't be here tonight."

"You saw this?"

"No. He was getting a taxi for me. He told me. His arm was cut—he had to go back and change."

"But you never heard any names, Mrs Weare. What made you think this Robert Leonard was talking about Jervis?"

"I don't know—I just knew it. Don't you ever know things like that?"

"I've had hunches," admitted Mr Fazackerley. "I shouldn't be here now if I hadn't."

"Well, that's what I had," said Nan—"a hunch."

"A hunch isn't evidence. You know, Mrs Weare, there wouldn't be much left of that story of ours if you took it into court. Any clever counsel would have you tangled up inside of five minutes so you wouldn't rightly know whether you were on your head or your heels. And then, what does he want to kill Jervis for? What's the motive? You must have a motive."

"The money," said Nan in a small frightened voice.

"But he doesn't get the money."

"No—Rosamund gets it."

"Don't you get it—after Jervis?"

She shook her head.

"I was in Mr Page's office—I know all about the will, because I typed it. I've got a settlement. I shouldn't get anything else. If Jervis had an accident, everything would go to Rosamund Carew." The last words only just reached him.

She pushed back the rose-coloured curtain and stood up. The big, still room was empty.

"I'm frightened," she said. Her eyes implored him.

Mr Fazackerley got to his feet. His brain teemed with questions. The gaps in Nan's narrative had not escaped him—very little ever did escape him. It did not escape him now that they had been here long enough if they did not wish to advertise a consultation. He darted a reassuring glance at Nan and said in his kindest voice,

"Jervis is a pretty tough proposition."

They crossed the room in silence. At the door Nan turned to him.

"If he asks you to come down to King's Weare, will you come?"

"And butt in on your honeymoon?"

"Yes—*please*."

"Well, as a matter of fact he *has* asked me," said Mr Fazackerley.

"And you said?"

"Well, I said I'd got more than enough to get through in London."

"Oh, but you haven't—not really."

"I have—and that's gospel. But if you want me to come—"

"Please, *please* come," said Nan.

"Well—I'd like to," said Mr Fazackerley.

XV

"WELL?" SAID ROBERT LEONARD.

He splashed a small amount of soda into a good deal of whisky with a jerk of the hand, picked up his glass, and turned to Rosamund Carew. She was standing by the window of her drawing-room looking out into the cloudy darkness of the August night. Her right hand held back the green and gold curtain, her left hung at her side. There was something in the pose that suggested strain. Without turning, she said,

"It's frightfully late."

Mr Leonard drank half the contents of his tumbler at a gulp. Then he set down the glass sharply.

"Hospitable creature—aren't you?"

"It's too late to be hospitable, Robert. You oughtn't to have come in,"

"Rubbish!"

She looked rather wearily over her shoulder.

"I have to be careful when I'm here alone—doubly careful just now. It's been touch and go over this business." She dropped the curtain and turned around. "I've squared Mable Tetterley."

Robert Leonard was lighting a cigarette.

"She seemed to be all over you."

Rosamund came slowly from the window. Her gold dress made the faintest slurring sound as she moved. She held herself rather stiffly upright, as if she was fighting fatigue.

"I confided in her," she said in a dry, toneless voice. "She was dying of curiosity of course, so I told her that when I found out by accident that Jervis was in love with this girl, I didn't feel that I could stand in their way. She simply lapped it up."

She came up to one of the big chairs and leaned against it.

"What about Jane Manning Temple?"

"I got off the same piece to her. She said I was a saint." Rosamund's brows drew together. There was a momentary look of Jervis in his black mood.

"Well, that's a bit of all right," said Leonard. "I noticed she made a beeline for old James Mulroy as soon as you left her, and between 'em they'll do all the broadcasting that's necessary."

He finished his whisky and stood with the empty glass in his hand, frowning down at it.

Rosamund sat down on the arm of her chair. A bright shot cushion of emerald and blue made for her a background like shoaling water. The light changed upon the gold of her dress and her drooping white shoulder. She looked past Leonard as if he were not there.

All at once he turned to the table and put down the empty glass.

"I suppose—" he said in a considering voice. "I suppose you couldn't work off that piece on Jervis, could you?"

Rosamund stared at him.

"Are you suggesting that I should try and persuade Jervis that I gave him up because he was in love with his typist?"

"Page's typist. Yes, something of the sort."

"Talk sense!" said Rosamund.

"My dear, you're not being very bright. I am talking the most excellent sense."

Rosamund laughed.

"Jervis married her to save the cash. In fact he took the cash and let the credit go. He wasn't in love with her, and he isn't in love with her—and whether he ever will be in love with her is on the knees of the gods.''

He blew a cloud of smoke.

''Now you're being high falutin. What's wrong with your making him believe—'' He paused, frowning.

''Well? What am I to *make* him believe?'' Her voice mocked him.

''Hold on—I'm getting there. Suppose the girl had told you he was in love with her—that they were in love with each other.''

''What are you getting at?''

''It would let you out—noble self-sacrifice, broken heart, and all that. And it would put his back up no end against the girl if he believed he'd been tricked into marrying her. I imagine the Weare temper could be counted on to do the rest.''

Rosamund lifted one hand and let it fall again.

''If!''

''Well, he might. These things stick, and when a man's been let down by one woman he's generally ready to believe the worst about the next one. You think it over. But don't take too long about it. What's wanted at the present moment is, 'A separation has been arranged between Mr and Mrs Jervis Weare, to take effect immediately.' We don't want any little Weares, you know. That would put the kibosh on the whole affair.''

Rosamund turned sombre eyes upon him. The blue seemed to have gone out of them, leaving them bleak and grey.

''It's time you went home,'' she said; and then, with a sudden tang in her voice, ''Oh, Lord! What a mess we've made of it!''

''Have we? That remains to be seen.''

Rosamund laughed. There was as much merriment in the sound as there is in a black east wind.

''Jervis offered me three hundred a year—he chucked it at me about as politely as you'd chuck a bone to a dog. I tried to get him to make it five hundred, but he wouldn't rise. I wish to heaven I'd gone through with it and married him!''

''Do you?'' said Robert Leonard.

He blew a perfect smoke ring and watched it rise and

melt outwards into the dusk above them. Only a single lamp
lighted the room. It stood behind Rosamund's chair. The
light came palely from under a painted and gilded shade; it
crossed Rosamund's shoulder and caught the gold upon her
breast. He saw that gold rise and fall, and rise and fall
again.

"Yes, I do," she said. "What's the good of pretending?
We've muffed it, and we're in the soup. You know it as well
as I do. Three hundred a year!" She threw back her head
and laughed again. "If it wasn't too late, I'd chance it
now."

Robert Leonard came deliberately over to her and put
heavy hands on her shoulders.

"That's enough about that!" he said roughly.

"That's for me to say."

"No, it isn't! You'll do what you're told."

He slid one hand behind her head, tilted up her face, and
kissed her. She did not cry out, but he felt her stiffen. Her
lips were hard and cold against his. He released her and
stood back.

"Now listen to me!" he said. "Jervis and this girl
haven't been living together, but she's going down to King's
Weare with him tomorrow—well, by now it's today. I'm
going down too. You can stay here if you like."

"Mable Tetterley has asked me down."

He seemed to consider that.

"Quite a good plan. We had better not be seen together
again for the present."

Rosamund put her hand to her head. She pushed back the
heavy gold of her hair and let her hand drop into her lap
again. Then she said without looking at him,

"What are you going to do?"

"Mind my own business."

She stood up at that.

"I think it's my business too."

She went to the table under the lamp and, jerking open a
drawer, pulled from it a sheaf of papers.

"Bills!" she said. "Today's little lot! Ever since the
seventeenth they've come pouring in. I tear them up, but I

kept today's to show you. Would you like to have a look at them?''

''No thanks—I've plenty of my own.''

''Exactly. And what are we going to do about it? I've got this house till the end of August. I've been paying the rent in advance on the first of the month. I'm overdrawn at the bank. And the minute the notice of Jervis' marriage is in the papers everyone I've ever dealt with sits down and sends me in a bill! And Jervis flings me three hundred a year!''

''Well, I haven't got that.''

''What are we going to do?''

''You are going to stay with Mabel Tetterley—and I am going down to Croyston,'' said Robert Leonard.

XVI

NAN SAW KING'S WEARE FOR THE FIRST TIME UNDER driving rain. They taxied from Croyston with the sky blue behind them and a heavy indigo cloud coming up out of the west. The road ran inland for a couple of miles and then, turning, zigzagged up the side of a bare hill covered with close sheep-cropped grass. As they came up the last rise, the wind met them and the rain—first heavy splashing drops, and then a solid shimmering fall.

They were running seaward again. Nan stared through the wet glass. She was frightened, but she was uplifted too. This was one of the great days of her life, whatever came of it in the end. She was with Jervis, and they were going home. She looked with all her eyes, and could see nothing but streaming rain and a blur of green grass half drowned by grey water. Then tall stone pillars, and straining trees lashed by the wind until they brushed the car as it passed. At last a grey house, and a portico under which they came to a standstill.

Jervis jumped out, and she followed him. Her new suitcases emerged; her new trunk came down dripping. There was comfort in them, and Nan needed comfort badly. She got none from Jervis. He hurried her up the steps and through a lobby into the hall with an air of gloomy abstraction. She felt very small and dreadfully alien in the new strange place which was full of the lives and the thoughts and the handiwork of Jervis' people. She could only come at them through Jervis. He must take her by the hand and bring her into his kingdom before she could be anything but a stranger in a strange land.

There was a suit of armour high on the wall to the right, and to the left a corselet, and greaves, and a morion. There were portraits. A sombre youth with Jervis' eyes and a Cavalier hat with a trailing crimson feather. There was an old man in a scarlet gown, and a lady with powdered hair and a pale spreading dress. Nan had a momentary impression of a family gathering looking down on her with dark critical eyes. They were not hostile—yet. They were searching her, appraising her, preparing to receive or to reject.

She turned, startled at Jervis' touch on her arm.

"Nan—this is Mrs Mellish. She has been housekeeper here for—How long is it, Mrs Mellish? Thirty years?"

Mrs Mellish, rosy and buxom, with severely parted grey hair and a black dress with a high stiff collar surmounted by white frilling and clasped by a large brooch of moss agate set in a pale gold rim, interposed in a firm, respectful voice.

"Thirty one years and six months in September, sir."

Just for a moment she looked at Nan, and there was no welcome in her look. She withheld, just as the portraits withheld. Nan was a stranger.

With the cold of it at her heart, she lifted her head and smiled prettily.

Monk, the butler, considered that she smiled very prettily indeed. He was a fat man, with small sunken eyes, sparse pale hair, and a voice so soft as to lend his most casual remark the air of a confidence. "A very pleasant young lady" was his comment to Mrs Mellish in the housekeeper's room later on. "A very pleasant young lady."

Mrs Mellish received the remark in a bridling manner. She drew back her double chin till it rested upon the neat white frilling. Not until Monk had repeated his remark for a third time did she make oracular response.

"That is as may be," she observed.

"Pleasant spoken, and pleasant looking," said Monk. "And favour being deceitful and beauty vain, that's as much as anyone is called upon to expect—and if she's been brought up religious, which it's too few is, it's a good deal more than most gentlemen get."

Mrs Mellish bridled yet more severely.

"You can keep your preaching for your chapel, Mr Monk," she said, "for I won't have it here. Whether other people have got religion or not is their own business, and as far as I'm concerned I was brought up Church of England and taught to order myself lowly and reverently to my betters, and to keep my tongue from evil speaking, lying, and slandering." She spoke in a composed, determined voice, sitting very upright and knitting with a brisk click of bright steel needles.

Monk blinked with his large pale lids.

"And who was I slandering or speaking evil of, if I may make so bold as to inquire?"

"Nobody," said Mrs Mellish firmly. "Not in this room, and not in my presence. Not whilst I've got my health and all my faculties—which, thank God, I've got and hope to keep."

When Nan was alone at last in the big room which had been Ambrose Weare's, she stood in the middle of it and looked about her with a mixture of passionate interest, shy pride, and a tremulous something akin to fear. Mrs Mellish had conducted her in state. A red-cheeked girl had brought hot water and been named, with a faint flavour of disapproval, as Gladys. Now she was alone, and she stood in the middle of the floor and looked about her.

The room was large and light. A big old-fashioned four-post bed with a maroon canopy and hangings stood against the long wall, with the door on the right. To the left beyond the bed was a built-out window nearly as wide as the room, and opposite the door another window, hung like the bed with dark red curtains. There was a great deal of dark red about the room—carpet, curtains, bed-furniture, the upholstery of a Victorian couch, and the covering of two deep armchairs set very formally one on either side of the hearth. The furniture dated from the forties—square solid mahogany wardrobe, chests of drawers, and mirror. The dressing-table had a crimson petticoat with transparent muslin over it, and a looking-glass with a great many little drawers. There was a very fat crimson pin-cushion with a frill. It was, Nan thought with alarmed dismay, very completely a grandparent's room, and very certainly not hers. She felt an abashed sense of being an intruder as she skirted the dressing-table to reach the large window.

One's first instinct in a strange room is to see what lies beyond it. Nan looked out and saw a wet green lawn. The lilac bushes that edged it bent in the wind, all beyond was mist. Overhead the heavy clouds drove across the sky. She could not see the sea, but she thought that she could hear it. The room stood at the corner of the house. Perhaps the other window looked on the sea. But when she reached it, though the sound was louder, the sea was still hidden. The view from this side of the house showed a paved terrace, then falling ground—at first grass with some flower beds, then shrubs irregularly planted, and finally a steep fall towards what looked like a ravine. To the left a kind of bluff or knoll covered with trees hid the sea. Nan felt sure that it hid the sea. She could hear the sound of waves against the cliff. She felt a great desire to go out into the rain and wind. Instead she washed her hands, looked at herself in the large mirror, and went down to tea.

Tea was to be in the library. She came into the hall and tried three doors before she found the right one—the dining-room, full of enormous mahogany furniture; the drawing-room, long unused and breathing faint ghostly camphor, lavender, and the smell of old calendered chintzes; the third room, a small comfortable place with books, shabby old chairs, and a writing-table. She found the library next to it, a pleasant room looking to the ravine, and Jervis sitting in the window with the largest dog she had ever seen standing gravely beside him. He had a head like a lion, and he was lion-coloured. He turned deep amber eyes on Nan and came padding to meet her. She put out a hand. He slid his head under it and sniffed her skirt.

"You're not afraid of dogs," said Jervis.

Nan threw him an indignant look.

"No. What's his name?"

"Bran. Tell him to shake hands with you."

Nan looked down into the amber eyes.

"Bran, shake hands," she said, and was aware of Jervis watching her quizzically.

She took her hand from Bran's head as she spoke and held it out. Immediately the huge mouth opened; her hand was taken gently but firmly and shaken from side to side. She felt the pressure of the great teeth, but it was a pressure which would not have broken an egg-shell. Then her hand was dropped and the velvet-soft muzzle moved across it with a caressing touch.

Jervis came over to them.

"You are free of Bran's affections," he said gravely. "He only shakes hands with people he likes very much."

Just for an instant Nan would have given everything she had in the world to know whether Rosamund was one of the people with whom Bran shook hands. The feeling was so irrational and so strong that it brought the blood to her cheeks. She walked to the window, Jervis behind her.

"Is the sea behind that bluff?"

"Yes."

"I thought it was—I thought I could hear it."

"You might today, but as a rule you'd hear the fall. The Weare storm comes down that cleft and takes a magnificent header just through there." He pointed as he spoke. "The fall is one of our sights. It will be worth seeing tomorrow after this rain."

The door opened, and Monk entered, bearing pontifically a large silver tray upon which, in order state, stood a massive and hideous tea-service. A tall pale youth followed with a cake-stand. In a hushed tone Monk issued orders. The tall youth, looking scared to death, set down the cake-stand with a clatter. In dignified reproach Monk lowered the heavy tray without the slightest sound. He then fixed the youth with an awful eye and withdrew. The door shut upon them.

"The wretched Alfred," said Jervis, "is in for it. He's new, and in a blue funk. What's the odds he drops the whole caboodle the first time Monk lets him carry the tray?" Here, you'll pour out the tea—won't you?"

Nan approached the tea with a good deal of fellow-feeling for Alfred. The heavy teapot, which she could hardly lift; the ornate and hideous urn; the sugar-basin, big enough to serve an early Victorian family of fifteen or so; the awkward high-shouldered milk-jug; and the tray itself, so weighty that it filled her with respect for Monk's muscular control, combined as a solid symbol of wealth and social position. There slipped into her mind the glancing thought that Mrs Grundy would be very fitly served from a set like this.

She looked up to ask Jervis if he took sugar, and caught his eye with a dark gleam in it.

"Hideous—aren't they?" he said.

XVII

NAN SAT UP IN BED IN THE DARK. SOMETHING HAD WAKENED her, but she didn't know what it was. At first the darkness seemed to fill the room, pressing in upon her so that the posts of the bed, the red hangings, which she had pushed back as far as possible, and the big wardrobe, which was somewhere on the opposite side of the room, were all lost in an even velvet dark. Then the curtain at the far window moved in some unseen current of air, and a pale luminous streak divided the darkness. The immediate effect was to make the room seem immensely large. A moment before, everything had been pressing in upon her; she could have touched the walls with her outstretched hand. And now, with a puff of wind, everything was immensely far away. The suddenness of it made her feel dizzy. She watched the streak of light, and tried to steady herself. It came and went, and came and went again.

Nan sat bolt upright, one hand hard on the bed and the other at her throat. She had waked like that, and she had not moved yet. Then, as the curtain was first sucked in against the window and then on a veering gust blown back into the room, her hand dropped and she took a long breath. It was bright moonlight outside. The blown curtain let the moonlight in, and it filled the room with an uncertain dusk. She could see the bed-posts against it, and the wardrobe like a black cave. Then everything was dark again as the curtain fell back into place. She drew another long breath. It must have been the wind that had waked her. She pushed back her hair and relaxed. It was rather horrid to find yourself sitting up in the dark and not know how you had got there. For a moment she had not known where she was—in what bed, in what room, in what place.

The curtain blew out again and fell slowly back. The light flickered and the curtain fell. A rumble of thunder sounded far away. This time she saw the curved end of the couch and the humped outline of one of the big armchairs. She was in the big bedroom which belonged to the mistress of King's Weare. It was absurd, and a little frightening—no, not a little—*very*. She wished with all her heart that they had given her the little room with the bright chintzes that was over the study. And then all at once she wondered if that was Rosamund's room, and she was glad to be here, and glad that Jervis had let them put her here. She knew that he was next door in the room which had always been his. It gave her confidence to remember that he was there.

She pulled up a pillow behind her back and watched the moonlight run across the floor like a wave flung up by the tide. Like a wave it ran back again. She could see all the furniture now, mysteriously soft and large. A pleasant drowsiness began to steal over her. She thought back to the evening before. Jervis had taken her over the house. She had made great friends with Bran. She wished people were as easy to make friends with as dogs. The thought of Mrs Mellish was rather daunting—so overwhelming respectable, so unyieldingly decorous. At dinner she had worn her grey dress and found it very supporting. Monk was not nearly so frightening as Mrs. Mellish though. She discerned distinct traces of humanity in Monk, and to the nervous Alfred her heart went out in sympathy. One could hardly imagine Mrs Mellish with a Christian name......Harriet perhaps—or Eliza. She wondered whether anyone ever called her by it now.

A drowsy warmth flowed over her; she slipped a little further down in the bed. She had wondered how the evening would pass, and she could hardly tell how it had passed. They had talked—and Jervis had read the paper. She couldn't remember what they had talked about, but it had been quite easy. He had read bits out of the paper and been very angry about something someone had said at a political meeting. She could remember the way he looked when he was angry, but she couldn't remember what the politician had said. The time had slipped away like pleasantly flowing water—water flowing softly. "Sweet Thames, run softly till I end my song." That was Spenser—or was it? She was slipping down into soft flowing waters of sleep, when all of a sudden they ebbed away and she was awake again, her heart beating and her eyes staring into the darkness.

It wasn't the flapping of the curtain that had waked her before, and it wasn't the flapping of the curtain that had waked her now. It was a sound—not in the room—somewhere else. Now that she heard it, she could remember that she had heard it before. The memory was like an echo just caught on the edge of sound. She did not yet know what it was that she had heard. And then, as she listened, it came again—a faint whining noise, followed by what sounded like a footstep. It was so faint that it puzzled her to guess why it should have roused her from her sleep.

She threw back the bed-clothes and sat on the edge of the bed, listening all the while. The sound came again—a long faint whine, and a distant padding step. The two things together said Bran; but instead of reassurance a wave of fear rushed in. Bran—downstairs in the hall—padding up and down and whining . . . It frightened her beyond her own power of knowing why.

She slipped down on the floor, went barefoot to the door, and stood with the wooden knob in her hand, summoning up her courage to open it. The knob was cold, and very smooth with age; it was mahogany like the heavy door. Just above her hand there was a bolt. She could slip the bolt and get back into bed again.

She turned the knob and opened the door; and as she did so, the curtain blew in with the draught and the moonlight ran across the floor. She stepped outside and closed the door behind her, holding to it. There was a soft woolly mat under her feet.

Her room was at the end of a short passage. The passage gave upon the stair head. The dog's whine and the sound of his padding feet came up the well of the stair.

She latched the door and went along the passage to the head of the stairs. It was not dark here. The moon struck through a long window set with painted glass, bleaching its colours and making them like colours seen in a dream. Nan leaned on the rail and looked over into the dark hall. The padding and the whining had stopped. She had a sense of the great beast standing down there, listening and looking up. She called softly,

"Bran—Bran—" and immediately she heard him take the stair. She saw him for a moment, huge, and black against the lighted window, said his name again, and then he was pressing against her, jerking his head up under her hand and whimpering.

"What is it?" said Nan. "What is it, Bran?"

He nuzzled her hand and whined.

"Don't you like the wind?"

This was a most reassuring thought. Some dogs hated wind. *But it wasn't so windy.*

All at once Nan was twice as frightened as she had been before. She wanted to get back to her room and bolt herself in. She took Bran by the collar, and he ran with her. She was breathing hard as she shot the bolt.

When she turned from the door, she saw Bran reared on his hind legs at the window with the curtain blowing round him. The moonlight threw a monstrous shadow almost to her feet. His nails scraped on the sill.

She ran to him and pulled away the curtain.

"What is it? What's the matter, Bran?"

He quivered and blew against the glass. With her hand on his neck she could feel his hackles rise. She pressed against him and looked out. The window looked to the south-west. It was open at the top. Bran pushed the glass with his nose and whimpered. It was a heavy old-fashioned window, and Nan strained as she raised it. The wind flooded the room—a soft, damp wind—and she and Bran leaned out together.

The moon was going down the western sky. By leaning far out Nan could see her in a clear dark pool ringed about with clouds that looked like icebergs. All the sky was wracked with cloud except for the one deep pool which held the moon, and between the cloud and the wet earth the wind blew joyfully. Nan could have run with Bran and the wind; she could have run barefoot over the grassy downs. She thought of this as she hugged Bran and felt the wind blow past them.

The terrace beneath the window looked like grey blotting-paper with symmetrical blots of ink at regular intervals. The blots were flower-beds full of crimson and scarlet and orange and flame-coloured snapdragons. They had been brilliant under the grey sweep of the rain; now, under the moon, they were blots of ink. It was queer to think of all those bright colours asleep.

The terrace was wide. A low balustrade guarded it. Then the grass fell away, shadowy, mysterious, to the unseen ravine, whose waters made a deep undertone to the soughing of the wind.

All at once the moonlight drained away. The pool of clear sky was gone. The clouds had fallen in upon it. Nan could see them move darkly as the wind drove them. And then under her hand she felt Bran's great throat muscles thrum to a growl too faint to reach her ears. She pressed closer to him and whispered,

"What is it?"

He flung up his head impatiently. The thrumming went on. A gleam of light slipped out between two hurrying clouds. A far off rumble seemed to answer Bran.

Nan rubbed her cheek against his ear.

"Darling lamb—don't you like thunder? Is there going to be a storm?"

He shook himself free and leaned forward. She could hear him growling now. A pale violet flare changed the sky, and was gone again. Bran quivered and snuffed the wind. Nan pulled at his collar, and might just as well have pulled at the hasp of the window.

A second flare lit everything with a sudden brilliance. Nan saw the black shadow of the ravine, the ink-black trees beyond it, and the curve of the cliff. It was when it was gone that she knew she had seen something else—a man on the edge of the ravine—a black shape on the edge of the dark ravine. And the shape was the shape of Robert Leonard. There was the forward thrust of the head, and the strong heavy frame.

Bran jerked under her hand and gave tongue with a deep, angry baying sound.

Another flash came, and showed no shape of any man at all. The storm went by far off with no more than the lowest rumble of thunder. It left the night to a formless dusk. If anyone moved in it, he would not be seen even as a shadow. Nan did not think that anyone moved in it now.

Bran had stopped growling. He snuffed at the wind, threw up his nose with a sharp sound, half bark, half howl, and dropped to the floor.

Nan became aware that she was very tired and very cold. She pulled the window down, and felt that if it had been to do again, she would have let it be; her hands were so chilled and heavy. She left the curtain drawn back, found the black, shadowy bed, and crept into it, huddling the clothes about her. She heard Bran throw himself down on the floor beside the bed with a heavy flop. She was asleep almost as soon as he was.

XVIII

THE DAY CAME UP IN A SEA FOG WHICH LIFTED BEFORE eleven. It left the grass grey with dew and every tree and flower hung with tiny brilliant drops which made rainbows in the sun.

Nan had slept late. She came downstairs to find that Jervis had breakfasted and gone out. When the fog lifted, she took a book out on to the terrace and sat on the low balustrade looking over to the ravine. The grey stone of the terrace was dry already, but the earth in the formal beds was dark. The snapdragons had lost their diamond points of dew; they made a rich pattern of colour against the grey background. The house was of grey stone too. There were creepers on this south-west wall—wisteria, clematis, and a climbing rose. The rose was not in bloom, but the bright violet stars of the clematis glowed like stained glass against the green of the wistaria leaves.

Nan looked up at her window and wondered if she had really stood there in the dead of night and seen Robert Leonard by a flash of lightning. A little shiver went over her. She had only to shut her eyes, and she could see him against the pale violet flare. She looked down at Bran lying on the stone at her feet with his nose between his paws.

Jervis hailed her from under the wall.

"Would you like to come and see the waterfall?"

She looked over the balustrade and saw him below her, bareheaded, looking up. A drop of three feet on the terrace side was a good ten to the path below. Jervis was gay and smiling. He had very much the look of being at home. He wore an old brown shooting-coat and knicker-bockers. Bran got up, put his fore feet on the balustrade, and looked over at him, pricking his ears. His nose quivered slightly. He made no sound.

"I'd love to come," said Nan.

"You'll want thick shoes—everything's sopping."

"These are the thickest I've got. I don't mind getting wet."

She ran down the steps in the middle of the terrace, and he met her, frowning.

"You'll get drenched. There are some gum boots in the cloakroom—I'll get them for you."

Nan looked from her feet to his and laughed irrepressibly.

"I'd fall out of them!"

"No, they're—I mean they'll fit you all right."

Then they were Rosamund's. Nan blushed to the roots of her hair with pure rage. Did he think she would wear Rosamund's shoes?

She ran across the path and down the wet green slope, calling to Bran. When Jervis caught her up, he said angrily,

"Why did you go off like that? And why on earth don't women have decent shoes? You'll get absolutely soaked."

"I don't mind. I haven't got country shoes, because I don't live in the country."

"You'll have to get some."

Her heart jumped. Would she? What did he mean? Did he mean anything? Did he want her to live here? And if he did want her to, could she do it? She didn't know.

She looked up at him with a faint smile which became suddenly tremulous. She felt like a child at a party where the other children were playing a game she did not know. She did not know Jervis' game, or how he wanted her to play it. She wondered how he would look, and what he would say, if she were to ask him just straight out.

They were walking down a steep slope. Sometimes it was so steep that it was difficult not to run. Once Jervis caught her arm to steady her, and once she turned her foot on a rabbit hole and grabbed at him with both hands. Bran kept ahead of them. Every now and then he looked back as much as to say, "This place is mine, and I'm showing it to you. Do hurry up!"

The sound of falling water came nearer every minute. On

the terrace it was an undertone; but as they went down the slope, it swallowed every other sound and rose to a dominant roar. There were trees between them and the water. The grassy slope ended with a three-foot drop to a path. They turned inland, and the path wound between the trees. The thundering rush of the water was below them now, but the trees hid the fall. Then the path twisted, and they came out upon a flat open space. From the right the headlong steam came hurrying down a steep rocky channel. A light bridge spanned it at its narrowest point a few yards from where they stood. Below them was the fall, the sound of it like the sound of an avalanche.

Nan stood by the railing which guarded the edge and looked over. A mass of foaming water fell forty feet sheer to a black pool. The ravine narrowed to a cleft, and within this cleft the water fell. The sides of it were dark and slippery. And beyond the black pool, which lay in shadow, the sunlight glittered on the sea. The spray came up into her face.

"It's high tide, so you're seeing it at its best. Watch that wave come in."

Nan watched, and saw a big wave rear itself and come driving through the mouth of the ravine, to break in foam and spray against the spray and foam of the fall. The black pool churned and flung up yellowish spume. In its violent movement it was no longer black, but a deep molten amber. The crests of its swirling waters were gold, and gold-orange, and white. The ebb of the broken wave dragged back a milky stream into the sea.

"You get the best view from the bridge," said Jervis.

"Does the sea always come up to the pool?"

"Yes—except at the ebb of a spring tide. A high flood tide will break half way up the fall. It's a fine sight. Come and see it from the bridge. Here, Bran! Hi over!"

Bran cocked his ears, lifted his head, and raced ahead of them to the bridge, where he turned with a joyful woof and then ran forward. But as he came on to the bridge, he checked so suddenly that he slid a couple of feet on the wet planks before he could stop himself. He came to a standstill with all four feet together, and immediately sprang back growling.

"What's up, Bran?" said Jervis. "What is it, you old fool? Hi over!"

The hair on Bran's neck stood up. He backed gingerly, lifting his feet as if he were on ice, and growling all the time.

Jervis strode forward and caught him by the collar.

"Hi over!" he said. "What's the matter with you?"

Bran beat with his tail, whined, and pulled away.

"He's frightened," said Nan rather breathlessly.

Jervis threw her an impatient look.

"Do you think he's a lap-dog? I won't have him made into one! He'll do what he's told. Now, Bran—what's all this? Hi over!"

Bran crouched down, cocked his ears, dropped them, and beat with his tail upon the ground.

"Over!" said Jervis.

Bran licked the air as near his master's hand as he could reach and thumped again.

"He's frightened of the bridge," said Nan in a choked voice. Her lips were dry, and something seemed to have closed her throat.

"He's been over it hundreds of times."

"Then there's something wrong with it today."

Jervis twisted his hand in the dog's collar, took a long stride towards the bridge, and pulled. Bran sat back on his haunches and resisted with all his strength.

"There's something wrong with the bridge," said Nan.

Jervis' eyes flashed.

"He's going over if I've got to drag him!"

"Don't!" said Nan. "There's something wrong."

"There's nothing wrong!"

He wrenched at Bran's collar, but without budging him.

"Jervis, there *is* something wrong!"

"Shall I show you there isn't?" He let go of Bran with a sudden contemptuous movement and turned to the bridge.

Nan felt the most agonizing certainty of danger. Her heart jumped, and before she knew that she was going to do it she found herself on the bridge ahead of him.

What happened after that was a horrible confusion. She did not hear the crack of breaking timber, because it was lost in the roar of the fall, but she felt the shuddering jar of it. The bridge seemed to be wrenched beneath her. She did hear Jervis' shout, and she felt his grasp like an iron clamp upon her shoulder. She thought she screamed, and the spray and the foam and the cold came up upon her face, and her hands, and her breast. She swung giddily above the torrent, and there was nothing between her and pool below—a long, long way below. The bridge was gone—everything was gone. She swung giddily, a frightful noise in her ears, and the water waiting for her. She had no thought for why she did not fall. She swung to and fro. It was all a confusion, like the broken bits of a dream.

And then suddenly she came shuddering out of the dream, to hear Jervis' voice above her:

"Can you lift your arm?"

The sound of the words had reached her before, but not their sense. She made a slow, weak effort to raise her right arm, but something clamped it down.

Then Jervis voice again:

"Your—left—arm."

She tried, reached up, and felt him grasp her wrist. Then she was being drawn up, slowly, dreadfully slowly, whilst the noise of the falling, churning water seemed to be right inside her head. She didn't seem able to think. The moment went on interminably. Then she felt a scraping sensation across her shoulders and back, and the feel of something solid beneath her. Something went round and round in her head. She gasped and struggled to sit up. She felt as if she had been wrenched in two. She got up on her knees panting.

The middle of the bridge was gone. A yard away the broken timbers stuck out over empty space. On her left Jervis was getting to his feet. Bran pressed against her and licked her cheek. She caught him about the neck and struggled up.

Jervis was breathing hard. His clothes were darkly stained.

"Are you—all right?"

She nodded, holding Bran tight. An extraordinary wave of emotion threatened her with tears. She did not cry easily. If she were to weep now, it would not be because she was afraid, but because her whole nature seemed to be dissolved in a flood of joy and thankfulness. She had saved Jervis. If he had walked out on to the bridge, he must have gone down with it—if she had not got there first, he would have gone down. She had definitely flung herself in front of him, with the knowledge that she was flinging herself into the danger which had been prepared for him. She felt again the frightful grinding vibration of the breaking bridge.

She clenched her hands and stood staring at Jervis. The wave of emotion spent itself against the force with which she thrust it back. When it had ebbed, she felt strangely shaken. She said, in a fluttering voice that was much less audible than she meant it to be,

"What happened?"

Jervis said harshly, "The bridge broke."

She said, "I went—down."

He threw her a curious look. It was almost as if he accused her—an angry look.

"You might have been killed."

"You saved me."

"I grabbed your shoulder. We came down together."

"Yes—tell me. I don't know a bit what happened. Everything broke."

"The bridge cracked—I grabbed you—and we both came down. Then the middle of the bridge went, and you were over the edge."

Nan's heart contracted. She might have pulled him over—she might so easily have pulled him over. The words said themselves aloud:

"I might have pulled you over!"

Jervis stood there frowning.

"You very nearly did. It was damned slippery. If I hadn't come down full length before the bridge actually fell, we should both have gone with it. As it was, I managed to hang on, and old Bran took hold of my coat and pulled for all he was worth. I got a good handful of your dress, and thank goodness the stuff was strong!"

That was why her right arm felt as if someone had been trying to cut it off. He must be very strong to have held her like that. It had felt like a long time, but perhaps it was only a moment. She found herself asking him this, as if it was something of great importance.

"Was it a long time? It felt very long."

"No. I couldn't have held you for more than a moment. I said 'Put up your arm,' and I got hold of it; but if it hadn't been for Bran, I don't think I could have got you up."

At the sound of his name Bran thrust his head under his master's hand, jerking it up. Nan felt an envy of him. He had saved them both, and he could *say* how glad he was. She couldn't. It came over her how strangely they were standing here, speaking cold conventional sentences on the ragged edges of death. She envied Bran very much. Perhaps it would have been better if she had cried her heart out.

She turned from the broken bridge and began to move stiffly down the path. Her knees shook a little, and before she had taken half a dozen steps Jervis' hand was on her arm.

"You're a bit shaky."

"A little. It's nothing."

He walked beside her with his hand under her elbow, and she was very glad of it. Bran kept coming up on her other side, pushing against her with his head and then falling back to heel again.

They came out of the trees, but instead of climbing the slope they followed the easier gradient of the path. The sound of the fall receded. After walking silent for some time Jervis burst out with a sudden,

"I can't understand it."

Nan wondered if he felt the accusing leap of her pulses.

"*He* did it," she said; and now her voice sounded unnaturally loud, as if she was still speaking against the roar of the fall.

Jervis stopped dead and swung her round to face him.

"What's that?"

He still held her by the elbow, and his grasp felt rough and strong.

"*He* did it."

"What are you talking about?"

"The bridge."

"You've got to say what you mean!"

"Yes—I saw him."

"What do you mean? Who did you see."

"Robert Leonard."

He let go of her so suddenly that she felt as if he had pushed her away.

She repeated, "I saw him." And then after a moment she added, "I *did*."

Jervis stepped back from her. There was an angry colour under his dark skin.

"We've got to have this out! You've got to say what you mean!"

"Yes, Jervis. I woke up in the night—something waked me—I don't know what it was. Then I heard Bran downstairs."

"You heard Bran?"—with angry suspicion.

"He was walking up and down and whining. I went to the top of the stairs and called him. He came into my room with me, and we both looked out of the window. He was very excited. I thought it was because there was a storm coming up."

"You seem to think he's a Pekinese! He doesn't mind storms."

"I know he doesn't. It wasn't the storm he was minding."

"No—I suppose it was Leonard!" Nothing could have been more incredulous than his voice; his eyes held a hint of fierce amusement.

Nan lifted her head.

"Yes. Bran is cleverer than you are—he knows when there's danger—he wouldn't go on to the bridge."

Jervis laughed angrily.

"Well—he was minding Leonard? And then, I suppose, you both saw him!"

"*I* did. I don't know if Bran did. I don't think he goes by seeing—he's got something else."

"You saw Leonard?"

"Yes, I did."

"Where?"

"Where the path goes into the trees."

Jervis laughed again.

"From your window! In the middle of the night!"

"Yes—I did. The moon went in, and there was a flash of

lightning. I could see everything *very* clearly, and I saw Robert Leonard. I *did* see him.''

Jervis' manner changed; it became colder and lost its rough edge.

''I'm afraid you have rather an obsession about Leonard. I hope you won't go about saying this sort of thing to anyone else—it might get you into trouble. You see, it's quite impossible that you could have recognized him at that distance by a flash of lightning.''

''I did recognize him,'' said Nan.

She began to walk on toward the house. Jervis came up with her.

''A man you've seen once!'' he said in a taunting tone.

''I've seen him more than once—and I should know him wherever I saw him.''

He gave an angry jerk of the shoulder and walked on in silence. The path entered a shrubbery, and presently came out upon the lawn. Just before they came to the house Jervis spoke again.

''What have you got against Leonard?''

She looked at him with a direct simplicity.

''He wants to kill you.''

Jervis was startled clean out of his angry impatience.

''You can't possibly mean a thing like that!''

''I do mean it.''

''You can't! I don't like the man—but it's a perfectly foul thing to say about anyone without proof.''

Nan looked away. There was a note of appeal in his voice that weakened her. She took a step towards the house.

''You've no proof,'' said Jervis.

She looked back over her shoulder for an instant.

''The bridge fell,'' she said.

She went into the house.

XIX

At lunch Jervis made the sort of polite conversation which he would have made to a guest, and immediately after lunch he went out. The day had turned to heat; the last of the haze was gone, and a fierce sun beat down upon the damp ground; far away on the horizon heavy piled up clouds suggested thunder.

Nan took a book to a seat on the shady side of the lawn, but she did not read. The book lay on her lap, whilst her thoughts moved restlessly about the broken bridge. She had had a shock, and it had left her shaken. Jervis had been as near death as he could ever be until death took him. She did not think of how near death she had been herself. She thought of Jervis taking that long step forward on to the bridge, of the bridge cracking, of the violence of its fall, and of the roar of the falling water. The water fell into the pool and was broken into foam and spray, and the bridge fell and was smashed. And Jervis—Jervis had only just not fallen. She had a horrible picture of the water battering him down into the pool. She shivered, cold in the midst of the heat, and tried to push the thought away. It kept coming back.

She opened her book at random and began to read. The words passed over her mind like water passing over stone; they left no mark. She shut the book, and saw Jervis crossing the lawn with Bran at his heels. He had a haughty, confident look. He stood at the end of the seat with his knee upon it and an arm along the back.

"Well—" he said. "I've had the men down at the bridge."

Nan turned to face him. Bran came over to her and put his head in her lap.

"The wood was rotten. The spray from the fall had rotted it. As a matter of fact Benham—that's the carpenter—reminded me that I had spoken to him about having it overhauled, but of course I didn't think there was any particular urgency."

Nan looked down at Bran and stroked his head. She did not speak. She had a picture in her mind of a lightning flash, and of Robert Leonard against a black background of trees.

Jervis lifted his head a little. Why didn't she speak?

"Benham made a thorough examination of the broken timbers. I think you suggested that they had been tampered with."

Nan looked up and said, "Yes."

"You suggested that Leonard had tampered with the bridge."

"Yes—I did."

"Then I think you ought to withdraw that suggestion. If the timbers had been partly sawn through, the marks of the saw would show. There aren't any marks. The timbers broke because they were rotten. The ends are all ragged and splintered, and the wood's so rotten that you can break it with your fingers. I can't think how it held so long."

Nan did not speak. She gave him a steady look, and then went back to stroking Bran.

A little dark colour showed in Jervis' face.

"You made what amounted to an accusation."

"Yes," said Nan.

He struck the back of the seat with his hand.

"Are you going to withdraw it?"

"No."

"After Benham's report?"

Nan flung up her head.

"He tried to kill you!"

"That's nonsense. The bridge fell because it was rotten and I'd put off having it seen to. As a matter of fact it was Leonard who directed my attention to it not a week ago—Benham reminded me. I don't like Leonard—he's not a man I've ever cared about, and he rather put my back up—but he's a family connection, and I think you ought to take back what you said."

Nan got up. She took a step towards him and stood still.

"This is the third time he's tried to kill you," she said.

She saw his face darken and then change. He was looking past her, and she turned involuntarily. Lady Tetterley and Rosamund Carew were coming across the lawn.

Nan braced herself. She wasn't ready to meet Rosamund— here, where Rosamund was at home and she was a stranger; she wasn't ready at all. Jervis was angry. She had the picture of the breaking bridge in the back of her mind. She felt taken unawares and defenceless, but she called on her courage, and it rose.

Alfred brought chairs, and presently Monk entered upon the imposing ritual of tea.

Lady Tetterley, a ginger-haired woman with pale eyes and magenta lips painted on crooked, shook hands without looking at Nan, and began at once to talk to Jervis about people Nan did not even know by name. Pogo was broke and was going to have a try for the Winkledon girl, but it wasn't likely she'd look at him, because Snorter was in the running too, and naturally he'd have a pull over Pogo.

Jervis preferring Pogo's chances, they became involved in argument, until Lady Tetterley produced a red herring in the shape of an extraordinary rumour about Bonzo's entry for the Cesarewitch.

Rosamund sat back in her chair with an air of complete detachment. Her beauty, her indifference, the skilful simplicity of her washing-silk dress, made Nan feel as if she herself was all wrong. She spoke to Rosamund, and Rosamund's replies left her with no more to say. Rosamund's manner conveyed perfectly the impression that she was being polite. Nan preferred Lady's Tetterley's frank rudeness.

She poured out tea, and presently Rosamund had joined the others in a quite unintelligible discussion as to whether Juju Fordyce was, or was not, mixed up in the Lansdell affair. Lady Tetterley was of opinion that he was. Her plucked red eyebrows went up into an exaggerated arch as she maintained her contention.

"Jinks told me he was, and Freddy told Jinks—and I suppose you'll admit that *Freddy* ought to know."

"Because of Dodo?" said Rosamund.

"*Naturally*. And as Tuffy said to me—"

"Dodo's the worst liar in London," said Jervis.

"Oh, not the *worst*!"

"By worst do you mean cleverest?" inquired Rosamund.

"Dodo hasn't the brains of a weevil," said Jervis.

Nan poured out tea. It was a useful function; apart from it, there seemed to be no reason for her existence. A spate of gossip swept past and left her on the bank. If it had not been for Jervis, she would not have minded. It would have amused her to watch Lady Tetterley, who was so thin that each of her restless movements threatened to break something. Having achieved a miraculous slenderness by the complete sacrifice of health, colour and bloom, she was inordinately pleased with the result. At intervals of ten minutes or so she opened a vanity case, peered into the glass which lined its lid, and applied powder to her bony features, and another touch of magenta to her thin lips. She talked without ceasing, and had something faintly unpleasant to say about everyone she mentioned. She appeared to amuse Jervis.

Rosamund sat, for the most part, lighting one cigarette from another and talking little. Once when Nan looked up she found herself meeting Rosamund's eyes. Behind their beauty and their wonderful dark blue a definitely hostile something met and then instantly evaded her. Nan felt a little shaken; she did not quite know why. She did not expect Rosamund to like her. An armed neutrality was the best that could be hoped for between them.

Lady Tetterley did not make a long visit. As they got up to go, Rosamund drew a little nearer to Jervis.

"I've got things all over the place here. I thought I'd blow in whilst I'm with Mabel and do some sorting and shedding."

"Oh, whenever you like."

"You don't mind if I leave some things here?"

"Won't you be wanting them?"

She made a very slight gesture with the hand which held her cigarette.

"Where can I put them? I've only got the Leaham Road house for another month. I shall have to look out for an attic in a slum, I suppose."

"My cue?" said Jervis. "I take it that this is where I ask, 'Why a slum?'"

"You needn't ask—because you know."

They had lowered their voices, and Lady Tetterley was listening with interest. It was not until Rosamund turned away that she made a restless movement towards Nan.

"Oh, by the way, Basher told me to be sure to ask you about your people."

Nan gazed at her. She did not repeat the word Basher, but she contrived to produce the impression of having done so.

Mabel Tetterley jerked her emaciated shoulders.

"Basher's my husband. He's got it into his head that you may be related to some Forsyths he used to know. I told him it was most improbable, but he said I was to ask. I believe he was in love with one of them. They used to live at a place called Glenbuckie, and one of the sons went off digging up Old Testament places in Chaldea. Basher says he was quite well known in his own line."

"Nigel Forsyth," said Jervis.

Mabel Tetterley nodded.

"That's it. He wrote books about it. You know—all sherds, and cuneiform, and bits of the Tower of Babel, and Abraham's cooking-pots, and Japhet's wife's nose-ring. I don't read them myself, but Basher gloats over them, and he particularly said I was to find out if you were related to these Glenbuckie Forsyths."

Nan's colour rose.

"Yes, I am."

"Not *really*!" Her tone made this an impertinence.

"Nigel Forsyth was my father."

Lady Tetterley knocked the ash off her cigarette and said, "Damn!" Then she repeated her "Not *really*!" and added, "Basher will be thrilled."

After which she turned with one of her abrupt movements and declared that they ought to have gone ten minutes ago.

Neither she nor Rosamund took any leave of Nan, who was left uncertain of whether to cross the lawn with them or to remain where she was. She made a tentative movement to follow them, but they were already some distance away; she would have had to run to catch them up. No one of the three looked around. She hesitated, stood looking after them for a moment, and then returned to the tea-table with a growing certainty that she had done the wrong thing. When, a few minutes later, she saw Monk and Alfred advancing to remove the tea things, she got up and walked to the house, her cheeks burning and her courage very low.

She met Jervis in the hall, and he looked at her with cold anger.

"Why didn't you come to see them off?"

"You went without me."

"You should have come too."

She said, with a simplicity that checked him, "I am sorry. You went off so quickly at the end, and I thought it would look foolish if I ran after you."

He passed on without another word, and she did not see him till dinner.

XX

THE EVENING WAS VERY HOT. MONK BROUGHT THEM ICED coffee in the library. It was still broad daylight, the terrace and the long slope to the ravine in full sun, and the shadows on the lawn dead still.

Jervis went out on the terrace, and Nan picked up a book. As long as Monk was in the room they had talked quite easily and pleasantly; when Monk was gone there seemed to be nothing to say—or too much. It was a relief to go through the pages of a book into another world. She had read no more than half a chapter, when she heard Jervis come back.

He rang to have the coffee taken away, and stood by the window smoking a cigarette until the door had closed behind Monk. Then he came over to where Nan sat by a window facing the shadowed lawn. He stood looking down upon her.

"Rather unwise of you to commit yourself like that to Mabel Tetterley."

Nan looked up. If she was startled, she did not show it. Her eyes had the wide, steady gaze which roused something in him. Anger? He took it to be anger.

"Dashing of course—but a bit unwise, don't you think?"

"I don't know at all what you mean," said Nan.

"Really?"

"Really."

"I'm afraid you've a bad memory. It was quite amusing to see you call Mabel Tetterley's bluff, but I think you'd better have held your tongue. You see, she's only got to look up an old *Who's Who* to score you off rather badly. And as it happens, Basher is the sort of fellow who would be sure to have cartloads of old encyclopedias and *Debretts* and *Who's Whos* knocking about the place."

"I don't know what you mean."

He sat down on the arm of a big chair and leaned towards her.

"Oh, I think you do. Mabel's as inquisitive as they're made. She'll go home, and she and Basher will look up the appropriate volume—I forget what year Nigel Forsyth died?"

"Nineteen-nineteen," said Nan.

"Oh, you've mugged it up?"

"You didn't finish what you were saying."

"Need I?"

"Please."

He laughed, got up, crossed the room, bent to one of the lowest shelves, and came back with a red book in his hand.

"All right—you've asked for it. Here we are! My grandfather was a bit of a collector too. Here we have *Who's Who* for nineteen-eighteen."

He flicked over the leaves. "Here goes!—'Forsyth, Nigel Darnaway. Third son of Alistair Darnaway Forsyth of Glenbuckie. Forfarshire. Born 1875. Education Winchester—Cambridge. Fellow King's Coll:—'"

"Why are you reading all that?" said Nan.

"You mean that it isn't news to you—you've been there already—you know all about the 'British Ass:' and 'Excav: Chal:'"

Nan had turned pale. She said.

"I would be likely to know."

He laughed.

"Meaning that it was premeditated, and you naturally got up the documentary evidence! But now we come to the important part—'Married 1908 Constance Lavington.' "

"Yes," said Nan—"my mother."

He clapped the book to and dropped it into the seat of the chair beside him.

"It won't do," he said. "You were a little fool to think you could pull it off."

Nan stood up.

"You don't believe me?"

He smiled.

"Why don't you believe me?"

He laughed.

"Let's drop it! But if I were you, I should leave the ancestry vague. Nigel Forsyth is just a bit too well known."

Nan put her hands behind her back. They were shaking, and she didn't want him to see them shake.

"Nigel Forsyth was my father, and Constance Lavington was my mother. My father's people were furious about the marriage because my mother was on the stage. She died when Cynthia was six months old, and my father never forgave his father for the things he had said about her. He went out to Mesopotamia, leaving us with a sort of aunt. Her name was Mrs Whipple—she was my mother's half-sister and the widow of a Major Whipple of the Indian Army. She brought us up. My father only came home once after the war. He died at Baghdad in nineteen-nineteen. There was only a very little money. Mrs Whipple—" She hesitated. "I can't be fair to her, because she made Cynthia very unhappy. I think she tried to do her duty. There was only a little money, and she wasn't fond of children. She wasn't fond of us, and she didn't understand Cynthia. That's why I went to Solano's as a dancing partner—I simply had to get Cynthia away."

The ash from Jervis's cigarette fell and powdered the carpet. He had been looking at her hard. His expression changed suddenly.

"You mean it's true?"

"It's quite easy for me to prove that it's true. I have my father's letters—I can show them to you."

His face changed again. The momentary embarrassment passed. He looked like a triumphant schoolboy.

"I've fallen on my feet! I congratulate myself—you're too angry to do it for me of course—but I'm about to apologize."

She took a step away from him and said in a low voice,

"Why didn't you believe me?"

He came nearer and took her by the arm.

"You saw Rosamund."

"Yes."

"What did you think of her?"

"She's beautiful."

"Yes. What else?"

"I don't know."

"I thought I did. I thought I'd known her for ten years. I thought I could have said just what she would do and just what she would say in any given circumstances. I thought she was beautiful, rather cold, fond of the good things of the world, indifferent to public opinion; not a great brain, but socially clever; truthful enough, and quite honest, as far as honesty goes; and with a decent family feeling for my grandfather and the place, and perhaps something a little warmer than that for myself. We got on well. We didn't make demands upon one another, but we behaved affectionately. I wasn't in love with her, and she wasn't in love with me; but we were pretty good friends, and I had a theory that friendship would make a better foundation for marriage than a lot of what passes for falling in love—and if I'd been the blindest young jackass that ever went chasing after a chorus girl under the impression that he was following an angel into the Garden of Eden, I couldn't have come a more colossal crash. To say that Rosamund let me down simply doesn't come within a hundred miles of it, and I'm not taking any more chances. She didn't break my heart, because she hadn't got it to break. And now I'll beg your pardon—provisionally—ratification to follow when I've actually seen those letters from your father."

He had been holding her lightly all the time he spoke. Now his hand dropped from her arm.

"Are you going to make me pay for what Rosamund did to you?" said Nan. She had not meant to say it, but the words said themselves hot and quick.

"Probably," said Jervis.

When his eyes laughed and the corners crinkled, Nan had it in her heart to pay her uttermost farthing without counting the cost. She said,

"And if I won't pay?"

Jervis did not answer in words. He frowned, turned abruptly away and, picking up the volume of *Who's Who*, went over to the shelf and put it back in its place. He stood for a minute or two looking at first one book and then another and whistling softly to himself. The tune bothered Nan because she couldn't put a name to it.

She would have given the world twice over to undo what Rosamund had done to him. She wondered whether she would ever be able to undo it. Just now, when his eyes had laughed, she had seen the bitterness and the hardness that were under the laughter. It hurt more than when he frowned. He frowned easily, and it meant very little; but when he laughed, her heart ached for him.

He turned away from the book-shelves and came back to the window. His face wore a bantering look.

"Well? What's the great idea? I should really like to know."

She said, "What do you mean?"

"Well, I'd like to know just why you married me, and just what's at the bottom of all this nonsense about Robert Leonard. A deaf and dumb idiot can see that you've got it in for him—and I must say I'd like to know why."

Nan tipped her head back, met his eyes, and said seriously,

"He's trying to kill you."

"Yes, you said that before—he rode me down in a taxi, and he arranged for the bridge over the ravine to rot in the spray. Come, you know, it's not good enough! But what I *do* want to know is why. What has poor old Leonard done to be cast for the part of first murderer? It seems a bit far-fetched, don't you think? And it would interest me quite a lot to know what put it into your head.''

"It's no use my telling you," said Nan—"you wouldn't believe me."

"I'm afraid I shouldn't. But you're probably of a very hopeful disposition—you might try."

She shook her head.

"It wouldn't be any use."

"How can you tell if you don't try?"

A smile just touched her lips and was gone again.

"You're never going to believe anyone again. It would be waste of time."

"You might convert me."

"Could I, Jervis?"

"I don't think so, Nan. But then that makes it all the more exciting for you. There's always an off chance."

She had been standing looking up at him; now she came a step nearer.

"He *is* trying to kill you."

"How intriguing! Have you any notion why?"

"It's something to do with the money."

"I'm afraid that's where you slip up. Poor old Leonard's not in the running—he wouldn't get a penny. It's distinctly to his interest to let me linger on and touch me for an occasional fiver."

"Does he do that?" (That meant that he was hard up—perhaps desperately hard up.)

"He does," said Jervis. "So you see I'm more use to him alive than dead."

"If he killed you—" said Nan. She stopped, because it was a dreadful thing to say.

"Yes—do go on. If he killed me?"

"Rosamund would get everything."

He gave her a sharp glance. So she was working round to his will. She evidently didn't believe in letting the grass grow under her feet.

He nodded.

"You seem to know all about it."

"I typed Mr Weare's will."

"Well?"

She looked at him in silence.

"You'd got as far as 'Rosamund would get everything.' Aren't you going on?"

"No—it's no use," said Nan.

Jervis laughed.

"Rosamund gets everything—so in case Robert Leonard should feel an overpowering urge to remove me and marry Rosamund, it might be a good plan if I put temptation out of his way by making a will in your favour. Is that it?"

Nan felt as if something in her must break. She didn't know whether it was her pride or her love. There was a feeling of anguished strain.

She said, "No!" with a little cry.

"Unfortunately my hands are tied, so I can't oblige you. I can make a settlement on my wife, but King's Weare and enough to keep it up on goes to Rosamund under my grandfather's will, failing a direct heir."

"I knew that."

"Then I don't quite see what you were driving at."

She came quite close.

"He is trying to kill you," she said. "I don't know why—I think it's because of the money. Perhaps he wants to marry Rosamund—I don't know. But I know that he's trying to kill you."

He looked down at her with hard amusement.

"You're very serious over it."

"I am very serious."

"And why? Don't you want to be a widow?"

"No," said Nan, very pale.

Jervis laughed outright.

"What an odd taste, my dear!"

Before she knew what he was going to do, he took her by the elbows, swung her off her feet, and kissed her on the mouth. He was still laughing when he put her down. She was as white as a sheet and trembling violently.

"Why, what's the matter?" he said.

She turned and ran out of the room.

XXI

JERVIS STOOD FROWNING AT THE DOOR. WHAT A TO-DO about a kiss! He threw up his head and laughed. He didn't know why he had kissed her, and he certainly didn't know why she had run away. One could not have expected a shrinking delicacy from the girl who had offered herself to a stranger for two thousand pounds on the nail and a settlement of five hundred a year. No—to do her justice, she hadn't asked for the five hundred a year; she had only stood out for her two thousand down. Still, she could hardly expect to be considered unapproachable. And after all, what had he done? Swung her off her feet, kissed her lightly, and put her down again. Yet he felt an undoubted sense of guilt, and it angered him. Her lips had been soft and cold; he had felt them tremble; when he put her down, she had the look of a child unbearably hurt. Preposterous! She had offered herself to him; he had married her—and she was to look like that for a kiss!

He stepped over the low window-sill and walked up and down the terrace smoking, until the sun went down into a rose-coloured haze.

Monk found him there watching the sunset. He presented a long envelope and a message.

"Mrs Weare has gone to bed with a headache, sir—and these are the papers you wished to see."

Jervis took them to the study.

So she had gone to bed with a headache. He wondered if he had made her cry. A faint tinge of triumph just touched his mood. He had lived ten years in the same house as Rosamund, and he had never seen her weep. He had kissed her a hundred times, and he had certainly never felt her tremble. Nan's lips had trembled when he touched them—she had trembled from head to foot and had run away—she had looked as if she was going to cry. Perhaps she was lying in the big four-post bed crying her heart out. He had a picture of her in his mind, lying there in the shade of the red curtains, with her head on her arm and her face hidden, weeping scalding tears. For some obscure reason the picture gave him a feeling of pleasure.

He tore open the long envelope which she had sent him. There were half a dozen letters on thin foreign paper, and a slanting pencil scrawl signed Nan. It said:

> Here are my father's letters—some of them. Please let me have them back.

There was a blister on the corner of the paper. It looked as if a drop of water had fallen there.

He sorted out the letters and read them through. They were the rather stiff letters which a man writes to children with whom he has no other than a formal relation.

> I hope you and Cynthia are doing well at school. There's nothing like a good grounding. Your aunt says Cynthia is very backward and does not try to learn. I am very sorry to hear this. You will both have to earn your living some day, as I have nothing to leave you. Life out here is precarious.

Jervis had a tenderness for children. He frowned at the letter as he read it. It was dated July 1919. Nan would have been eleven. Good Lord! What an exhilarating letter for a kid of eleven to get from a father on the other side of the world! It must have been about the last letter he wrote her too.

He turned to another.

> Your aunt says Cynthia is troublesome. I don't know what to do about it. I can't possibly get home until the war is over—and one can't say when that will be. I can be of use here because the Arabs know me. You must

try and manage Cynthia and not let her worry your aunt, for if she doesn't see her way to continuing to take charge of you, I do not really know what I can do.

That was May 1918. Nan would have been ten.
There was another, written a few months earlier.

MY DEAR NAN,

I have had your letter, and the snapshots of you and Cynthia. In answer to your questions—You are not at all like your mother. I am afraid you take after my side of the family. Your mother was very lovely, and everyone loved her. She took love and admiration as a right. Cynthia has a look of her.

All the letters were signed in the same way:

Your affectionate father
NIGEL FORSYTH.

Somehow Jervis found them pathetic. Outside of the signature there was not much affection in them. He got a picture of the man, worried and without an idea of what to do with two little girls in England. And he had a picture of the child who had hoarded these letters—a child who wanted to be like her beautiful mother, and wasn't; who had to shoulder the responsibility which Nigel Forsyth was laying down. It was Nan, obviously, who had to placate "your aunt," to manage Cynthia, and to bear in mind that she had got to earn her own living. He was prepared to bet that she had had to earn Cynthia's living too.

He put the letters back in their envelope and went upstairs.

He stood listening at the door between his room and Nan's, and then knocked upon it. There was no answer. And yet he was quite sure that it was not sleep that was behind the door; he had the feeling that the whole room was waiting to hear him knock again. Instead, he tried the handle, and found, as he expected, that the bolt was fastened on the other side. As the handle moved with a faint creaking sound, he heard the soft padding of feet and the merest ghost of a growl. Next instant Bran was snuffing at the crack.

Jervis was conscious of an ironical amusement. His wife locked her door and suborned his dog to guard it against him!

He knocked again, a good deal louder, and became aware of a movement that was not made by Bran. It was a very soft, almost inaudible movement. It suggested to him that Nan was sitting up in bed—putting back the bed-clothes—slowly, slowly. Bran pushed against the panel and snuffed the key-hole.

With his lips against the crack, Jervis said,

"Nan—are you awake?"

There was a silence. Then he heard her move. She came barefoot to the door and leaned against it, whilst Bran beat with his tail upon the carpet.

"Nan—" said Jervis.

She said, "Yes," in a whisper. It was an uneven whisper, and it told him for certain that she had been crying.

"I didn't mean to wake you."

There was no answer to this.

"I've brought you your letters."

Again no answer.

"Won't you open the door and take them?"

He knew that she was leaning against the door. He heard her hand slip on the panel, but she did not speak. He wondered why her hand had moved. It was not to open the door.

An impatience of her silence gave him a touch of bravado.

"I've come to ratify the apology. Aren't you going to open the door?"

She said, "No"—or he thought that she said, "No." Afterwards he wondered whether her silence had said it for him.

"Won't you open the door and take the letters?"

Nan had wept until she could weep no more. Those scalding tears seemed to have washed everything away, like a flood that obliterates all landmarks and leaves behind it an even desolation. There had been a moment when she could have killed Jervis for that light kiss. The hot rage was gone.

There had been a moment when she could have flung herself into his arms; and that too was gone. There had been shame, and shrinking, and terror, and the surge of something in her own nature which she had not known before. They were all gone. Her burning tears had carried them away. There remained a grey, desolate loneliness, and she was very tired.

She was not sure whether she had spoken when Jervis asked her to open the door. Bran pressed close to her in the dark, and when his warmth touched her she knew that she was cold.

Her silence and the darkness touched Jervis with a vague apprehension. He had come into his room without switching on the light. The windows stood wide and uncurtained, and there came from them a faint, dusky half light in which the accustomed furnishings of the room took on a strange aspect. The sky beyond the windows was pale with the rising moon.

All at once the strangeness was in his own thought. He had for an instant the sense that all this had happened before—in a dream—in some strange place. He and Nan, with darkness between them; and Nan weeping in the darkness. It touched a deep unknown spring and released a rush of some emotion which rose in him and then ebbed again. The whole thing passed between one breath and the next. It left him with the feeling that he had just waked up and did not quite know where he was. He said, in a changed voice.

"Are you all right?"

And this time he heard her say, "Yes"; and he heard Bran push against the door.

Nan straightened herself a little. They could not stand here like this. It would be better to open the door and take her letters—only she couldn't do it. If she opened the door, he would know that she had been crying. No—he had no light in his room; there was not the faintest thread of light at the foot of the door. Why were they standing like this in the dark with the door between them? She had no strength to go away. She leaned against the cold panel, and very faintly her lonely desolation felt the stir of a desire that he should speak, that he should go on speaking; because, when she heard his voice, she did not feel quite so dreadfully alone.

His voice came to her through the panel.

"What is the matter?"

She drew a breath that returned in a sigh.

"Nothing."

"You've been crying."

"No."

"Then won't you open the door?"

A little warmth crept up in her. She had cried for such a long time. It would be nice to make friends. She was very tired. She put up her hand and slipped back the bolt, and at once she was afraid.

The door opened into Jervis' room. As he turned the handle, Bran threw all his weight against and plunged joyfully through the opening, mouthing Jervis and butting him with his head. Nan could see him, huge and black against the three pale windows on the far side of the room. She could see Jervis too, tall and black. Bran ran back to her, whining.

She stood quite still where she was, and Jervis took a step forward as far as the threshold and stretched out his hand with the letters in it. He did not cross the threshold, and when she had taken the letters he stepped back. Then he said in a constrained tone,

"I've read them. I'm sorry for what I said. I'd no business to say it."

Nan put the hand with the letters to her breast. Her hand was cold, and the letters were cold. She did not speak.

All at once Jervis said,

"Good-night."

He stepped back and shut the door.

XXII

FERDINAND FAZACKERLEY CAME DOWN NEXT DAY, ARRIVING in time for dinner with an extraordinary assortment of luggage, including the yellow Gladstone bag, a canvas holdall, a uniform-case scraped and battered down to the bare tin, a wash-basin with a leather top, and some assorted parcels. All except the parcels were plastered over with labels of every shape and colour.

When dinner was over, they had coffee on the terrace, with the heat dropping out of the day and a breeze blowing in from the sea. Mr Fazackerley's bright brown eyes looked appreciatively from his coffee to a bed of flame-coloured snapdragons, from the snapdragons to Nan in a green frock, and from Nan to Jervis.

"This rural solitude," he said, "is a very refreshing thing. I don't mind telling you that I find it very refreshing indeed. It reminds me forcibly of the Garden of Eden."

Nan laughed at him.

"Are you the serpent?"

"No," said F.F. "I take it this is the Garden of Eden before the serpent got there—and, as I said before, I find it mighty refreshing."

He fished a lump of sugar out of his coffee and crunched it. Then, putting his cup down, he said,

"No more accidents?"

There was a little dragging silence before Jervis said in a casual tone,

"Only the old bridge."

Ferdinand jerked round in his wicker chair.

"What do you mean, the old bridge?"

Jervis, sitting sideways on the balustrade, waved a hand in the direction of the ravine.

"Only the old wooden bridge above the fall."

"Great Smith! Above the fall? And it fell? Is that what you're giving me?"

"What a dramatic mind you've got, F.F.! The timbers were rotten with the spray."

"Rotten, were they—and with the spray?"

Jervis nodded.

"It's going to cost a lot to build another—more than I can afford."

Ferdinand sent a dancing look at Nan, and received a definite impression. He went back to Jervis.

"The bridge fell. And was there anyone on it when it fell?"

Jervis got up and stood half turned away, looking down towards the ravine.

"Nan had a narrow escape," he said. "She'll tell you about it if you want to know."

Ferdinand certainly wanted to know. He looked at Nan, and found her changing colour.

"There's nothing to tell, Mr Fazackerley."

"Oh, I guess there's something."

"No, there isn't." Then, as Jervis looked over his shoulder with a sardonic gleam in his eye, she coloured and said stumblingly, "I ran on to the bridge. It cracked, and then it fell. Jervis pulled me up."

"Great Mississippi!" said Ferdinand. "Can't someone do better than that? That's the baldest thing in stories that I've struck since they taught me to read! The—bridge—broke. The—bridge—fell. He—pulled—me—up. Haven't you got a few extra syllables about you, Mrs Jervis? I just feel as if I could do with them if you have."

Nan's head went up.

"Ask Jervis what happened."

She had hardly seen him all day; he had been out and busy about the place; she had breakfasted and lunched alone. She had a sense of temerity when she saw how black a frown her words provoked.

"Nothing happened. The bridge was rotten, and it broke."

"Bran wouldn't cross it," said Nan only just above her breath. "I knew there was something wrong when Bran wouldn't cross it."

"I'm not an inquisitive man," said Ferdinand, "but I'm feeling the strain of this conversation pretty badly. If someone don't tell me what happened soon, I'm going to be a first-aid case."

"Oh, Nan'll tell you—what happened, and a bit over. The bit over is the interesting part of course—it always is. And, being a pressman, you won't worry over its being fiction. The bigger the lie, the better the story. That's it, isn't it, F.F.?"

"That's where you're wrong. The Press wants facts, but it don't want plain facts. It wants facts viewed through the medium of imagination. You take a bit of dry stone. That's a fact—isn't it? You take a handful of dry stones. Well, you've got a handful of dry facts, and there's not a bit of interest in them—they're just dry—you're going to yawn your head off looking at them. But you take your handful of dry stones and put them at the bottom of a stream and let the water run over them, and what have you got? They're still facts—you're not going to deny that. They're just as much facts as they were when you'd got them dry in your hand—but you're not yawning over them any more—they're not dry any more—they're a handful of jewels—they've got light and colour, and movement—the water's made them come alive. Well, that's what imagination does to facts—it makes them come alive. And the Press wants live facts—not dead ones that are going to make people yawn their heads off."

Jervis had been listening in a careless attitude, one knee on the balustrade. His sudden smile came and went again. It gave his face an extraordinary charm. He looked at Ferdinand with affection.

"Very nicely put, F.F. I'm afraid I only deal in dry facts—that's why I'm not competing. Nan will turn on all the imagination that's required."

Nan's cheeks burned with a sudden scarlet. Everything in her was reacting violently from the moment when she had stood with the door between herself and Jervis and had not had a word to say. That was last night; but it might have happened in another world. She had felt drained and dumb, a sort of ghost in the dark. She did not feel in the least like that now. She wanted to convince Ferdinand, to get him on her side. She felt warm, and alive, and sure. She leaned toward him with her elbow on the arm of her chair.

"I'll tell you what happened."

"That's better," said F.F.

Jervis got up and strolled away.

"When the thrills are over you can wander down to the ravine and view the remains," he said.

He went down the steps and on down the grassy slope.

"*Now*, Mrs Jervis," said Ferdinand.

"Jervis doesn't believe—anything."

"Well no—he wouldn't. Suppose you try me—I'm a whale at believing."

"There's so little to tell. There's nothing that you can prove—there's only the feeling, the frightfully strong feeling."

Ferdinand nodded.

"You mean you've got a hunch. Well, I take a good deal of stock in hunches myself. You go right on and tell me all about this bridge business."

Nan went on. She told him about waking up in the night and looking out of her window and seeing Robert Leonard by a flash of lightning.

"And what does Jervis say to that?"

"He says I couldn't possibly have recognized him all that way off."

"Well, there's something in that."

"I saw him. First there was a moon, and then the clouds went over it and it was quite dark—and after that there was a flash of lightning, and I saw him."

"Where?"

She turned and looked across the balustrade to the ravine.

"There—just where Jervis is now, where the path goes in amongst the trees."

Ferdinand whistled through his teeth.

"It's a long way off."

"I saw him," said Nan.

"All right. Now what about the bridge?"

"Jervis took me down to see the fall, and when we came

to the bridge Bran wouldn't cross it—he wouldn't go onto it at all. He *knew*."

Ferdinand nodded.

"I've seen an elephant do that in Burma—it just stood there and trumpeted. Go on."

"Jervis was angry with him. He tried to drag him on to the bridge—" She stopped abruptly.

Ferdinand laughed a little.

"Keep right on," he said.

"Well, the bridge went—and I'd have gone too, only Jervis grabbed hold of me and pulled me up."

His bright brown eyes mocked her a little.

"I never did care for an expurgated edition—it puts too much strain on the imagination."

"That's all," said Nan hastily.

"George Washington! All? And how did you come to be on the bridge? Bran wouldn't cross, and you *knew* there was something wrong, *and so* you went onto the bridge yourself just to see what would happen."

He had the satisfaction of seeing her cheeks burn.

"Well—that is so, isn't it?" he said.

Nan jumped up.

"You'd better go down and look at the bridge."

"If I'd got a hat on, I'd take it off to you, Mrs Jervis!" said Ferdinand Fazackerley.

XXIII

THEY LUNCHED NEXT DAY WITH THE TETTERLEYS. MABEL Tetterley rang up and invited them in a casual, inconsequent manner. She said Basher was dying to meet Nan. She extended her original invitation to include Ferdinand, and finished up by hoping that they wouldn't be poisoned, because she had a new cook and Basher said she had a Lucrezia Borgia sort of look about her.

The heat held. After a time their road lay along the cliffs. The blue of the sky and the blue of the sea swam together in a trembling haze. The car was an open one. The sun flooded down upon them, and there was no breeze but what they made themselves.

Jervis drove at what seemed to Nan a break-neck pace. It made her giddy. She closed her eyes, and heard Ferdinand laugh behind her.

"Road hog! Isn't he? You should have seen him push the old Ford we had in Anatolia. We had the local brigand after us, and when I wasn't getting shell shock over the bullets that were flying, I was having a heart attack at what the speedometer was registering. After the needle had run twice round the dial it cashed in its checks, and I was wishing I'd cashed in mine and got it over."

They skimmed down a steep hill and tore up the other side. Nan felt exactly as if she were in a lift; but there was something exhilarating about it too. She laughed as they raced at the hill, and Jervis looked sideways at her and smiled.

"Jolly view here."

The road was on the edge of the cliff. The sea was blue beneath them; the water sparkled in the sun.

"Beastly bad bit of road on that hill, F.F. Quite like old times! I can't get anyone to do anything about it, and what it'll be like after another winter, Lord knows." He turned to Nan. "That's your friend Leonard's chicken farm."

Nan sat up straight. She saw a green field dotted with hen-houses, and a neglected garden that had grown right up to the walls of an old stone house. The whole place looked uncared for.

"What a *frightful* place!" she said.

Jervis laughed.

"A bit untidy! It's been empty for ever so long. I must say he doesn't seem in a hurry to get things straight."

"It's a hateful house," said Nan, looking at it. "I'm not surprised it was empty a long time—I shouldn't think anyone would want to live there ever."

Jervis slowed down as they went past.

"It belonged to a famous smuggler called Old Foxy Fixon. He lived about a hundred years ago, and after his grandson died people said the place was haunted, and nobody would live there. It's still called Old Foxy Fixon's house. It belongs to the Tetterleys, and I expect they were very glad to get it let."

Nan went on looking at the house over her shoulder until a turn of the road hid it.

A bare quarter of a mile farther on they turned in at the Tetterleys' gate.

Basher, alias Sir George Tetterley, proved to be a massive, silent person. He had kind eyes, and a ridiculously soft voice which he used as little as possible. Lady Tetterley talked enough for a half a dozen.

Rosamund did not appear until lunch had been announced, when she strolled in looking exquisitely cool.

"Robert's going to be late. Something's the matter with that damned car of his. It just got us here and no more. He's tinkering with it down at the garage. I say the scrap-heap's the only cure. The brute nearly killed us yesterday, and I've told him I'm not going out in her again."

Mr Leonard came in half way though lunch. He looked hot, and explained that he hadn't been able to get his car going. Nan had been placed between him and her host. She had, therefore, an empty chair on one side of her for the first twenty minutes or so.

Sir George made one remark about the weather, and another about the crops. Before, after, and between these remarks he ate his lunch. Oddly enough, Nan did not find this silence unpleasant. It was a companionable silence; it did not exclude, but admitted her an intimacy in which one spoke if one had something to say. At the moment, Sir George had not anything to say to her. He looked at her kindly and seemed to take it for granted that they should both listen to the flow of conversation from the rest of the party. He smiled appreciatively once or twice, frowned when Lady Tetterley produced a piece of unpleasant gossip about a neighbour, and did more than justice to the efforts of the new cook.

When Robert Leonard took the empty chair beside her,

Nan would have preferred a more conversational neighbour on her other side. In desperation she leaned towards Sir George and said,

"Lady Tetterley said you used to know my father's people."

Sir George nodded and said,

"Long ago."

"Will you tell me about them? They quarrelled with him about his marriage, and I've never seen any of them."

"Haven't seen them for years," said Sir George—"twenty years. Used to stay there when I was a young fellow—very kind to me and all that."

Nan looked disappointed.

"I know my grandfather's dead," she said.

Sir George nodded again. He took up his glass, emptied it, and signed to have it refilled.

"All gone," he said. "Place sold. Great pity for an old place to go out of the family."

"My father had a sister," said Nan. "I'm called after her."

"Yes," said Sir George. "That's why I thought you belonged to the family. She wasn't Anne, you know; she was Nan—christened Nan."

"So am I," said Nan. "Am I like her?"

"Yes," said George Tetterley—"very." His face and his voice were quite expressionless. He helped himself to a vegetable that was being handed to him and then remarked that it was too late in the season to expect decent peas.

When the dish had gone on its way, Nan said,

"Do tell me about her. Is she alive?"

He shook his head.

"Did she marry?"

"Yes—quite a good chap."

From the other side of the table came Ferdinand Fazackerley's voice:

"When I was in Mexico in '24 . . ." He proceeded to tell a lively story of an encounter with a guerilla band. The name of Pedro Ramirez emerged from it. It appeared that Ferdinand had been uncommonly lucky to have escaped the undesired role of providing entertainment for a temporarily idle band. "They'd got a really high-class show all fixed up, with me for the star performer. There was a kind of

William Tell turn, with all the best shots seeing how close they could shave me without actually putting me out of action. And there was a Mazeppa turn, with me for Mazeppa, and the worst-tempered bronco in the bunch for the Wild Horse of the Ukraine.''

"How *divine!*" said Mabel Tetterley.

"Well, that's not the adjective I should use myself—but I was brought up a Primitive Methodist, and it rather cramps my style when it comes to really adequate alternatives.''

"Did you do Mazeppa?"

"Well, no. I reckon I wouldn't be here now if I had.''

"But you're not telling us what happened,'' said Mabel Tetterley.

"Well,'' said Ferdinand, "this is a very instructive tale— one of the real mother's-knee kind, all around the text of 'If you do a good turn, it'll come back to roost.' I'd done my good turn getting on for eight years before and forgotten all about it. I'm not going to tell you what it was, because I've got a real modest disposition, but just when those bright boys were going to get going with their quick-shooters, that good turn came home to roost—*deus ex machina*, same as in the Greek plays when they want to get the mess cleared up at the end. I don't want you to think I'm a Greek scholar, but I've a profound admiration for the translations of Professor Gilbert Murray.''

This was the occasion for one of Sir George's smiles.

"You're not telling us how you got away,'' said Mabel Tetterley.

"Pardon me, Lady Tetterley, that is what I am doing.'' He paused and looked around the table.

Sir George was smiling; Rosamund Carew lighting a cigarette with an air of calm detachment; Jervis—well, just Jervis; Mabel Tetterley faintly bored at the digression into Greek plays; Robert Leonard in the act of lifting a tumbler of whisky and soda to his lips; and Nan an eager child waiting for the end of the story.

"My *deus ex machina* was a man called Hermann Eisenthal.''

Robert Leonard's glass continued its upward way. He drank as if he was thirsty and set it down.

Ferdinand was looking at Lady Tetterley. But those glancing eyes of his certainly had the faculty of being able to see two things at once. He had most certainly seen the knuckles whiten on Robert Leonard's broad red hand. Ferdinand judged that the glass it was holding had missed being a casualty by a fairly narrow margin. He finished his story.

"Hermann Eisenthal remembered the good turn which F.F. had forgotten. He had the guerilla chief in his pocket, and it was pull for the shore, sailor, pull for the shore. And if you've ever been all trussed up and ready to take the floor as a high-class target with a nasty half-breed monarch-of-all-he-surveys waiting to give the word for the shooting to begin, you'll know just how glad I was to see Hermann. I tell you he'd got Mr Pedro Ramirez feeding out of his hand. It's no good your asking me why. He'd got him sitting up for sugar like a circus dog. Well, I've often thought it would be interesting to know what the sugar was."

Ferdinand's bright brown eyes went past Robert Leonard to Nan. Perhaps they were looking for something as they passed. Perhaps they found what they were looking for.

"Your husband wasn't with me that time, Mrs Jervis," he said, "or I'd have put the whole thing down to his luck. He's the sort that falls on his feet, you know, and if there's any bad luck going, it kind of richochets off him and lands back where it came from."

XXIV

WHAT DID F.F. MEAN? DID HE MEAN ANYTHING AT ALL? OR were his words just an echo of something in her own mind? Nan couldn't make out. Or were the words nothing, and she was just reading into them the accusation which filled her thoughts? It was as much as she could do to sit next to Robert Leonard without crying this accusation aloud—"You've been trying to kill Jervis!" She caught the inside of her lip in her teeth to hold it against those words. What would everyone say if she called them aloud?

Sir George Tetterley was giving her a potted version of his last game of golf; to such a mellow mood had lunch and her likeness to that earlier Nan Forsyth brought him. Curiously enough, some delicate extra sense informed her that of all the people around the table Sir George would be the least surprised if she were suddenly to say what was in her mind about Robert Leonard. Quite definitely Sir George did not like him—oh, quite definitely. Neither did he like Rosamund—much. This surprised Nan. She was young enough to give beauty too many points in the game.

Rosamund had begun to smoke before she had begun to eat. She ate very little, and she lit one cigarette from another all through the meal. She wore a straight, plain dress of heavy white washing silk. In contrast to Mabel Tetterley, whose thin neck was hung with beads like small golf balls, Rosamund's throat was bare. Seen through a bluish haze of smoke, she had the air of beauty withdrawn behind its own impalpable veils.

Nan's heart hurt her very much as she looked across the table at this beauty of Rosamund's. Jervis' very anger against her was the measure of his love and his loss. Having loved Rosamund, it could not be possible that he should ever love Nan.

She shrank away from these thoughts, and gave Sir George so earnest a listener that he not only played out that round of golf but began upon a previous one and took her through it without omitting a single stroke.

They went out into the garden after lunch and had coffee under the shade of two enormous cedars. As they crossed the lawn with the sun pouring down upon them, the party broke up into twos and threes. Nan found herself walking with Ferdinand.

"What did you mean?" she said without looking at him. "I?"

"Yes, Mr Fazackerley."

Ferdinand stopped dead, rumpled his hair, and looked at her with a half shy, half bold expression which reminded her of a sparrow looking at a crumb.

"I just hate you to call me that," he said.

Nan blushed a little with pleasure, and he threw out his hand in an odd gesture.

"I'd hate it worse if you were to think me fresh."

"Fresh?" said Nan.

The queer bright eyes twinkled at her.

"That's just American for forward. I shouldn't like you to think I was pushing myself into being friends with you—but I'd like it mighty well if we *were* friends."

Nan said, "Oh—" It was a little sound with a quiver in it. Her eyes were soft and misty. "Oh, how *nice* of you!" she said.

Mr Fazackerley stuck his hands into his pockets.

"That's for fear I'm going to take right hold of your hand and pretty near shake it off."

"How nice of you, F.F.!" said Nan.

They began to walk again. The sunlight dazzled round her. She didn't feel afraid of Rosamund any more. Here was a really, truly friend of Jervis' who wanted to be friends with her. She found it immensely strengthening. Ever since she had married Jervis she had felt as if she were walking through a strange, empty desert place alone. F.F. wanting to be her friend was like suddenly finding out that the desert wasn't quite empty. She came back to her first question.

"What did you mean at lunch?"

"Perhaps I didn't mean anything."

"You did—you told that story on purpose, and you looked at *him*—Mr Leonard. What did you mean?"

Ferdinand turned and waved a hand in the direction of a most undeniable view. The trees had been cut away to frame a glimpse of the sea.

"That's pretty good—isn't it?" he said.

Nan hadn't anything at all to say about the view.

"Who was Eisenthal?" she said.

Ferdinand turned in a leisurely fashion and let a roving glance travel about the lawn. Lady Tetterley and Mr Leonard had reached the shade and were already disposed in comfortable chairs. Sir George was in the act of joining them. Jervis and Rosamund Carew had taken a wide circle away from the cedars and were entering upon a shady path overarched by tall rhododendrons. A footman had just emerged from the house bearing the coffee-tray.

"Who is Eisenthal?"

It certainly seemed safe enough to answer her.

"A fellow I met out there."

He got a frown, and a clear indignant look.

"What *was* he?"

"A chemist," said Ferdinand.

"You mean—an experimental chemist."

"Yes—that was quick of you."

She shook her head.

"Why could he make the guerilla chief do as he liked?"

"Chemists are sometimes useful."

"How was Eisenthal useful?"

"A handy fellow," said Ferdinand.

"Don't you *know*?"

"Well yes, I know."

"Are you going to tell me?"

"Well, that's what I don't know."

"Why?" He saw a faint sensitive clouding of those eager eyes. Her lips parted. "You're not going to tell me—"

He told her what he hadn't meant to tell anyone—yet.

"Eisenthal was a genius gone wrong. I don't know what he'd done, but he'd made his own country a hundred degrees or so too hot to hold him. He looked like any other professor, only more respectable, and he'd a fierce brain. Well, he'd got an invention that had been mighty useful to that guerilla chief."

"What was it?" said Nan.

"What'll you do if I tell you?"

"I won't tell *anyone*."

"Certain sure?"

"I won't—really."

Ferdinand had another look about him. Jervis and Rosamund had disappeared. The coffee was half way across the lawn. Lady Tetterley was flirting with Mr Leonard. Sir George had retired behind *The Times*.

He began to speak in the sort of voice that barely carries a yard:

"About a month before he'd copped me, Mr Pedro Ramirez had brought off a mighty useful little coup. He was carrying on operations in the Madalena district and harassing the government quite a bit. Then they turned nasty and sent up some real troops—and that's where he brought off his coup. There were three trains, and they left Madalena at three-hour intervals. The first of them ran off the line on the edge of the big pass where it enters the hills. It went down a couple of hundred feet, and there weren't any survivors. The second train crashed through the parapet of the bridge over the Madalena River about five miles short of the hills. And the third ran off the track only ten miles out of Madalena."

"How?" said Nan.

"Eisenthal," said Ferdinand.

"Yes—but *how*?"

F.F. waved his hand toward the sea.

"I'm not a chemist, but I got away with the idea that Eisenthal had invented a thing that disintegrated certain substances. The man who told me said he'd seen the sleepers where those three trains left the line, and they were just mush."

Nan looked at him with eyes like saucers.

"But, F.F.—the first train got as far as the hills."

He nodded.

"Why didn't it crash sooner? It must have run over the places where the other two trains went off, and the second train must have run over the bit of line where the third one crashed."

"Yes. You're bright—aren't you? I was bright too. I said to the man who told me, 'Look here, what are you giving me?' He said, 'I don't know—but as I told you, so it happened.' Afterwards I asked Eisenthal. I'm not an inquisitive man, but I kind of like to know how things happen, so when I got a chance I asked him, and he told me it was all a matter of careful timing. You spray the stuff on, and it takes just so long to make a thing dicky, and so much longer to rot it right through. It must all be calculated very carefully—so much stuff to the square inch, and it takes just so long to work. Well, the place where the first train crashed was done first. It ran over the other two places before they'd got dangerous. He said he'd experimented most carefully and timed the whole show to the minute.''

Nan looked away to the distant blue of the sea. She said under her breath,

"The stuff made wood rotten?"

"So I'm given to understand."

"Jervis' bridge was rotten."

"That's when I began to think about Eisenthal."

Nan turned round quickly.

"What happened to Eisenthal?"

"I'm not quite sure. I think he's dead."

"He's not . . . ?"

"Leonard? Not on your life! It's not so easy as that. The nearest I've got to it at present is that they were both in the South American continent at the same time—but that's not very incriminating for Mr Leonard."

"Will you tell Jervis?"

He shook his head.

"Not a bit of good telling Jervis. I shall keep my eyes open. Don't you want any coffee? I've got a hunch we've been admiring the view just about as long as we'd better."

They crossed the grass slowly. Ferdinand talked about Constantinople. South America was a long way away. Eisenthal was dead. They came out of the sun into the shade.

Robert Leonard was sipping his coffee. He looked cool and comfortable. He smiled pleasantly at Nan and engaged her in conversation whilst Lady Tetterley transferred her attentions to Ferdinand. Sir George kept *The Times* firmly between himself and the outside world. After a little while he ceased to turn the pages; the sheets crumpled and sank lower, and a steady rhythmical sound came from behind them.

XXV

THE PATH UNDER THE RHODODENDRONS WAS COOL AND dark; a faint breath of damp rose up from between the twisted stems. There was water not very far away. Jervis walked beside Rosamund Carew, but he didn't look at her; he looked into the green gloom ahead of them. When they came to the place where a couple of planks crossed a runnel of water, he stood still and said,

"What do you want to say to me?"

"Quite a lot of things."

"Well, suppose you get down to it."

"I'm not in any hurry."

Jervis looked at her in order to ensure the direction of the portentous frown.

"If you've really got anything to say to me, I think this would be a good place to say it, and then we can go back and join the others."

Rosamund, as usual, was smoking. She withdrew her cigarette and blew out a cloud of smoke before she said,

"Won't she let you speak to me? Poor old Jervis!" There was a light drawling contempt in her voice.

Jervis smiled, that sudden, dangerous smile of his.

"You are too attractive," he said. "You always were. One must defend oneself."

Rosamund drew at her cigarette.

"I've been wondering where on earth I'd seen her before, and I've just got there. Used she to dance at Solano's?"

Jervis nodded.

"I believe she did. Have you anything to say about it?"

"No—I just wondered whether you knew."

"Certainly I knew. Is that all you wanted to say to me? Shall we go back and have our coffee?"

"It isn't nearly all. Your coffee will have to wait. I've got a lot of things to say to you."

"Say them," said Jervis.

She threw away the end of her cigarette. It fell into the water and with a little hiss went dead.

"Why did you get engaged to me?" she said suddenly.

"Why does one get engaged to anyone?"

"You weren't in love with me."

He shrugged his shoulders very slightly.

"Or you with me. Is there any object in digging up these ancient remains?"

"Yes—I'd like to know why you ever thought of marrying me."

She was lighting another cigarette, and she looked, not at Jervis, but at the spurting flame of the match. Jervis looked at it too. It licked the paper and blackened it; infinitesimal red points strung themselves together where the edge of the paper had been; a tiny spiral of smoke went up.

"One thinks about marrying—and when you've got as far as that you look round for someone to marry. You were adjacent, you were heavily backed by the family, and you appeared to be quite pleased with the idea."

Rosamund threw her head back and looked at him out of half-closed eyes.

"I was thrust on you against your will? Is that what you're trying to say?"

"Not in the least! You might know by now that I don't try and say things—I say them. It was a matter of mutual convenience. We both got something out of it."

Rosamund drew rather a long breath.

"Did you wonder why I broke it off?"

"Oh no—it was perfectly obvious."

"You think I did it to get the money."

Jervis' eyes met hers for a moment. Their expression was one of amusement. It stung her into a hot protest.

"What a foul mind you've got! No wonder you were livid, if you thought I'd done a beastly thing like that!"

Jervis laughed.

"Perhaps you'd like to explain why you did do it."

"I can't. But it wasn't anything to do with the money. You can't possibly believe a thing like that!"

"Can't I?"

"No, you can't. It's not true anyway. And if you hadn't rushed off and married the first girl who vamped you, everything would have been all right."

"It must have been a nasty jolt for you. Pretty good staff work—wasn't it?"

Rosamund swung round and stood with her back to him for a moment. Then she said over her shoulder,

"You needn't rub it in."

"I don't want to talk about it," said Jervis—"I never did. Don't you think we might go back to the others?"

"No."

"Is there anything else you want to say to me? Because if not—"

"Of course there is!"

"Let's get on with it then."

Rosamund turned round. Her face never varied from its even pallor, but a still paler line seemed to have been drawn from nose to mouth. It ran from the nostril to the corner of the lip on either side, and it made her look ten years older.

"You're as hard as nails," she said. "It's no use trying to work on your feelings, because you haven't got any."

"Yes?"

She made a slight gesture with her cigarette.

"Jervis—I've got to have some money. I can't go on— the situation's impossible—I owe about five hundred."

Jervis frowned at the running water.

"You can send the bills to me. I'll settle them this time, but not again. After this you'll have to make do on your allowance."

"Three hundred a year?"

He looked at her, and looked away again.

"If I make it four, will you keep within it?"

"No—I can't. It's no good pretending that I can. If Uncle Ambrose had meant me to live on four hundred a year, he ought to have brought me up differently."

Jervis was smiling again.

"I think you were twenty before you were here, except on a visit. It strikes me you were pretty thoroughly brought up by then."

"Whoever brought me up, it wasn't on the four hundred a year standard. I can't do it. If Uncle Ambrose had known you were going to marry someone else, he'd have left me properly provided for. He talked about it once before we were engaged, and he said he'd leave me twenty-five thousand."

"What's the good of talking like that?"

"Give me that twenty-five thousand and let me clear out. I don't bring you very good luck—do I? Well, let me clear out. I've got a good opening that I could take if I'd some capital. Let me go, and I've an idea that it'll be better for all of us."

"My dear Rosamund," said Jervis, "I'll see you at Jericho before I'll give you twenty-five thousand pounds!"

Rosamund drew at her cigarette. The pale lines were a little paler.

"Jericho?" she said, "You won't get rid of me as easily as that. You'd better think again—second thoughts are best."

Jervis laughed.

"I'm afraid I might think forever without your getting any nearer that twenty-five thousand. And now I think we'll go back to the others."

He turned as he spoke, and set a brisk pace back along the path. Rosamund walked beside him in silence. Just as they came to where the shade ceased, she laughed and said,

"It would have saved a lot of trouble if we had married each other—wouldn't it?"

Jervis stepped out into the sunlight.

"Do you think so?" he said.

She could not see his face.

XXVI

Nan got up to say good-bye at a quarter to three. Her heart was like a hot burning coal. She had had to sit by Robert Leonard, to take her coffee from his hand, and to listen whilst he talked. Her burning anger lit a bright colour in her cheeks and made her eyes brilliant. She felt as if anything she touched would be liable to scorch or go up in a little puff of smoke. It was a dreadful feeling of course, but it made her very sure of herself.

When she got up to go, Mr Leonard looked at his watch and exclaimed.

"I'd no idea it was so late! You've beguiled me from my duties, Mrs Jervis. I ought to be attending to my incubators at this very moment. Give me a lift as far as my gate, will you, Jervis? My car's a fixture till I can get someone out from Croyston."

Impossible to refuse of course. Nan wondered whether Jervis would have liked to refuse.

He said, "All right," with an air of complete indifference.

At any rate she wouldn't have to sit next to the man. F.F. would have that pleasure. F.F. wouldn't mind of course. It was only she who felt like an exploding bomb when Robert Leonard was anywhere about. She got in beside Jervis, and heard the other two settling themselves behind her, F.F. full of amiable chatter.

"Did you have a car in South America? I forgot where you were. Were you ever in Mexico? Shocking roads, but not as bad as San Pedro. The Madalena roads are pretty hard to beat. I had an old flivver there. She was a wonder. She jumped the potholes like a bird."

They moved off, slid down the drive, and coasted as far as Mr Leonard's gate. He got out and made his farewells.

"You must come and see my place some day, Mrs Jervis. Thanks for the lift, Jervis. Good-bye, Mr Fazackerley."

"'Av revoir," said Ferdinand.

The afternoon was very hot. There was nothing surprising in the fact that Robert Leonard found it necessary to pass a handkerchief across his forehead. Ferdinand, looking back, admitted this, but could not quite understand why Mr Leonard should have quite so shaky a hand. He began to speculate about Mr Leonard. The man had had his hand clenched on the seat between them. When he took hold of the handle to open the door, the hand shook—most undeniably it shook. As he stood mopping his brow and watching the car out of sight, it was still shaking. And he had drunk nothing but lemonade, so it wasn't that.

Jervis wasn't thinking about Robert Leonard. He looked once at Nan, and was aware of distinct relief. She had not golden hair, sea-blue eyes, regular features, or a statuesque figure. He was feeling a strong distaste for all these things. Nan's firm round chin, her brown hair, her steady grey eyes, and the rather childish contour of her face were as complete a contrast as could be found to the charms of his cousin Rosamund. His gaze dwelt upon his wife with approval.

They began to descend the hill, and before they came to the steepest part he put the car into bottom gear. For a couple of hundred yards the gradient was about one in seven, and the surface bad. They had on their right a high bank out of which the road had been cut, and on the left a narrow strip of rough grass with an occasional scrawny bush, and beyond that a low parapet of loose stones which defended a sheer drop to the sea below.

Jervis had scarcely changed down, when amongst his other thoughts there slid into his mind a conviction that there was something wrong with the car. The conviction became a certainty and took entire possession of him. The steering was behaving oddly; the wheel wobbled, and there was a drag to the left. A drag to the left was a drag to the cliff. The wheel kicked in his hand. He wrenched it over and jammed on the brakes, and as he did so a number of things happened all at once. The near front wheel came off and went bounding down the hill, its scarlet and black catching the sun. The front axle came down with a heavy bump on the left. The car swung round, slid, tilted, and fell over with a crash. Robert Leonard heard the sound of it as he walked up the path from the gate to his house. He stood still. Then he walked on again.

On the three people in the car, two were taken entirely by surprise. Ferdinand Fazackerley had a moment of wondering why the road should be so much rougher going down than it had been coming up. Then he saw the black and scarlet wheel go bowling down the road like a child's hoop gone crazy. And then the car turned over and threw him clear. Nan did not see the wheel or notice the jolting. She was looking over the steep edge of the cliff. She had never seen anything so blue in all her life. The tide was high, and the water came up to the foot of the cliff. The first thing she knew of the accident was a violent jolt, and then the side of the car dropping away from her on her left. She gave a little cry and put out both her hands. Something struck her right shoulder. Then the car turned right over with a sound of smashing glass, and she was on her hands and knees on the rough grass with the leather seat pressing down upon her back.

Ferdinand Fazackerley picked himself up out of the dust of the road. He felt rather dazed. He wasn't sure whether he had been thrown clear or whether he had jumped, but he was in the middle of the track with the knees of his trousers torn and the car across the road, very neatly upside down, her bonnet hitched up on the stone parapet. He couldn't see Jervis, and he couldn't see Nan. He felt grateful for the parapet, because if it hadn't been there, the car wouldn't have been there either, but at the bottom of the cliff like a smashed egg. He came out of his daze with a jerk and ran forward just as Nan crawled out from under the front seat. She pulled herself up by the wall and said,

"Where's Jervis?"

Ferdinand ran round to the other side of the car.

She said, "Where's Jervis?" again.

She couldn't run, because her legs didn't feel as if they belonged to her. She crawled round the car, holding on to it. It looked so odd upside down. The sides were smooth; her fingers slipped on the paint. She got round to the other side and saw Ferdinand dragging Jervis clear. Jervis did not move or help himself at all. Then she saw his face. And when she saw his face, she forgot all about her legs not belonging to her, and she let go of the car and ran to him. There was a most dreadful moment when she thought he was dead. Everything stood still. Her thoughts wouldn't move. She couldn't take her breath, and a blackness like the darkness of a nightmare made a wall all around her. It was like being buried alive. She did not know how long it lasted.

Ferdinand's voice came through the blackness. His hand shook her arm.

"Nan! *Nan!*"

Nan became aware that she was sitting on the grass with her back against the stone parapet. There was something heavy on her lap, and as she became aware of it, it moved. She looked down through the blackness that was thinning away, and saw that it was Jervis' head that had moved. A moment later she realized that she was crying. The tears were running down her face and wetting Jervis' hair. She began to look for her handkerchief, not to dry her eyes but to dry his hair; but before she could find it he muttered something unintelligible, opened his eyes, put his hand to his head, and sat up. His coat was torn, and a great smear of blood and dust ran all down one side of his face. He put his hand to his head again, frowned at Nan, and said,

"What are you crying for? Are you hurt?"

The tears ran down Nan's face. They ran into the corners of her mouth and tasted salt; they ran down on to her neck and trickled away under her dress. She didn't want them to run down like that, but they just came. And she couldn't find her handkerchief. She complained about it out loud.

"I can't find my handkerchief." The last word was split in two by a choking sob. It was a devastating depth of misery to be sitting drying in the dust, with Jervis scowling at her, and not to be able to find a handkerchief.

"Is that why you're crying?" said Jervis.

"I thought you were dead!" said Nan; and as she said it Ferdinand's hand came over her shoulder with a clean folded bandanna.

It was of a lively shade of purple, with an orange and green thunderstorm in the middle and some rather lurid scarlet lightning. Nan mopped her eyes with it. As soon as she had a handkerchief she didn't want to cry any more. You can't dry yourself very well with silk, but she did her best.

Jervis looked at her with gloomy dissatisfaction. What was she getting at? It would be a very good thing for her if he was dead, because she would be free and quite well provided for. It was ridiculous to cry about it. But she had been crying. The wet on his cheek was blood, but the wet on his head wasn't. She must have been crying all over his hair.

He had got as far as this, when Ferdinand addressed him.

"Anything broken?"

Up to this moment there had been a closed door between him and everything that had happened before he sat up and saw Nan crying. Now this door suddenly burst open, and he looked through it and saw the near front wheel of his car go bouncing and bounding downhill with a kind of demented *joie de vivre*.

"Broken?" he said. Then he scrambled on to his feet. "What made that damned wheel come off?"

He stood staring at the car, with her three wheels in the air and her bonnet hitched up on the parapet. Her last drunken lurch had carried half of it away. The stones had gone down two hundred feet into the sea.

"If I hadn't yanked her round a bit, she'd have gone too," said Jervis.

Ferdinand agreed.

"That is so," he said soberly. "It was a mighty near thing—a mighty—near—thing. I'm not an inquisitive man, but I'd like to know what made that wheel come off."

XXVII

No one was any the worse. Jervis had a scratch on the cheek and a bump on the back of the head. Nan had the consciousness that she had made a fool of herself. Ferdinand had a pair of trousers which would never be the same again. And the car had a broken windscreen, a buckled mudguard, and a badly dented bonnet—negligible injuries when contrasted with what might have been.

A breakdown tender came out from Croyston, retrieving the missing wheel at the bottom of the hill. Three dusty and disreputable people walked back to the Tetterleys' to use the telephone and wash.

Mr Leonard, who was emerging from a hen-house, saw them pass. He did not think that they had seen him. He stepped back into the house. Presently he saw Walters, the King's Weare chauffeur, drive past in the old Napier saloon, and a little after that again he watched him return with Jervis, Nan, and Ferdinand Fazackerley.

Jervis and Ferdinand went into Croyston to see about the car. Nan had a bath and tried to forget that she had told Jervis she was crying because she thought he was dead. She put on her grey and silver dress and sat on the shady side of the lawn waiting for them to come home. They were late for dinner.

When the fruit was on the table and the servants had left the room, Nan leaned back in her chair and said,

"Why did that wheel come off?"

She spoke to Ferdinand, and with a lift of the eyebrows and a wave of the hand Ferdinand passed the question on.

"Well, that's for Jervis to say."

"I don't know," said Jervis. "Walters swears he went over the wheel-nuts with a brace only yesterday—but then of course he'd be bound to say that."

Ferdinand picked up a grape, looked at it, and bit it neatly in half.

"How long's he been here?"

"Fifteen years."

"Methodical guy?"

"What do you mean by methodical?"

Ferdinand removed the seeds from the other half of the grape and swallowed it like a pill.

"Well—take me. I'm not methodical—if I've got a car, I run her till she stops, and then I get hold of the nearest expert and I put it up to him to say what's wrong. That's my way, but I'm free to confess that it's not methodical. Now Walters looks to me like one of those guys that's got a place for everything and everything in its place—a day when he oils her, and a day when he greases her, and a day when he takes her to bits, and a day when he goes over her with a spanner tightening things up—to say nothing of powdering her nose and touching her up with lipstick. Isn't that so?"

Jervis nodded.

"But the wheel came off," he said.

"A spanner can be used for loosening nuts as well as for tightening them up."

"What do you mean?"

"Hasn't it struck you that you've been having rather a lot of accidents lately?"

"What do you mean by that?"

Ferdinand took another grape.

"That you're having too many accidents. They kind of get me asking why."

"What accidents have I had?" said Jervis in a challenging voice.

Ferdinand finished his grape. He pushed one of the seeds up on the rim of his plate.

"That's number one," he said. He pushed up a second seed. "Two." Then two more, and finished counting, "Three—four."

"What are you playing at F.F.?"

Ferdinand prodded the first seed with the point of his fruit-knife.

"This one's way back in the mists of antiquity, but I reckon it's important. You get the back of your head stove in, and you're left drowning in a pool with the tide coming up—and Mr Robert Leonard is seen coming away from the spot."

Jervis flung up his head with a jerk.

"What are you talking about?"

"I'm talking about that accident you had ten years ago, when you were left to drown."

Nan watched them with her steady eyes.

"*Left* to drown?" said Jervis.

"By Mr Robert Leonard."

"What are you saying F.F.?"

"He was seen leaving the spot."

"Who was?"

Mr Robert Leonard."

"*Seen?* By whom?"

"By a very credible witness."

Jervis hit the table with his hand.

"Witness? What witness? Where have you been getting all this balderdash?"

Ferdinand bit another grape in half and proceeded to remove the seeds.

"Well, I'm not giving my witness away just now, but as far as I remember Mr Robert Leonard skipped out of the country p.d.q. whilst you were still unconscious. It might be worthwhile asking yourself whether he wasn't afraid you might have seen something before he knocked you out."

Jervis pushed back his chair.

"I think everyone's gone crazy about Leonard!" he said angrily. "I've no use for the man—never have had any use for him—but good Lord, F.F., why on earth should he try to murder me? If he's a homicidal maniac, he's kept it pretty dark—and short of being a homicidal maniac, I can't lay my hands on any reason why he should want to murder me."

"Can't you?" said Ferdinand. "Well, I guess we'll leave that and come down to present day."

"What about it?"

Ferdinand turned his bright brown eyes on Nan.

"What about it, Mrs Jervis?" His look teased, probed, and defied the anxiety which came like a cloud across her clear gaze.

"Oh, if you've been talking to *Nan*!" said Jervis with harsh contempt.

"Why shouldn't he talk to me?" said Nan quite gravely.

Jervis laughed.

"You've got an *idée fixe* about Leonard; but I thought F.F. had more sense. All this bores me rather, you know."

"I'm coming right down to present day," said Ferdinand, "and you'll just have to put up with being bored. How many accidents have you had this last week or so?"

"One," said Jervis.

Ferdinand shook his head mournfully.

"I'm a bit of a liar myself! You can't get away with it—not in front of me and Mrs Jervis. You've had three accidents this week, and you're darned lucky to be alive."

"Three?"

"There was a taxi that knocked you down at the corner of your own square after Mrs Jervis had heard Mr Robert Leonard offering a taxi-driver five hundred pounds for a job that was going to risk landing him in prison."

"Why don't you call her Nan?" said Jervis irrelevantly.

"Well—" said Ferdinand, "I've got a lot of respect for her, and I wouldn't like her to think I was getting fresh."

Nan had two dimples. They made her little air of dignity very attractive.

"You may call me Nan," she said.

"That's real nice of you." He turned back to Jervis. "You're trying to push me off the track. But there's nothing doing—I'm not easy skidded. We'll get back to that accident. There mayn't be enough evidence for a jury, but there's enough for me. And then we come to your broken bridge—"

"Good Lord, F.F.! I can't put that on Leonard!"

"Well, I'm afraid I can't. But I knew a man called Eisenthal who invented stuff that could turn wood rotten in anything from six to twenty-four hours—it went on looking all right until you put a weight on it, and then it crumbled and splintered away like an old stump that's been left rotting in the ground. Eisenthal's dead. Last I heard of him he was back of the Madalena with an Englishman, and by and by the Englishman came down the river alone. I never met him. He called himself Brown. He had a chin that stuck out, and a head some few sizes too big for the ordinary hat—and that's just about all I could rake together about him. It's not very much, but that's none of it that don't fit Mr Robert Leonard. That's as far as I've got up to date, but if you were looking at Robert when I was talking about Eisenthal at lunch, you may have tumbled to it that he wasn't deriving any very keen pleasure from my remarks."

"What an imagination you've got, F.F.!"

Ferdinand shook his head.

"Imagination nix!" he said.

"So Leonard put your friend Eisenthal's stuff on the bridge, and then—did you happen to think out how he was going to arrange that it was Nan and I who would cross the bridge at the psychological moment?"

"It didn't take much arranging. You brought Nan down here on a pouring wet evening. It was a dead cert that you weren't going to wander round and show her the sights in the rain. It was pretty much a dead cert that the rain wouldn't last for ever, and that as soon as it stopped you'd be showing her around, and one of the first things you'd show her would be the waterfall. And what does everyone do when they're being shown the fall? Don't they stand plumb in the middle of that bridge and look down into the pool? Mr Robert Leonard is liable to know that just as well as I know it, and I figure it out that he'd only got to slip over to the bridge any time in the night to fix things so that the next person who walked over that bridge or stood there to point out the view would be likely to give an exhibition of high diving. That's the way I figure it out."

"You only want that convenient witness of yours! Can't you produce him? He ought to have seen Leonard at the fatal spot."

"I did see him," said Nan. "I told you I did."

Jervis laughed.

"Oh, yes—I forgot—Nan saw him! The case is complete!

She looked out of her window in the middle of the night, and she saw him by a flash of lightning! He must have been the best part of a couple of hundred yards away—but what is that to the eye of faith? We couldn't have an accident without Leonard, so somebody's bound to have seen him hanging round! Come on, F.F.! It's going to be a bit of a job to saddle him with the wheel coming off my car, but I suppose you're going to have a sporting try.'' He tilted his black head and looked at them both. His frown was gone. His look had a surface brilliance of amusement, but under it Nan, at least, was aware of something fiercely challenging.

She thought, "He hates me. I can't help him."

And then Ferdinand was speaking.

"Well," he said, "if Robert wanted to monkey with your car, you made it real easy for him."

"Attaboy!" murmured Jervis.

"Well, didn't you? After you'd put us down at the front door you ran way back into the shade. I located the place after I'd cleaned up. Your oil had dripped some. Well, there you were, half way down to the garage with the near front wheel bung up against one of the best lot of bushes for cover that anyone could find in a day's journey. And where was Robert till about the middle of lunch? Messing about with his car in the garage, wasn't he? And what was to prevent him stepping into the bushes on his way up to the house and operating on that wheel of yours with a spanner? A spanner's a fine thing to carry in your pocket—handy without being compromising. An archbishop might carry a spanner. I've got a hunch that Robert carries one. He was going to be late for lunch anyhow, so he wouldn't be in a hurry. As a matter of fact he wasn't in a hurry."

"Go on, F.F., you're doing it awfully well."

"I am going on. I'm going to tell you how I know he wasn't in a hurry. I stepped down to the garage and I had a look at his car. There were a couple of chauffeurs there, and they hadn't much opinion of her—about due for the scrap-heap was what they opined. I'm a good mixer, and we got chatty—conversation flowed. I wanted to find out just how long Robert had really wasted over his old wreck. Well, I guess I got what I wanted. He didn't waste so very long. He left that garage at one-fifteen precisely. The second chauffeur happened to notice the time, because he'd got a date with a girl—at least that's what I guessed from the way he looked when the other one chaffed him about being so sure of the time. So you see Robert didn't hurry."

"Don't you wash your hands when you've been tinkering with a car, F.F.?"

"That's where Robert has me cold. I've a good deal of respect for Robert as an organizer. No one's ever going to be able to prove anything about Robert. He's methodical—he don't leave proofs lying about to be picked up. I can't prove that he stood in the bushes and loosened the nuts on that wheel, but I'm pretty well sure that's what he did."

"Well played!" said Jervis. "That's a very good effort, but I'm afraid it's not quite good enough. If Leonard had been up to any hanky-panky with the wheel, the last thing he'd do would be to ask for a lift in a car that might go to glory at any moment."

"Say first instead of last, and I'm with you."

Jervis gave a short laugh.

"So he's suicidal as well as homicidal?"

Ferdinand sat back in his chair and put his hands in his pockets.

"We've got to take some risks in this world. That was his risk, and he took it. It wasn't a very big risk anyway. He'd have fixed that wheel so that it wouldn't come off at once. There wouldn't be anything to make it come off down that smooth stretch of road between the Tetterleys' house and where you shed him. What did he want with a lift anyway? It wasn't going to save him more than five minutes. I don't know a thing about incubators, but you're not going to make me believe that five minutes one way or another is going to make them lie down and die—and if it was, why didn't he make tracks just as soon as you set him down? He didn't—he just stood there and mopped his brow and watched us out of sight. In my opinion he didn't think it very likely that he was going to see any of us again. It's my opinion he was bidding us a lingering farewell. If there is a place in this countryside where a loose wheel is liable to come off, I should say that piece of hill with the potholes has it every time—and if you hadn't braked when you did and pulled her round a bit, well, I don't think Robert ever *would* have seen any of us again. No—Robert hasn't had any luck, and I reckon he's beginning to feel a bit sour about it. Three real good accidents, leaving out the one ten years ago, and nobody a cent the worse. It's real discouraging. But is he going to be discouraged? Is he downhearted? Is he going to give it up as a bad job? Or is he one of those strong, persevering, painstaking guys that just keep on until they get where they want to? It looks to me as if that was the sort he was, because if he had his first try ten years ago and he's still going strong, it kind of looks to me as if it would take a good deal to make him quit.''

Jervis turned his eyes upon Ferdinand with a searching directness.

''Can you give me a single reason why he should have had a try at all, either now *or* ten years back?'' The banter had gone out of his voice; it was quiet and level.

Ferdinand shot a glance at Nan; but Nan was looking down into her lap.

''Come, F.F.—have you got a single reason why Leonard should want me out of the way—why he should ever have wanted me out of the way? Motive and opportunity—that's what you've got to prove against any criminal. Well—you're alleging opportunity. But you can't run on one leg. Where's your motive—or rather, where's Leonard's motive?''

Ferdinand Fazackerley pushed his chair a little farther from the table. He still had his hands in his pockets. He contemplated the pattern of the carpet—rather a lively blue and green pattern upon a crimson ground. Mr Ambrose Weare had liked bright colours, and plenty of them. The wall-paper was sealing-wax red after the fashion of thirty years ago. Perhaps it was all these bright colours that made the room feel so hot.

Jervis spoke again.

''You must have a motive, unless you're going to fall back on his being a homicidal maniac. Are you going to do that?''

''Well—no,'' said Ferdinand slowly. ''I'm of the opinion that folks don't plan murder unless they've got a kink—but

I'm not going to say that Robert isn't accountable for his actions in the ordinary sense of the word.''

"Then, on your own showing, what's his motive?"

Ferdinand took his right hand out of his pocket and hitched the arm carelessly over the back of his chair.

"You don't know of one?" he said.

"It's not up to me to produce that motive, F.F.; but I may mention that if I'd gone over the cliff this afternoon, Leonard wouldn't have stood to gain a halfpenny."

"Who would?" said Ferdinand.

Jervis smiled with sudden sweetness.

"You, if you'd been a survivor. Did you have a spanner in your pocket this afternoon? You're down for two thousand pounds in my will. Did you have a go at those wheel-nuts by any chance? There's about as much evidence against you as against Leonard, it seems to me. You did know the compromising chemist in Mexico, and that's more than you can prove that Leonard did. You might have come down here stealthily and sprayed the bridge. You were in town when I was knocked down by that taxi. And you were certainly knocking around on Croyston beach ten years ago. I believe I could get you hanged if I was the public prosecutor, but I'm pretty sure I couldn't get a verdict against Leonard."

"I'll give you Robert's motive if you want it," said Ferdinand. "You say you've left me two thousand pounds. It's mighty nice of you, and I hope I never get it. But if you'd been a casualty any time this week, who comes next for King's Weare? Isn't it Miss Carew?"

Jervis nodded.

"Under my grandfather's will—yes."

"You can't make a will and cut her out?"

"Not unless I have children of my own."

"And if you'd been a casualty ten years ago?"

"Rosamund would have come in."

"And hasn't it ever occurred to you that Robert takes a romantic interest in Miss Rosamund Carew?"

"Nonsense! They're cousins."

"There's nothing to stop cousins marrying each other—is there?"

"That's pure imagination."

"No!" said Ferdinand. He swung round in his chair and addressed Nan. "What do you say? Haven't I given him his motive?"

Nan stood up. She stood with one hand just touching the table and looked across the grapes and oranges at the two men.

"Jervis won't listen to either of us," she said. "Perhaps he wants Robert Leonard to kill him. He doesn't want to hear anything against him. Perhaps he thinks that you loosened the wheel, so that we might all go over the cliff together—or perhaps he thinks that I did. Do you think that I had a spanner in my pocket this afternoon, Jervis? Perhaps you do." She leaned a little on her hand, and a brilliant rose burned in her cheeks. "Someone is trying to kill you. If it isn't Robert Leonard, who is it? Is it F.F.? Or is it I? It's one of us, you know. You say Robert Leonard hasn't got a motive. Don't you know that there's something between him and Rosamund? I don't know what it is, but there's something. I knew it the very first moment I saw them together at the Luxe. If Rosamund were to get King's Weare, Robert Leonard would get it too. Why didn't Rosamund marry you? Has she ever told you that? You asked her—didn't you? That was waste of time—you ought to have asked Robert Leonard." She stopped speaking, but for a moment she still leaned on her hand, while Jervis looked at her, and she at him.

Suddenly he flung out of his chair, strode to the door, and opened it. Then he stood back, holding it conventionally.

Nan went out with her head up, and the burning rose in her cheeks.

XXVIII

When he had shut the door on Nan, Jervis came back to the table.

"We'd better shift out of here, or Monk will be coming in. Come into the study."

He did not speak until they were shut in together. Then he walked to the window, which was open towards the sunset, frowned at the blue and golden sky without seeing it, turned round, and said,

"What's behind all this?"

Ferdinand sat on the arm of a shabby leather chair.

"Robert," he replied succinctly.

"Damn Robert!"

"Well, that's not *my* business."

"Look here, F.F.—" He broke off. "There are things I can't say, even to you." He walked to the end of the room and back again. "That business ten years ago—you say Leonard was seen coming from the place where I'd fallen?"

"Well, I didn't say *fallen*. It's my belief he laid you out."

"And left me to drown?"

"You've said it."

"What grounds have you—"

"I'm going to tell you, because I think it's about time you knew."

"How long have *you* known?"

"For about a week."

"Well, what is it?"

"It's a very curious thing. The child who saved your life by holding you up in that pool when you were unconscious—

well, she just happened to have seen Robert coming away after he'd laid you out.''

"What did she see?''

''She saw you go around behind the rocks, and she saw Robert come down the cliff close beside her. He didn't see her. He went after you, and by and by she saw him again, walking away. That's why she knew his back view when she saw it again—it's peculiar, you know, the way he walks with that big head of his pushed forward. He went up the next path on to the cliff, and when she got worried about your not coming back, she went behind the rocks and found you lying in the pool with a hole in the back of your head.''

"This is very convincing—ten years after!" Jervis laughed. "I could make up a better yarn than that if I'd ten years to do it in!''

''There's no one making up a yarn. That kid was plumb straight.''

"Why didn't she say all this at the time?''

''She was down at Croyston with some kind of an aunt, and they were leaving that afternoon. She was late for the train and soaked through, and the aunt punished her. And when they got back to where they lived, she poor kid was in a fever and was sick for weeks.''

''And you've met her again?''

"Last week.''

Jervis paused. The room filled with silence. Ferdinand Fazackerley did not break it. He kept his bright dancing eyes on Jervis' face, and saw the colour rise in it to the roots of the black hair. After one of the longest minutes he had ever known, Jervis found his voice.

He said, "Nonsense!" sharply.

''Have it your own way.''

''What are you talking about?''

''Nan,'' said Mr Fazackerley.

Jervis made a step towards him.

''If you're fooling—''

''I'm not.''

"Nan!" said Jervis. "You mean it was Nan?''

''I recognized her right away. She don't look any older to speak of, and when I saw the scar on her arm, that clinched it. I've told you about that before. She'd cut herself pretty well to the bone holding your head off the rocks every time a wave came into that darned pool. It was her arm or your head. Well, she made it her arm every time. There was bound to be a scar, and when I saw that scar on your wife's arm at the Luxe, I thought I'd butted in on a very pretty romance.''

Jervis stood for a moment with a perfectly blank face. Behind it his mind, like a shuttered room, was being violently shaken as if by an earthquake. His thoughts slid together, collided, broke. With a violent effort he turned about and walked to the window. The sun was gone; a kind of golden haze tinged the dusk. There was no wind at all; each tree and bush stood up dark and solemn without the slightest movement. The whole scene might have been painted on glass. The contrast between its stillness and the turbulent confusion of his thoughts gave him a sense of being in some remote and unfamiliar place.

He did not know how long he stood there. The gold went out of the air and left it yet more gravely still. A very faint green light came from the horizon. This too faded. An impalpable stream of darkness flowed between him and all the world.

Suddenly he crossed to the door and switched on the light. The room had been quite dark. As the light came on, the windows seemed to recede. All the shades and degrees of the outside darkness vanished. The straight crimson curtains framed blank, black windows.

Ferdinand Fazackerley had not moved. He was sitting on the arm of one of the big chairs with his hands in his pockets.

"You weren't fooling?" said Jervis.

"Great Washington—no!"

"You're sure it was Nan?"

"Everlasting certain sure."

"She told you so?"

"No, she did not. I recognized her. And then, when we were at dinner, I told the story of the plucky kid who saved your life, and you bet I watched her. She didn't give much away—she don't, you know—but I could see she was scared, and I tumbled to it that you didn't know, and that she didn't want you to know. I'm not an inquisitive man, but I thought I'd like mighty well to get to the bottom of why you didn't know, and why she didn't want you to know. I haven't rightly got to the bottom of it yet.'' Those bright yellow-brown eyes of his twinkled with questions. He crossed one leg over the other and leaned sideways against the back of the chair. ''Well?'' he said.

Jervis stood by the jamb of the door. He looked at a bare, blank window and spoke.

''Did she know—when she married me?''

Ferdinand twinkled more noticeably.

''Holy Niagara! What do you think?''

Jervis made a gesture. There was no expression on his face.

''Why not ask her?'' suggested Ferdinand.

''I'm asking you,'' said Jervis. ''You seem to be well behind the scenes. Did she know when she married me—or did she find out afterwards?''

''Know? Of course she knew! Why do you suppose she married you?''

Jervis set his jaw and was silent.

''Better ask her!'' said Ferdinand with a short laugh.

Jervis turned abruptly, flung open the door, and went out. Ferdinand watched him with a quizzical smile. He went impetuously through the hall and out at the front door, shutting it hard behind him.

XXIX

JERVIS WENT STRIDING DOWN THE DRIVE AND, ONCE OUTSIDE the gates, left the road for the downs. He could have found his way blindfold, but out here under the sky and away from shadowy trees, it was not so dark. The cloudless expanse above his head was luminous and already pricked with stars. The moon had not yet risen. The short grass was smooth under foot, and on the long swelling curve of the down he walked fast and far.

As he walked, his thoughts cleared. If it was Nan who had saved his life ten years ago at the risk of her own, and if she had known this, their whole relation was on a different basis; it was profoundly affected—so profoundly, in fact, as to alter his entire point of view.

He went back to the stinging shock of Rosamund's defection on the eve of their marriage. He had believed then, and had since had this belief intensified, that it was a shameless and callous manoeuvre to supplant him at King's Weare and as his grandfather's heir. To counter this, he must be married by the date fixed in Ambrose Weare's will. Nan had stepped into the breach with her quiet proposal that they should marry as a matter of business. She had been very businesslike. She must have something for her trouble—a percentage. She had, in fact, put herself up for sale for two thousand pounds. He remembered that he had offered five hundred, and she had raised him very coolly to two thousand. He had not known then that the money was not for herself—old Page had let that out afterwards. It had gone to the sister, who was on her way to Australia. Page had said he believed Nan had been supporting her. A decent old thing Page—scandalized by the marriage of course, but anxious to be scrupulously fair to Nan.

Jervis was aware that he himself had not bothered his head about being fair. By marrying Nan he spoilt Rosamund's dirty game, and that was all he had cared for at the time. In the last twenty-four hours he had experienced a disposition to turn his back on the events which had led up to his marriage. They made a background so incompatible with Nan as he was beginning to know her that he had desired to detach her from it—to detach them both—not to look back at all—to blot the whole thing out. F.F.'s story made it impossible to detach himself, or to detach Nan, or to blot things out. He felt instead an overwhelming desire to rake things up, to know what had been at the back of Nan's mind when she proposed that business arrangement. He had set her down as a shrewd opportunist catching at a marriage above her hopes. But, then, why not play her best card— why not show her scar and claim her gratitude? Why not give the thing a decorative gloss of the "I saved your life, and now I can help you save your fortunes" order? The shrewd opportunist would surely have done this. But Nan, according to F.F., had been scared to death lest he should know. She had hidden her trump card instead of playing it. She had hidden her parentage too. No opportunist worth the name would have neglected to claim Nigel Forsyth as a father. What *had* been in her mind?

Something glimmered amongst his thoughts like a will o' the wisp. It was a dancing point of light that turned a flickering gleam here and there and was gone. The child who had saved his life—the gleam touched that. Did she remember? F.F. said that she had remembered. He recalled the headlong fury of his resolve to beat Rosamund at her own game. The gleam touched that too. It illumined possibilities—the depth of the abyss into which he might very easily have plunged. He would have married anyone, and picked her up anywhere. He had certainly been mad, and it was Nan who had stood between him and the abyss. The gleam touched that.

None of these things presented themselves to him in words. It could hardly be said that he recognized what the gleam showed him. His conscious thought had not greatly altered as yet. There was behind it a pressure which would compel it to alter.

He walked on, and presently the moon came up out of the haze at the horizon's edge. It cast a faintly golden trail upon the smooth, dark sea.

Jervis turned and began to walk back by the way he had come. One thing at least he could now explain to his own satisfaction, and that was Nan's extraordinary obsession with regard to Robert Leonard. He didn't, of course, believe the story of Leonard coming down the cliff and passing the pool. That was nonsense—part of the obsession. No—what had happened was quite obviously this—Nan had seen

Leonard somewhere on the beach either that day or some other day. F.F. said her aunt had taken her away that afternoon, and then she had been ill. Well, it was quite obvious—she had had a shock, and she was feverish, and she had got Leonard mixed up with her fever. It was the simplest explanation in the world. She had had a bad dream about Leonard and had tacked it on to the things that had really happened.

Jervis felt much better when he had settled this. It let Nan out, and it let Leonard out. It explained everything perfectly.

He got back to King's Weare to find the house dark except for a light in the hall. Monk had standing orders never to sit up. It was a relief to find that F.F. had had enough sense not to sit up either. To be sat up for was the most irritating thing in the world. He put out the hall light and went up in the dark. As he passed Nan's door, he heard the thump of Bran's tail and a faint snuffing sound. He said "Lie down, Bran!"

As he opened his own door, the sounds ceased. He put on his light and undressed. Before he got into bed he drew the curtains back, and fell asleep whilst he was wondering why moonlight made everything look so still.

He waked with a start, he did not know how much later, and at first he did not know why he had waked. Everything was dark and quiet as sleep; only the window framed the moonlight. Then he heard a sound—Bran moving in Nan's room. Restless brute! But that wouldn't have waked him. He raised himself on his hand, and as he did so, he heard a choking cry and in a moment was out of bed and at the door between the two rooms. If it was bolted. . . . . But it gave to his hand. He switched on the light, and saw Nan sitting up in bed under the crimson canopy, her eyes wide and blank with terror, and her lips parted on a gasping cry. Bran, with his forepaws on the bed, whined and licked frantically at her hair, her shoulder, her arm. As the light went on, he growled, flung round, dropped to the floor, and bounded to meet Jervis, thrusting at him with his head and making anxious sounds in his throat.

Jervis bade him lie down harshly. His first thought was that the dog had frightened Nan. Then, as he reached the bed, he saw that her gaze was fixed neither on him nor on Bran. It had no focus; it saw nothing. It was just a wide gaze of fear. She was sitting stiffly upright with her hands pressed down upon the bed. Her short brown hair was wildly rumpled. Her face was of an agonizing pallor, her eyes all staring pupil. She had on a childish white night-gown, rather high at the neck, and beneath it her breast rose and fell with each sobbing breath.

Jervis sat down on the edge of the bed and put a hand on her shoulder.

"Nan!" he said. "What is it? *Nan!*"

At the sound of his voice she gave a convulsive start and woke. It was only then that he realized that that blank gaze had been fixed upon something in the world of dreams. His hand and his voice waked her. She turned terrified eyes upon him, and said his name in a choking whisper.

"Nan—what is it? I say, don't be so frightened—you're all right. It was just a beastly dream." She trembled, and he put his arm about her. "All right in a minute. Just hold on, and it'll go. Would you like a drink of water? . . . No, I won't go till you want me to."

She was small and light to hold. Another of those dreadful shudders passed over her. He felt her struggle with it, stiffening herself against his arm until she was rigid. A sudden awkward tenderness for her fear came up in him. Under his impatient temperament he had a soft heart for children, animals—anything weak, defenceless, frightened. He patted her shoulder and tightened his grasp.

"Look here, there isn't anything to be afraid of. It was only a dream."

She turned then, straining back against his arm so that she could look at him.

"Did you—dream it—too?"

"No. Look here, it's nothing—a dream's nothing—it can't hurt anyone—you've only got to wake up. Here's Bran telling you the same thing. He's most awfully upset about you."

Bran had his forepaws on the bed again. The tip of his tail moved deprecatingly. He pushed his head forward and blew warm puffs of air at her hand, her arm.

"She's all right," said Jervis. "You dream too—don't you, old boy? You think you're catching a rabbit, and then it does the dirty on you and disappears just as you've got your teeth into it. Now she's all right, and you can get down."

Bran stood his ground with just a flick of the ear to show that he had heard. His eyes went to Nan.

She said, "Down, Bran!" in a shaky whisper, and he dropped to the floor.

"Feeling better?" said Jervis. "What was it? Would you like to tell me?"

Leaning against his arm, and looking up at him with those unnaturally wide eyes, she said,

"I thought—you were dead."

Her voice was the lost ghost of itself. He hardly heard the words; yet they reached him, releasing some emotion which he did not understand. He did not try to understand it, but it reinforced that old tenderness.

"I thought—you were dead." said Nan.

"Do I feel as if I were dead?" His arm tightened about her.

"I saw you—in a dark place. You were—dead."

He remembered the tears running down her face when she sat by the wayside. She had wept then because she had thought him dead; but now she did not weep. He said on an impulse.

"I don't know why you should mind."

At once she drew away from his arm, sitting up stiffly and turning her head away.

"Would you mind, Nan?" he said.

There was a silence. He wished that he had not asked her that. When he had been wishing it for what seemed quite at long time, she drew a sobbing breath.

"I'm sorry," he said. "I'm not—used—to anyone—minding about me."

She looked round at him then with something in her eyes which blotted out everything that he had thought or believed about her before this night. It was something quite impossible to mistake. There were tears in her eyes, and behind the tears a shining.

He got up in confusion, went over to the washstand,

poured out a glass of water, and came back with it in his hand. Nan took it gratefully, but her hand shook. He found himself guiding it. She drank about half the water and gave him the glass again. When she spoke, it was in her natural voice.

"Thank you, Jervis." Then, after the slightest pause, "I'm all right now—it's gone." She threw out her hand with a childish gesture. "Oh, isn't it lovely when bad dreams go like that?"

"It's quite gone?"

"Yes."

"Can you go to sleep again?"

She said, "I'll read."

"Have you got a book?"

"Yes."

He stood there, not knowing quite what to do. He felt as if he had never seen her before, and yet as if he had known her all his life.

He said, "Nan," in a tone which she had not heard from him before.

She pushed back her hair and smiled at him.

"I'm *really* all right now. I'm dreadfully sorry I woke you."

"Would you like me to leave the door open?"

"Oh no—I've got Bran."

A perfectly absurd anger flared up in him. She'd got Bran, had she? Well, let her have Bran! He certainly hadn't the slightest desire to force himself upon her. He frowned, said good-night in a stiffly polite voice, and strode to the door. As he shut it, he caught a glimpse of her settling herself against her pillows.

His room seemed very dark. He went over to the bed and sat on the edge of it, watching the line of light under the door through which he had just come. His spirit of anger died. He was moved and puzzled. He could not remember anyone having cried for him before. It moved him a good deal that Nan should have cried for him this afternoon. She had sat on the dusty grass and cried because she thought he was dead. It was an astonishing thing to have happened; and yet it was less astonishing and less moving than the look which she had given him just now. When he thought about that look of Nan's, a sort of piercing sweetness and warmth penetrated to the very depths of his consciousness. He was quite unable to think clearly about it, or, indeed, to think about it at all. The whole experience was as yet a matter of feeling; it had not been transmuted into thought.

He sat quite still for a long time, watching the line of light beneath the door. When at last it went out, he got up, stretched himself, and got into bed. He lay on his right side and watched the moonlight. The moon was not full, and the light was pale, not bright. The window framed it, and one black bough of the tall cypress at the corner of the house; the bough crossed the window like an outstretched arm. He lay looking at it, and all the time that warm sweetness pierced deeper and deeper. He began to slip away from the moonlight into a more enchanted place. There was a dream waiting for him—a warm, sweet dream, full of colour and light. But when he had almost reached it, something pulled him back.

He woke with one of those violent starts which come on the edge of sleep. In a moment he was out of bed and at the door between his room and Nan's. If opened on a dark room peaceful with sleep. He said her name under his breath, but there was no answer except the faint thudding of Bran's tail upon the floor. He frowned in the dark and shut the door.

As he turned and stood for a moment facing the window, something came through it and hit the floor with a sharp rap. It sounded like a pebble. He went to the window and looked out. It faced towards the drive. The curving belt of trees took the moon. The sky was luminous over them, the moon itself unseen. The shadow of the cypress was black upon the house. The blackness made a pool beneath him as he leaned out.

Out of the blackness someone said his name.

XXX

"JERVIS—"

Jervis stared into the black pool of shadow under the window. Instead of waking up he must have walked straight into the maddest dream. He said,

"Who's there?"

"Jervis—" said Rosamund Carew.

It was Rosamund—of course it was Rosamund. But it could only be Rosamund in one of those dreams which turn everything topsy turvy and hurry you from one absurdity to another. *"Rosamund!"* he said.

"For the Lord's sake don't go shouting out my name like that!"

"I wasn't shouting."

He could just see her now—or rather, not her, but a shadow that moved, amongst other shadows that were still. Then she turned her face up to the window, and he could see it like a pale oval reflection in dark water.

"Jervis—I'm in a hole. Can you come down?"

"What is it?"

"I'll tell you if you come down. Don't wake anyone."

He hesitated, frowning furiously. What was this all about? He turned his wrist and looked at the luminous dial of his watch. It was two o'clock. What on earth was Rosamund playing at?

"Jervis. I'm in a perfectly damnable hole."

He said, "All right—wait a minute," and turned back into the room.

He got into some clothes—a tennis shirt, flannel trousers,

blazer, socks, and shoes. Then he went down to the study, opened the window, and got out.

Rosamund was waiting for him.

"What's the matter?" he said.

"My car broke down."

"Where?"

"About three miles away, on the main road."

"Well, I'll knock up Mrs Mellish. She'll have a room got ready for you."

"No—no—I don't want to do that." She came quite close and put a hand on his arm. "I want to get back. Mabel Tetterley doesn't know I'm out."

"What have you been up to?" said Jervis.

"That's not your business."

"What do you want me to do?" said Jervis angrily.

"Make less noise to start with, and then lend a hand with the car."

"What's the trouble?"

"I've ditched her. We could get her out together, but I can't budge her alone, and there isn't likely to be anyone passing for the next four hours or so."

Jervis did not know what prompted him to say,

"You're alone?"

"Well, would I come and dig you out in the middle of the night if I wasn't? I don't walk three miles in evening shoes for fun."

"All right I'll get the car out and run you back."

Rosamund's hand closed on his arm—a strong hand for all its whiteness.

"No, you can't do that—it'll give the whole show away."

"What is there to give away?" said Jervis.

"Well, to be quite frank," said Rosamund, "I can't afford another scandal on the top of turning you down. It isn't all jam as it is. Mabel's under Basher's thumb, though you wouldn't think it. Basher's a prude of the first water when it comes to his own womenfolk. If he knew I'd been out all night, he'd never have me in the house again."

"And it's not my business where you've been?"

"Well—is it?"

"How can you get back without someone finding out?"

"It's as easy as mud. The second chauffeur sleeps over the garage. You couldn't wake him if you drove a lorry through the room. I've got a key, and I can take her in the same way I took her out, without anyone being a penny the wiser."

So she couldn't have gone out much before midnight. Queer business this. He felt an impatience to get quit of it.

"Well, we'd better be getting along," he said.

Rosamund moved, let go of his arm, and stepped out of the shadow. The moonlight touched her uncovered head and took all the gold out of her hair. It looked grey with threads of silver in it. Her face, her hands, and the column of her throat were like ivory seen through water. She was wrapped in a black Chinese shawl whose embroidered flowers were like faint ghosts whose colour and sweetness have died and been forgotten.

She moved beside him, walking quickly and in silence. She could keep pace with him without effort. She produced, as always, an effect of graceful ease which was in sharp contrast to the habitual bluntness of her speech. She did not speak now until they were past the gates. Then she said in a mocking voice,

"Don't you want to know where I've been?"

"Not particularly."

"No wonder I jilted you! You don't care who I've been meeting?"

"Why should I?"

"Do you?"

"No, I don't."

"No healthy curiosity?"

"I'd like to know what you're driving at."

"I'd like to know myself," said Rosamund, her voice harsh on the words.

They walked on without speaking for a couple of hundred yards. Then Jervis said,

"Are you going to marry Leonard?"

"Should you mind if I did?"

"Not in the least. But I should think twice before I did it if I were you."

"Why?" said Rosamund.

"The man's an outsider."

"Thank you—he's my cousin!"

"Everyone's got some dud relations. Are you going to marry him?"

"No," said Rosamund.

"Well, that's damned sensible of you."

Rosamund moved a little farther away from him.

"You've made such a sensible marriage yourself—haven't you?"

Jervis said nothing. Quite suddenly, when she said that, he saw Nan as he had seen her settling back against her tossed pillows; her rumpled hair, soft and brown; her little tremulous smile; her eyes clear shining after rain. Sensible? That wasn't the word for the marriage that had brought Nan into his life. Who wanted to make a sensible marriage? He had taken a leap in the dark, and it had landed him in a place of extraordinary enchantment. You weren't sensible in an enchanted place. He threw back his head and laughed. What a jest fate had played on him! What a gorgeous, rollicking, enchanting jest! Gusts of laughter shook him. He wanted someone to share it with him. But he couldn't very well share it with Rosamund. It was just like fate to thrust Rosamund upon him at this juncture.

She had got right away on to the other side of the road. They had reached a bend where half a dozen wind-driven thorn trees stood above the hedge on one side and a row of elms cast a dense shadow across the road from the other.

"Here's the car," said Rosamund.

"We haven't come three miles."

"It felt like four in these shoes."

The road dipped into the shadow. The car stood in at an angle towards the hedge. The place was as black as overhanging boughs could make it.

"You ought to have left your lights on," said Jervis.

Rosamund didn't answer. He heard her move, but he couldn't see her.

He opened the door of the car and leaned forward to switch on the lights.

XXXI

NAN CAME EARLY TO BREAKFAST, AND FERDINAND FAZACK-
erley late, with his red hair sticky and rumpled from the sea.
He had made some attempt to brush it, but except for the
colour it looked a good deal like the coat of a Scotch
terrier. Jervis did not come to breakfast at all.

"Alfred says he went out early," said Ferdinand over his
bacon. "It's going to be hotter than ever, so I guess he's
wiser to get through with anything strenuous before the
thermometer breaks."

By eleven o'clock Alfred was being questioned.

"Did Mr Weare say he was going to be late?"

"No, ma'am."

"Well, did he say where he was going?"

"No, sir."

"Did he say anything at all, Alfred?"

"No, ma'am."

"Well, did you see which way he went?"

Alfred looked agonized. He was a shy lad with a strong
objection to committing himself.

"No, sir."

Nan made a flashing guess.

"Did you see him at all, Alfred?"

"No, ma'am, I can't say I did."

"He wasn't there when you went to wake him?"

"No, ma'am, I can't say he was."

There wasn't anything more to be said. It was the most
ordinary thing in the world for Jervis to get up and go out
before the servants were afoot. He would go down to the sea

for a swim at three in the morning if the fancy took him. Since Nan had been at King's Weare he had been out every morning. Once he had walked into Croyston and breakfasted there because he wanted to see a man about a deal in sheep. He might have done the same thing again, and he would certainly be frightfully angry if he were pursued by fussy inquiries.

Lunch time passed. Ferdinand and Nan sat down half an hour late. Nan found it difficult to eat, but she would have found it still more difficult to refuse what was offered to her, because that would mean that there was a reason why she should not be able to eat. She ate therefore with determination. Everything seemed to require a great deal of biting, and nothing had any taste. It was like eating lumps of sawdust.

At four o'clock she got up from her chair as Ferdinand came into the library, and went to meet him. When they met, she looked at him, and then looked quickly away.

"We've got to do something," she said.

"Well, what do you want to do?"

"I don't know. I'm—frightened."

"Oh, I wouldn't be frightened."

"He'd never stay away like this—*would* he?"

"Well—he might. But we'll do some ringing up and see if we can't get him. If he went into Croyston, he'd go to the George."

Jervis had not been to the George, nor to any of the other places that they tried. They rang up the Tetterleys, and Rosamund answered.

"Did you want Mabel? She's away. She and Basher went off last night to put in a couple of days with his sister. Jervis? No, he hasn't been here. Has he gone off? Well, he does, you know—he always has. I expect he's forgotten he's married. I shouldn't ask too many questions if I were you—he won't like it." She laughed. "That's putting it mildly! When you've known Jervis as long as I have—"

Nan's voice came small, and steady, and clear.

"You haven't seen him?"

"Not since yesterday."

Nan hung up the receiver. She turned a composed, colourless face on Ferdinand.

"What are we to do?"

"What did she say?"

"The Tetterleys are away. She says they went away last night. She says she hasn't seen him. She says he goes off—suddenly—like this. Is that true?"

F.F. ran his hand through his ginger hair.

"Well—he's sudden. Jervis has always been mighty sudden. It's his temperament. If he gets an idea, he don't want to wait and turn it over in his mind—he wants to get going and do something about it mighty quick. I've known him start off across Europe without any luggage. Look here, he's all taken up with improving his breed of sheep—well, isn't he? And suppose he went into Croyston and met someone that told him there was a prize ram he'd be a fool to miss—in Northumberland, or anywhere as far as you can get on the map where they do breed sheep—well, he'd be quite liable to board the next train—"

"Without letting anyone know?"

Ferdinand rumpled his hair again.

"Well, he might give a telegram to someone to send, and they might forget it. That's a thing that's very liable to happen. But I was thinking I'd run down into Croyston and make some inquiries."

Jervis had not been seen in Croyston. He had not been seen at the railway station. There was an early train to town at seven-forty-five. They tracked down the two porters who had been on duty. Neither of them knew Mr Weare by sight—but the train had been quite crowded as there was a day excursion. The most of the passengers were ladies; but that wasn't to say that there weren't some gentlemen too. This was the porter who had clipped the tickets. No—he hadn't taken particular notice of any of them, not knowing anyone by sight—"Only got my transfer a week ago, and I'm sorry I can't help you, ma'am."

The other porter, a long melancholy man with a thin neck and an embarrassingly mobile Adam's apple, proved to be the type of witness who responds instantly to any suggestion. Asked if he had noticed a tall gentleman with black hair, he fingered his Adam's apple and looked vaguely over Nan's head.

"Tall gen'leman? Black hair?"

"Yes," said Nan. "Did you see him?"

"Well, I might have done."

"But did you?"

"Very tall gen'leman?"

"Six foot," said Ferdinand firmly.

The porter's eyes came down an inch or two. From his manner it appeared that if they had wanted a gentleman of six-foot-three or upwards, he could have obliged them—but six foot . . . He shook his head mournfully.

"Well, I can't say as I noticed anyone of that description."

"You'd be liable to notice Mr Weare—he's kind of noticeable. Quick walk—strong build—very black hair—holds his head up and looks as if he'd bought the earth."

"Foreign gen'leman, sir?"

"No," said Nan—"Mr Weare of King's Weare."

"Oh—*him*?"

"Did you see him?" said Nan quickly.

"Well, I couldn't rightly say I seen him."

"Would you have known him if you had?"

"Well, I couldn't rightly say I'd know him."

"Was there anyone on the train who might have been Mr Weare?"

"Well, there might have been." The porter brightened slightly.

"A tall gentleman."

"Well, there might have been."

"Was there?" said Nan.

The porter seemed to think so. He stopped fingering his Adam's apple and scratched his head in a melancholy, ruminative manner.

"There *was* a tall gentleman on the train?"

"Well, there might have been."

They had to leave it at that.

Whey they were driving back from Croyston, Nan said in a suffocated little voice,

"I dreamt—last night—that he was—dead."

"Well, I guess that means he's alive," said Ferdinand. "Dreams go by contraries." But he didn't look at her.

"Stop the car!" said Nan rather breathlessly.

Ferdinand pulled up at the side of the road. They were out of sight and hearing of the sea, in a lane with a straggling hedge on either side. The sky over them was veiled with something between haze and fog. The hedges were powdered thick with dust. It was very hot and very still. The light was pitiless—glare without sun.

"I guess there's going to be a storm," said Ferdinand.

Nan took no notice.

"I dreamt—last night—that he was dead." She looked straight in front of her, and neither face nor voice had any expression. "It was—a dreadful dream. There was a dark place—and I saw him—he was lying on wet stones—it was quite dark."

"How could you see him if it was dark?" said Ferdinand. Nan was affecting him very uncomfortably. He made his voice as brisk as possible.

"I don't know—you can in dreams. I saw him. He was lying on the wet stones—and his eyes were shut. I woke up screaming, and he came in."

"Jervis did? When did you say this was?"

"Last night."

"What time was it?"

"I don't know. I looked at my watch afterwards—it was a quarter to two."

"Afterwards?"

"After he'd gone back to his room."

"Was he just as usual then?"

Nan's chin quivered for a moment.

"He was—kind."

"Oh, you poor kid!" said Ferdinand to himself.

He did not say anything out loud, but he took his left hand off the wheel and laid it on her knee.

"Well, that means he was up and about at two o'clock. It might mean that he dressed and went out then. We ought to find out which of his clothes are missing."

"I've asked Alfred—he sees to them."

"What does he say?"

"He doesn't seem sure. He says there's a pair of grey flannel trousers and a blazer gone—and he thinks a blue serge suit, but he isn't sure whether Jervis brought it back from town. I made him ring up and find out, and they say it's not there.''

''Anything else missing?''

''I don't know. I told Alfred to go through everything whilst we were out. We'd better go on.''

They got back to find Alfred tolerably sure that there were quite a number of things missing—the doubtful blue serge suit; evening trousers and dinner jacket; shirts, socks, and pants; and, most important of all, tooth-brush and razor.

''No pyjamas?'' said Ferdinand.

Alfred was very dubious about pyjamas. No—Mr Weare hadn't taken his dressing-gown or his hair-brushes. But Alfred was prepared to swear to a dozen pocket handkerchiefs, because they were new and Mrs Mellish had had them to mark.

''Now that's mighty strange,'' said Ferdinand. ''He's taken his handkerchiefs and left his hair-brushes. And if all these things have gone, what have they gone in?''

''Oh, there's a suit-case missing, sir,'' said Alfred.

''Where from? Where did he keep it?''

They were in Jervis' room, Nan sitting on the edge of the bed, Alfred on his knees in front of piles of clothes, and Ferdinand moving restlessly about the room. Alfred got up and dusted himself.

''Mr Weare likes to keep his suit-cases handy, sir. He wouldn't have them taken to the box-room in case of wanting them in a hurry.'' He opened a door in the wall near the head of the bed, and disclosed a deep cupboard. There were three or four suit-cases in it, and some hat-boxes.

''Are you sure one is missing, Alfred?'' said Nan.

Alfred appeared, for once, to be on really firm ground.

''The new Revelation, ma'am.''

''And you're sure it was here?''

''Oh yes, ma'am. He brought it down new from town. Mr Monk will tell you the same.''

Downstairs again, Nan and Ferdinand faced one another.

''It looks as if he'd gone away,'' said Nan.

''It surely looks like it.'' Ferdinand's eyes avoided hers.

''Why didn't he leave a message?''

Ferdinand looked out of the window.

"He might have given a telephone message or a telegram to someone to send off. I've done that myself—and sometimes it's all right, but sometimes you're liable to get let down."

"Why didn't he leave a note *here*?"

"Well—he seems to have been in a mighty hurry."

"Why did he taken all those handkerchiefs and leave his hair-brushes?" said Nan.

XXXII

THERE WAS NO LETTER FROM JERVIS BY THE POST NEXT day. Nan did not know that she was counting on one until the post had come and brought nothing. She looked at Ferdinand, and Ferdinand exercised some ingenuity.

"Now look there, there's a thing he might have done—a thing I've done myself when I've had my mind all taken up with something. He might have written a note to leave here, and have gone away with it in his pocket. If he finds it, he'll send a wire—but he mightn't find it till he gets back home. It's a thing might happen to anyone. Why, in my own home-town there was the case of Shucks Lawson. Poor old Shucks had got it bad. He wasn't a man any more; he was just a shadow—Cornelia Van Bien's shadow. And then all of a sudden he lit out and everyone would have bet their bottom dollar that Cornelia had given him the mitten. By and by Cornelia began to look kind of shadowy too. She'd never been what you'd call robust, but she got so poetic-looking that she pretty nearly wasn't there at all. And then one day she got a cable from Melbourne, Australia—and I know what was in it, because I knew the operator pretty well, and he told me. It was one of the longest cables we'd ever had in our town, and he was kind of proud of it. It said: 'Letter proposing marriage just found pocket winter suit can you forgive love you to distraction cable reply or shall go plumb crazy Shucks.' ''

Nan had been looking down at her plate. She had made a very fitful breakfast. She heard Ferdinand's voice, but she did not really hear what he was saying, because her own thoughts were speaking so loudly all the time. She felt suddenly as if she could not sit there and listen to them any longer. Her face changed, her mouth quivered. She pushed back her chair and got up.

"I must go and see Mrs Mellish," she said.

Since she had come to King's Weare she had daily interviewed Mrs Mellish. It was really Mrs Mellish who conducted the interview, but Nan hoped that with a little practice she might yet arrive at ordering beef when Mrs Mellish had proposed mutton.

She proceeded to the housekeeper's room, and was received with Mrs Mellish's usual austere respect—a respect not in the least personal, but indicative of the fact that Mrs Mellish knew her manners. Today Nan approved the menu without so much as reading it. She stood, and Mrs Mellish stood. She said, "Yes, that will do very well," and continued to stand, looking past Mrs Mellish in a manner which was secretly resented—"There's places where one should be, and there's places where one shouldn't be; but to be looked past as if I wasn't there—in my own housekeeper's room—*well*!" Nan continued to look past her until Mrs Mellish, in her own phraseology, "Could abear it no longer."

"Was there anything further, ma'am" she said in such a politely controlled voice that anyone less absorbed than Nan could scarcely have missed the offence behind it.

Nan did not start, but she came out of her abstraction and turned her eyes upon Mrs Mellish's face.

"Yes," she said. "I wanted to ask you whether you or the maids heard anything on the night Mr Weare went away. We think he has written, and that the letter has been mislaid."

"Yes, ma'am?" Mrs Mellish's tone was not really a very encouraging one.

"If anyone noticed anything," said Nan, "it would be a help. Someone may have heard him moving about. It would be a help if we knew what time it was when he went out. We are—" She paused for a long time, and then said, "anxious."

"Yes, ma'am," said Mrs Mellish.

Her plainly banded hair made the neatest possible frame to her plump, pale face. The hair was iron grey. In the morning Mrs Mellish dressed to match her hair, in a strong iron-grey material which suggested in the most insistent manner reliability and moral worth.

"Will you ask if anyone noticed anything?"

"Certainly, ma'am," said Mrs Mellish.

She left Nan to a feeling that she had been knocking imploringly upon a door that was not made to open. Then, as she stood waiting for Mrs Mellish to return, it came to Nan that it was not so much that the door was not made to open, as that it had been deliberately slammed in her face. She stood there and thought about this. Why do people slam doors? Either because they are angry, or else because they have something to hide. There wasn't any reason why Mrs Mellish should be angry with her. Had Mrs Mellish by any chance got something to hide?

Mrs Mellish came back into the room with the slow walk of a comfortably covered woman who is concerned with her dignity. It appeared that nobody had noticed anything. Gladys had slept all night—"and hard enough to get her up in the morning, ma'am." Fanny had waked up with the cocks crowing, but she hadn't been awake more than five minutes and she "hadn't heard nothing."

"And you, Mrs Mellish? Your room is the nearest."

"No, ma'am."

Her eyelids came down over her rather pale and prominent eyes. There was the effect of a blind being pulled down. First the door of the house had been slammed, and now the blinds were down. In a civilized country you cannot break into somebody else's house. Nan turned and walked out of the room with the sense of defeat heavy upon her.

She found Ferdinand Fazackerley in the study.

"I want to go and see Rosamund," she said.

"Why?"

"I want to."

"Why do you want to?"

Nan put her hand to her cheek.

"She talked too much."

"When?"

"On the telephone—I suppose it was yesterday."

"How do you mean, she talked too much?" Ferdinand's eyes darted questions.

Nan pushed back her hair.

"She doesn't talk—much—to me—as a rule. She wouldn't say three words to me if she could make two do. She wouldn't speak to me at all unless she simply had to. But when I telephoned to ask her if she had seen Jervis, she talked a lot."

"What did she say?"

"I think she was trying to make me angry. I can't remember what she said—it wasn't worth remembering." Her chin lifted a little. "I just wondered why she said so much."

Ferdinand frowned, looked as if he was going to speak, checked himself on an indeterminate vowel sound, and then said,

"Do you want me to drive you up there?"

Nan nodded.

They had a silent drive. When they came to the place where the wheel had come off Jervis' car two days before, Nan, on the seaward side, looked down over the cliff with a steady, thoughtful gaze. The sea came up against the cliff. It was deep enough to have hidden the car if it had gone over. The water would have stood above it—green water shading to blue. The car would have been drawn by ebb into the race that sets round Croyde Head, and there, amongst the rocks, they would have been battered to pulp or sucked down into the soft bubbling quicksands beyond the head.

She turned her eyes from the sea to the square ugliness of Robert Leonard's house.

"He's been away," said Ferdinand, as if she had named the man.

Instantly Nan flashed round on him.

"When did he go? Where has he been?"

"He went away on Thursday."

"This is Thursday," said Nan. She paused. "Isn't it?"

The sense of strain that loses count of time made it difficult to be sure of where they were in the week. It was between the Tuesday night and Wednesday morning that Jervis had gone out and not come back.

"Yes, it's Thursday all right. It was Tuesday we lunched with the Tetterleys. Leonard had crocked his car, you remember. Well, he got it going enough to take him into Croyston that evening. He ran it into Brown's garage for repairs, and he dined and slept at the George. He had breakfast there Wednesday morning very sharp at eight, and he hired a motor-bicycle to take him out here in time to save his incubators from going cold. He's got a perfectly water-tight alibi, you see."

"No, I don't," said Nan. "If he was planning anything wicked, isn't that just what he'd do—go away and pretend he wasn't here?"

Ferdinand looked at her quickly sideways.

"I went to the George. He was playing billiards until half-past eleven. The chambermaid called him at seven. His car was in Brown's garage out of action—I went there and made sure of that."

Nan's lips made an unwontedly hard line. She held them close over something which she didn't want to say, because if she said it, the spoken words might break her self-control, and she would want it all if she was going to see Rosamund.

Ferdinand did not press her. He did not in fact speak until they reached the Tetterleys. Then he looked quickly at her again, thought how pale she was, and said,

"Well, I'm not on in this scene, I guess. I'll put her in the shade and wait."

Nan was shown into the drawing-room, a big formal room which Mabel Tetterley used as little as possible. It was still furnished after her mother-in-law's taste, Basher having proved extraordinarily obstinate when pressed to get rid of an ebony grand piano, two ormolu cabinets, an immense pale carpet with bunches of pink and yellow roses festooned with blue ribbon, and a quantity of water-colour paintings executed by the late Lady Tetterley in a frigid classical style.

Rosamund was standing at the far end of this room. She held a cigarette in her right hand. She was dressed in pale yellow linen. As Nan came towards her, she turned away to pick up a match-box.

Nan stood still a couple of yards away, and watched the tip of the cigarette redden to the flame of the match. Rosamund's strong white hands were perfectly steady. She blew out her first mouthful of smoke before she spoke.

"Wanderer returned?" she said.

"No," said Nan.

Rosamund drew at her cigarette.

"He's not here. Did you think he was?"

Nan said, "No," again in the same quiet voice.

Rosamund laughed.

"I haven't seen him, and I haven't got him here. And if you'll take my advice, you'll stop hunting round after him. Good Lord, my dear! This is the twentieth century, and a man does occasionally go away for twenty-four hours without taking his whole family with him!" She tilted back her head and blew a passable smoke-ring. "Jervis has always been an erratic creature—if he thinks of a thing he likes to do it at once."

"Yes," said Nan—"Ferdinand said that too."

"It's bound to be true if Ferdinand said it!" Her voice was insolent. Then suddenly she curbed it. "I know Jervis pretty well, and if you want my advice—which I don't suppose you do—I should say let sleeping dogs lie." She paused, blew another and a better smoke-ring, and added with drawling emphasis. *"Every time."*

She had remained standing. A long window let in a brilliant panel of sunshine which slanted to her feet. Nan was standing too. She came a little nearer and said,

"Do you know where Jervis is?"

Rosamund's beautiful eyebrows rose.

"That's a little crude, isn't it?"

"Yes," said Nan. "I'm not worrying about being crude—I'm worrying about Jervis. If he's all right, he may be anywhere he likes, and he may be with anyone he likes. If you know where he is, will you tell me?"

"I've told you that I don't know."

"Yes," said Nan. "But you keep hinting that you do. I should be very glad if you would stop hinting and say what you mean."

Rosamund gave a short laugh.

"I don't mean anything. If I'm to be quite candid, I think you're making a damned fuss. Men *will* go off on their own—and, knowing Jervis, I should say there'll be the devil to pay when he finds out that you've been sending the town-crier round after him."

"Yes," said Nan. She fixed her steady eyes on Rosamund. "You say men go off—but do they generally go in the middle of the night without any luggage?"

Something odd happened; but it happened so quickly that it would have been difficult to swear to. Nan had only an impression that Rosamund had begun to say something, and that before the words reached her lips the cigarette which she was holding slipped sideways so that the red-hot tip burnt her finger. It was just an impression.

The cigarette slipped, and Rosamund said, "Damn!"

Nan thought that she had been going to say something else. She didn't say it. She tossed the cigarette out of the open window and began to light another.

"Didn't he take any luggage?" she said. Then she went on without waiting for an answer. "That doesn't mean very much—does it?"

Nan said, "I don't know."

"Do you want me to dot the 'i's? I don't mind if *you* don't."

"I would like you to say what you mean."

Rosamund laughed again.

"Perhaps he picked up what he wanted at Carrington Square."

"No," said Nan.

"You've been ringing them up?"

"Yes," said Nan.

Rosamund blew another smoke-ring.

"Well—they're Jervis' servants," she said.

Nan let that go.

Rosamund walked to the window. The movement brought

her into the full sunlight. She turned. Her hair shone in the sun like bright, pale gold; her eyes were sharply blue.

"There is an alternative of course. If a man pays the rent of a flat, he very often keeps some things there."

"You don't seem to have a very high opinion of Jervis," said Nan.

Rosamund shrugged her shoulders.

"I don't expect him to be a plaster saint. If you do, I'm afraid you're going to get a good many jolts. If I had married him, I should have been quite philosophical about that sort of thing—but of course *I* never pretended to be in love with him." The stress on the "I" was of the slightest, but it was there.

Nan's colour rose a little. She kept her voice quiet.

"You are trying to make me believe something that you don't believe yourself. I'm wondering why."

The ash fell from Rosamund's cigarette. It made a dusty patch on the fine primrose linen of her dress. With an abrupt movement she turned and dropped the stub on to the gravel below the window. With a still more abrupt movement she turned back again.

"Would you rather believe that he was drowned?"

The colour in Nan's cheeks drained away. Her voice did not change.

"It's not a question of what either of us would rather believe—it's a question of the facts. I want to know what is true."

Rosamund stood with her hands behind her. They held the jamb of the window. She leaned back upon them.

"You're very detached," she said. "Well, then, here are your facts. Twice this summer, whilst we were bathing together, Jervis had cramp pretty badly. The last time I had to help him in. I don't think he'd have got in if he'd been alone. Well—you would have it you know."

A little more colour ebbed away. Nan said,

"Is that true?"

"Certainly."

"Then the servants would know about it."

"If you think Jervis would be likely to go round telling people that sort of thing—"

"Did *you* tell anyone about it?"

"Why should I? I didn't particularly want to make Jervis wild with me just then."

"I see. Then nobody knew about this cramp but you?"

"And Jervis," said Rosamund.

"Yes, of course. Jervis would know if he had had cramp," said Nan.

She watched Rosamund's face, but it showed nothing. The sun dazzled behind her.

"You can't tell me anything else?"

"I'm afraid not. Ring me up if you hear anything."

"Yes," said Nan. "I'll ring you up when he gets back."

She said, "Good-bye, Rosamund," and turned and walked out of the room.

XXXIII

"WELL?" SAID FERDINAND FAZACKERLEY AS THEY TURNED out of the Tetterleys' gate.

"I don't know," said Nan. "Don't talk to me for a little."

They drove in silence along the cliff road. It was very hot, but there was a breeze from the sea. When they turned inland, they lost it.

"What don't you know?" said Ferdinand after a while. "In my opinion it's always a whole sight better to tell what you don't know, because that's the sort of stuff that's liable to go sour on you."

"I'm going to tell you," said Nan. "I'm only sorting it out."

"Well, I'm not curious, but I like to know things—and when there isn't anything to know, I'm a whale at guessing.

Did you get anything out of the beautiful lady? Is she still talking too much?''

"Yes, she is."

"Now that's very interesting. I'd like to know what she talked about."

"She tried to make me angry," said Nan. "She tried to make me jealous. And then she tried to frighten me."

"That's not very original. Will you tell me what she said?"

Nan looked at the dusty hedgerow sliding past. A little straw had caught on the lowest branch of an overhanging thorn-tree. The shining stalks held the sun as Rosamund's hair had held it.

"What she said doesn't matter. She wanted to make me think that there was—someone Jervis might be with." She paused, and added, "Some woman. I told her she didn't believe what she was trying to make me believe. Then, I think, she was angry—but I'm not sure if she was really angry. She turned right round and tried to make me believe that Jervis—was drowned." She stumbled over the words, and her hand took hold of the edge of the seat and gripped it.

"What did she say?" said Ferdinand quickly.

Nan forced her voice.

"She said he'd had—cramp. She said he'd had it—when he was bathing—with her. She said—she'd had—to help him in."

"Jumping Mississippi I wish she'd said it to me!"

"Why?" said Nan.

"So I could tell whether she was lying. I've had a heap of practice at telling whether folks are lying. It takes a real smart liar to put it across with me."

"Oh, it wasn't true," said Nan.

"Sure?"

She gave a half impatient nod.

"Yes—quite sure. I'm not worried about that—I'm worried about why she said it—I'm worried about why she said any of it. It—it frightens me."

"Great Hoover! Why?"

"I don't know why."

Ferdinand looked at her.

"You're scared to death. Can't you tell me about it?"

He had slowed the car to a bare ten miles an hour. She put her hand to her cheek and pressed it there.

"If she knows—anything—" She paused.

"Yes?" said Ferdinand encouragingly.

"Perhaps she doesn't," said Nan.

"But if she does?"

"She might—want—" She stopped, flung her hand down in her lap, and said in a choked voice, "I can't!"

"Try!"

"If they—if she—knew—where he was—" She broke off again. "They might want him to do something—there might be—a choice." She beat with one hand upon the other, hard. "They might let him go if he gave them enough money—but if he wouldn't—if he *wouldn't*—they could say—they had always thought—he was—drowned." She faced round on Ferdinand and said passionately, "I'm wicked to think a thing like that! Tell me I'm wicked, F.F.! Tell me it couldn't be true!"

"Now when you say 'they'?" said Ferdinand.

"Leonard," said Nan—"Robert Leonard and Rosamund."

"Robert has got a mighty good alibi. It's a good seven miles from Croyston to King's Weare, and his car was in Mr Jeremiah Brown's garage with the cylinder head off. I like to know about things, so I collected that."

"He could hire a car."

"Well he didn't—not in Croyston—nor a motor bicycle."

"He might have borrowed one," said Nan.

"Who would he borrow it from? He's got no friends around here—folks don't cotton to him much. Who's he going to give himself away to by borrowing their car to do the meanest sort of criminal job? *Borrowing?*" He took his hand off the wheel and jerked the word away. "Nix on borrowing!"

"Rosamund," said Nan.

Ferdinand darted a sideways glance at her. He saw a pale, composed profile, lips colourless but firm, hands folded. He nodded. The car was moving slowly between the high banks of a sunk lane.

"She certainly was alone in the house—Tetterleys away, servants in a separate wing. But then, I did a bit of searching round when you were paying your call. I had a real nice talk with the second chauffeur. His name is Hoskins. He's some talker. I should say he's of the opinion that I nourish a grand passion for Miss Rosamund. The servants' wing looks out over the road to the garage. They've room for four cars in the garage, and Hoskins sleeps up over it. I said I thought I'd seen Miss Rosamund's car in Broyston Tuesday night, and he said she hadn't been out. He stuck to that, and what's more, he said he could prove it. For one thing, he'd cleaned the car that afternoon, and she certainly hadn't been out in the dust; and for another, he'd filled her up with oil and petrol, and next day when Miss Carew took her out he had a look at the petrol-gauge, and full up she was."

"Perhaps he wasn't telling the truth," said Nan.

"In my opinion he was."

"It isn't difficult to fill up again," said Nan—"and I expect Rosamund knows how to clean a car. Don't you see—" she lifted one hand and struck the other with it—"don't you *see* that that clean car and that full petrol tank were her alibi? *You* haven't got an alibi for Tuesday night, and neither have I. Why have she and Robert Leonard got such beautiful alibis?"

Ferdinand drove on without speaking.

"You think she got Jervis to come away with her?"

"I don't know. She could have fetched Robert Leonard from Croyston."

"And when she'd fetched him, what was he going to do? Jervis didn't like either of them well enough to go promenading around with them in the middle of the night. No—that's something I don't see."

"He's gone," said Nan. "*Someone* got him to go."

Ferdinand did not answer this at all. In spite of himself he was thinking of a warm, dark sea, with the moon going down in the west and the first gold flame of the dawn brightening the east. He could see the water, and a black moving speck which was Jervis' head. And then the speck was gone, and he could only see the wide grey sweep of the water.

The day dragged on its way, and with every hour it grew hotter. By five o'clock the sun had almost disappeared behind a thick haze. It was as if the very fierceness and heat of its burning had sent out a shrouding veil of smoke. Under it the sea was oily and lead-coloured.

Ferdinand had gone into Croyston. He had made up his mind that if Jervis had neither written nor returned by next morning, they must go to the police. Beneath the surface of his thoughts there floated an uneasy doubt as to whether they had not already delayed too long.

Nan stayed in the house. She had the feeling that something might happen at any moment. Impossible to move from the spot which might be the scene of this happening. She stayed in the library. There was a telephone there, and she was waiting for the bell to ring. It might ring *now*, whilst she was over by the window, or *now*, when she had turned and almost reached the door. A few quick steps would bring her close enough to snatch up the receiver, and then she would hear Jervis' voice. She never got beyond that first sound of his voice. He had not to explain why he had gone away; he had only to be there—a living voice. It did not matter at all what the voice said—no, it didn't matter at all.

She paced the room with an even step. From the door to the table where the telephone stood was about half way. She made a little pause there as if she were waiting for the bell to ring. Then from the table to the window—and here it took all her self-control not to hurry. She must touch the window-seat with her knee before she turned and walked back to the table again. As she walked, she braced herself against that possible sound of the bell. And the bell might ring without its being Jervis who was waiting at the other end of the line. Ferdinand might ring up from Croyston, or Rosamund, or—or anyone. She went on pacing the room.

An acute strain is rather like very severe frost; for just as a frost sharply defines physical objects, and at the same time renders them immovable, so a certain degree of mental strain has the effect of sharply defining thoughts and fixing them in an unnatural rigidity. In this condition an impression which would ordinarily be of the most fleeting nature becomes as indelibly impressed as an image cut in ice.

Nan had walked perhaps fifty times from the door to the table, from the table to the window, from the window to the table, and from the table back to the door, when she became aware of such an impression amongst her frozen thoughts. At first her awareness of it was vague and inattentive, but gradually her attention began to focus itself. It puzzled her, and, her attention once focussed, she felt a slight relief in having something definite to think about.

The impression was the impression of Mrs Mellish looking at her with eyes like windows with the blinds pulled down. She had asked Mrs Mellish whether she had seen or heard anything between Tuesday night and Wednesday morning. Mrs Mellish had said no. The very tone of that dry "No, ma'am" beat at Nan's ears. She had asked Mrs Mellish to find out whether the maids had seen or heard anything; and it was whilst Mrs Mellish was out of the room that the impression had been made—a slammed door, eyes with the blinds drawn down—something to hide. Mrs Mellish came back, and reported that nobody had noticed anything. Between two and half-past seven Jervis had walked out of the house. No one had seen or heard him go—no one had seen anything—no one had heard anything. Then why had Mrs Mellish slammed her door and pulled down her blinds? The impression that she had done so was clearer now than it had been at the time. The ice had set and defined it sharply.

Nan paused by the table, as she had paused there fifty times; but this time, instead of going on towards the door, she turned half-left, walked quickly to the hearth, and rang the bell. Then she faced round towards the door and waited until Alfred appeared.

"Will you ask Mrs Mellish to come and speak to me here, please."

She would see Mrs Mellish here. In the housekeeper's room, with its photographic enlargements of Mrs Mellish's husband and Mrs Mellish's respected and respectable parents, with Mrs Mellish's workbox in Tonbridge ware and Mrs Mellish's photograph album on a small rose-wood

table, and a large illuminated text hanging over the mantel-
piece, Nan had been made to feel an alien and an intruder.
The very china dogs, white poodles with baskets in their
mouths, had gazed at her aloofly from either end of the
mantelshelf. The old-fashioned wall-clock had a disapproving
tick. Here she could meet Mrs Mellish upon neutral ground.
This was Jervis' room.

Alfred went away, and presently came back again. Mrs
Mellish had just stepped out.

"I would like to see her when she comes in."

Nan went back to her pacing.

At seven o'clock the telephone bell rang with a startling
loudness and set her heart thumping. She was by the door.
She turned, ran back, and picked up the receiver.

"Who's there?"

"Ferdinand."

"Yes?"

"Look here, Nan, there's something I want to follow up.
I'm getting a move on with a hired car. It mayn't be
anything at all, but I feel kind of bound to follow it up. You
won't get rattled?"

"What is it?"

"It doesn't amount to much. There's a new garage the far
side of Croyston. Well, the man says a Morris-Cowley
stopped to fill up at seven o'clock Wednesday morning. He
was about because he was doing a job on his own car. He
says there were two men in the car, and from the description
one of them might be Jervis, but it's very vague. It was the
other man who did the talking. He was the driver, and he'd
red hair, so it oughtn't to be hard to trace him. He talked
about going to London, so I'm off looking for him. Don't
you go worrying."

Nan felt dazed and weak. The receiver was heavy in her
hand. She said.

"Jervis hasn't got a Morris."

"The car was the other man's—*he* was driving. They
may have met by appointment, or Jervis might simply be
getting a lift—or it mayn't have been Jervis at all. The
garage man only said, 'a gentleman with black hair.' That's
about all he noticed—his front name isn't Sherlock."

Ferdinand rang off, and Nan began walking up and down again. She walked for a long while, and then sat down by the window and let time flow past her like a sluggish stream, so slow that though it moved, the movement was imperceptible.

At seven the dressing-bell rang, and Alfred came in. He hovered for a moment by the door and then came nearer. Mrs Mellish had missed her bus from Croyston—and would it be convenient for Mrs Weare to see her after dinner?

Nan said, "Yes—it doesn't matter," and Alfred withdrew.

When the dinner-bell rang, she realized that she had not changed. She went upstairs, washed her hands, and came down again, to sit alone at the big table in the dining-room and take a spoonful from each dish that was offered to her.

XXXIV

MRS MELLISH CAME INTO THE LIBRARY. NOBODY WOULD have known that she had been cooking. She wore her black afternoon dress, with a medallion brooch depicting a pink church leaning a little sideways against a background of bright blue sky. She had an air of dignity and leisured calm as she came to a standstill at a respectful distance and waited for Nan to speak.

"Please sit down," said Nan.

"I'd rather stand, ma'am."

Did she do it on purpose? Did she know how difficult it was to talk to someone who stands literally, as well as morally, on her dignity?

Nan braced herself.

"I'd like you to sit, Mrs Mellish." She indicated a chair near her own.

After a momentary hesitation Mrs Mellish advanced another

chair—one without arms and straight in the back. Upon the extreme edge of this chair she seated herself, her body stiffly erect, and her hands neatly folded. After a suitable pause she said,

"Yes, ma'am?"

Nan leaned forward.

"I want you to help me."

Mrs Mellish registered a blank inability to understand how she could possibly be of any assistance to Mrs Weare. After a further pause she again said,

"Yes, ma'am?"

At the same time her folded hands moved slightly and displayed the square of a clean linen handkerchief as stiff, as blank, and as blameless as Mrs Mellish herself.

"We're in great trouble about Mr Weare," said Nan.

Mrs Mellish said "Yes, ma'am?" for the third time.

Nan got up abruptly. If she were to sit still and listen to Mrs Mellish saying "Yes, ma'am?" anything might happen. She felt a passionate desire to pick up the nearest book and send it crashing through the window, or, better still, straight at Mrs Mellish's head. She stood for a moment at the window, holding back the heavy curtains and staring at the dark. It came right up to the glass. It was heavy and solid. She couldn't see anything at all.

She let the curtain fall and turned round again.

"You've known Jervis a long time."

"Yes, ma'am."

"You knew him when he was quite a little boy."

"Yes, ma'am."

"You've known him all those years. We're in dreadful trouble about him—we think—that something—must have happened."

"Yes, ma'am?" said Mrs Mellish.

There was a little heavy brass box on the telephone-table; it was used to hold stamps. Nan wrenched her eyes away from it. She wanted to pick it up and throw it at Mrs Mellish—*hard*. With an effort, she stood where she was.

"Do you know of anything that might have taken him away suddenly?"

Mrs Mellish considered this in silence. She had been

brought up to tell the truth, and classed lying with dirt, unpunctuality, gossip, and voting anything except Conservative. There were worse sins, such as stealing, atheism, and immorality; but they hardly came within the purview of the respectable. After a suitable pause she compromised by saying,

"I can't say that I do."

"You'd tell me if you did—wouldn't you? Mr Fazackerley has gone to London to make inquiries there, but—I don't feel as if Jervis had gone to London—I *don't*."

Mrs Mellish said nothing. Her hands rested on the linen square. The thin wedding-ring which Albert Mellish had placed on a slim finger forty-five years ago had now become sunk between two rolls of firm pink flesh. The finger was no longer slim; the gold just gleamed when it caught the light, like a hidden secret, like the gleam of past and gone romance.

Nan turned away and walked to the end of the room and back again.

Mrs Mellish never moved at all. She was sitting there because she had been ordered to sit; otherwise, she would have risen when Mrs Weare had risen; but, having been ordered to sit, sit she would until she was ordered to rise. A stubborn sense of her own superiority upheld her. She knew her place, if Mrs Weare didn't know hers. She looked up and saw Nan standing over her.

"Mrs Mellish—you know something. What is it?"

Mrs Mellish reinforced her dignity. This wasn't any way for a mistress to behave, and she didn't hold with it.

"You know something—"

"Indeed, ma'am—"

"Yes, you do!" The urgency of the tone melted into appeal. "Oh, won't you tell me?"

Mrs Mellish sat up a little more stiffly.

"If I may put the question, ma'am—what makes you think as I have anything to tell?"

"You have—haven't you? I want you to tell me what it is. It mayn't seem an important thing to you—it may even seem a very, very little thing—and you may have some reason for not wanting to tell me; but won't you please put all that on one side and just tell me what it is? We've got nothing to go on, and it's like being shut up in a pitch dark room—even the least little glimmer of light might show us where the door is. Don't you see that?''

There was another pause, and Mrs Mellish said,

''No, ma'am.''

The tears rushed into Nan's eyes. They were so hot with anger that they burned there. She stepped back because the impulse to take Mrs Mellish by those plump cushioned shoulders and shake her until her eyes bulged and her teeth rattled was simply overpowering. After a moment she said,

''You *do* know something—I *know* that you do! Why won't you tell me what you know?''

The subtle air of offence which had accompanied Mrs Mellish to this interview became more noticeable. It wasn't for anyone that knew her manners to colour up and behave hysterical like Mrs Weare was doing. Mrs Mellish thanked Providence that she was not as other women were. She thanked Providence that she'd been brought up respectable, and to know her manners and have a proper control of herself. She had had her troubles, and she'd known how to behave herself. At her husband's funeral she had shed a widow's decorous tears, but she had been careful not to let them spoil her crape. She despised Nan a good deal for her changing colour and the quiver in her voice. She did not speak.

Nan went back to her chair and sat down. It was no good appealing to Mrs Mellish. She knew very well that she was being despised, and the Forsyth pride stiffened her back. She allowed the silence to lengthen. Then she said, in a voice which Mrs Mellish had not heard before,

''I'm waiting.''

''I beg your pardon, ma'am?''

''I'm waiting for you to tell me what you saw or heard on Tuesday night.'' Nan's voice had a quiver in it now. It was hard with authority.

Mrs Mellish looked up, a little surprised, and met steady eyes with something behind them that demanded an answer. The change flurried her a little. Unconsidered words sprang to her lips.

"Nothing that was to say anything, ma'am."

"Then you did see something?"

Mrs Mellish recovered herself.

"I couldn't say, ma'am."

"I think you must say."

Mrs Mellish bridled.

"I'm sure I'm the last to keep back anything as 'ud be any help," she said. With the fingers of one hand she pleated a fold on the white linen handkerchief on her knee.

"Yes. What did you see?"

"I'm a poor sleeper," said Mrs Mellish, "and when I don't sleep, it's my 'abit to make myself a cup of tea." She paused, and added, "On a spirit lamp."

"Yes?" said Nan.

"I'd run out of tea," said Mrs Mellish. "I make so bold as to keep some handy—I've a caddy that was give me by Mr Weare for the purpose. Come Tuesday night, my caddy was empty, and I went down to fill it. It might have been three o'clock or thereabouts."

"Yes?" said Nan. "Go on, please."

Mrs Mellish meant to take her own time.

"I went down the back stairs, and so I come up. I had my candle in my hand, and when I came up to the first floor, the door through to the landing was half open. I put my hand on it to bring it to, and I heard a door open along the corridor."

"Yes?" said Nan. "What door was it?"

"It was Mr Jervis' door—Mr Weare, I should say—so I blew out my candle—it being an awkward time of night to meet a gentleman, and me in my dressing-gown."

"Yes?" said Nan rather breathlessly.

The black curtain that had fallen between Tuesday night and Wednesday morning was going to be lifted; she was going to get a glimpse of what lay behind it.

"I shut the door," said Mrs Mellish, "and came away up to my room and made my cup of tea."

Nan straightened herself again. She had leaned forward involuntarily to catch the first glimpse of what was behind that curtain.

There was no glimpse.

She choked down her sick disappointment and forced her voice.

"You didn't see Mr Jervis?"

"No, ma'am."

Nan caught the tone of relief. Now why should Mrs Mellish be relieved? She hadn't seen Jervis. Why should she be relieved about that? The next question was across her lips before she knew that she was going to ask it.

"Whom did you see?"

Mrs Mellish was so much startled that her hand closed on the linen handkerchief and crumpled its neat folds.

"I went up to my room, and I made my cup of tea," she said; but her voice had lost its balance; it hurried over one word, and dragged on another.

Nan gave her no time.

"You saw someone. Whom did you see?"

"I blew my candle out, and I shut the door."

"You blew out your candle. Mr Jervis' door was open. Did you see a light? Was there a light in Mr Jervis' room?"

Mrs Mellish looked up, and down again.

"There might have been."

A tingling triumph came up in Nan.

"There was a light—you saw it! What else did you see?"

"I couldn't hardly say." The words were almost inaudible.

"You *must* say," said Nan.

"I'd rather you didn't ask me, ma'am."

"I'm afraid you must say what you saw."

Why didn't she want to? What was she hiding?

Mrs Mellish rallied her dignity.

"It'd be best for all parties if you'd let me go now, ma'am."

"You must say what you saw," said Nan.

Mrs Mellish made a curious sort of jerking movement.

"Well then, I did see someone—and I wouldn't have mentioned it if I hadn't been driven. There's never been no evil speaking, lying, nor slandering in my kitchen—no, nor in my housekeeper's room neither. But if you *will* have it, ma'am—"

"Yes, I will have it," said Nan.

"Well then—I saw Miss Rosamund."

So the curtain had hidden Rosamund. Nan did not know what she had expected, but it was not this. The shock had numbed feeling, but it left her voice quiet and level.

"You saw Miss Rosamund. Will you tell me just what you did see?"

Mrs Mellish put the linen handkerchief to her chin for a moment, and then to either temple. The moisture stood on her pale skin.

"I blew out my candle, and so soon as it was out, I could see there was a light somewhere. And I looked round the crack of the door—and there was Mr Jervis' door open and a light in the room, and Miss Rosamund coming out with a suit-case in her hand. And just as I looked, the light went out, and I shut the door quick and come away."

Nan sat there pale and straight. She had brought this humiliation on herself. Mrs Mellish would have spared her, but she had forced her to speak. Well—since she had come so far, she must go the whole of the way.

"You're sure you saw Miss Rosamund?"

"Yes, ma'am."

It was no use—she couldn't go on. If there were more questions to be put, then someone else must put them—Ferdinand, or Mr Page. She would have to send for Mr Page tomorrow if there were still no news. *Rosamund*. Rosamund, with the suit-case in her hand. She felt very sick and giddy, but she managed to get up and to speak steadily.

"Thank you, Mrs Mellish. You won't speak of this to anyone?"

Mrs Mellish recovered her poise.

"It's not by any wish of mine that I've spoke of it now," she said, and withdrew without haste, and with the consciousness of high moral worth.

It was some time later that Nan realized she was still standing as she had stood to see Mrs Mellish go. The realization came with a slight sense of shock. It was some time since the door had closed, but she did not know how long. Everything had stopped when the door shut; now it went on again with a little jerk, but slowly, unevenly, and as if it might stop again at any moment. The sense of strain and of expectation was gone. Jervis had gone away with

Rosamund. She felt humiliated into the very dust. They had gone away secretly, and Rosamund had lied to her. All the time she had talked about drowning and about Jervis getting cramp, she was lying. She had been in Jervis' room at three o'clock in the morning. She had stood in the door with his suit-case in her hand.

Nan was too numb to feel hurt. The thought of Rosamund was like a heavy weight that numbed her. Jervis had come into her room and been kind. Was he expecting Rosamund then? Was that why he was awake? Had he only been kind because she must not be awake? She must sleep and know nothing because Rosamund was coming?

Her mind filled with pictures. They came up like bubbles in dark water. She could see them coming, but she could not stop them. As each one reached the surface of her mind, it floated there, showed its iridescent colours, and broke in a spray like tears.

She saw herself and Rosamund side by side. Jervis loved Rosamund.

She saw Jervis comforting her—the curtain blowing in the draught from the open door—the door between his room and hers. He wouldn't have left it open if Rosamund had been there. She trembled against his shoulder and was comforted. The door was open, and the curtain blew.

She saw Rosamund with a suit-case in her hand.

She saw other things.

After a long time no more bubbles rose. Her mind was dark and empty. She went up to her room, and at the first sound of her foot on the stair, there was Bran, keeping step with her. She locked the door upon them both; she locked the door into Jervis' room. Then she undressed and lay down on her bed. A heavy weight of fatigue made all her limbs feel like lead. She lay down and covered herself with the sheet. With no interval at all, she dropped into the deepest depths of sleep.

XXXV

JERVIS WEARE OPENED HIS EYES. HE MIGHT AS WELL HAVE kept them shut, because he could see nothing. An even blackness with no shading in it confronted him. He dropped his lids and slipped back into a vague half consciousness. Presently he moved, threw out an arm, and groaned. The sound of this groan was the first to reach his ears since he had heard Rosamund move beside him in the dark just before he leaned forward to put on the lights of her car. He heard his own groan, and opened his eyes again. He was still in the dark. But where was Rosamund, and where was the car?

He sat up and felt his head. There was a lump on the back of it like a tennis-ball. He frowned furiously. His head was swimming, and the darkness was full of fireworks. He put his head in his hands and leaned forward. The fireworks grew paler, and his head began to clear. He became aware of something hard running into him. His right leg felt numb. He put down one hand gropingly, and touched stone. The damp cold of it roused him. He moved his leg. It was not injured; it was only numb.

He scrambled up, and once more the darkness filled with rockets and catherine-wheels. He had to sit down again. His mind cleared momentarily. He was in the dark, sitting on wet stone, with a lump on his head. But a moment ago he had heard Rosamund move beside him in the darkness, and he had leaned forward to switch on the lights of her car. She had no business to leave a dark car by the side of the road—it was damned dangerous.

He put his hand to his head again. You couldn't raise a lump like that in a moment. Had they been run into? He remembered leaning forward to put on the lights. He couldn't remember the lights going on—they hadn't gone on—his hand had never reached the switch—he had leaned forward, and someone had knocked him out.

Who? That was the question.

And *why?*

Someone had most undoubtedly knocked him out—unless there had been an accident. Someone might have run into that dark car.

Jervis fingered his head. He had been leaning forward to switch on the lights—his head was already inside the car. If there had been a smash, he couldn't see how he had got off with a bump on the head. And then, how had he got *here*—and where was he?

He felt about him again. . . . Stone . . . not a stone floor . . . damp . . . uneven. He got over on to his hands and knees and felt farther afield. One groping hand passed roughened ridges and came down into a slimy hollow; the other, feeling ahead, went over a rounded edge and found nothing beyond it. For a moment Jervis stayed like that, his left hand slipping, and his right over the edge of an unknown drop. Then a sharp splinter of rock cut his knee, and half involuntarily he drew himself back into a sitting position. What place was this? A dark place, and damp with the passage of water. With his mind awakened to this, his ears caught a sound which had not meant anything until now, when he became aware that it had been present all the time. It was the sound of water.

He sat there listening. The sound was the sound of water, but it was not the sound of a stream. It neither flowed, nor rushed, nor tinkled; it had none of the notes of running water. It was the sound most familiar to him of any sound on earth. It was the sound of the sea.

Everything stood still in his mind for a moment. Then the sound of the sea again. His hand went down and touched the damp stone. He put a finger to his mouth, and found it salt. The sound of the sea—and rock with a salt dampness upon it. . . . The sea had been over this stone, and not so long ago. Then if there was a way for the sea to come in, there must be a way by which he could get out. He wasn't going to stay here to be drowned like a rat in a trap. Only he must have light. This intense darkness puzzled him. It must mean many winding turns. But then, of course, it was the middle of the night. Or was it? How long had he been unconscious?

He began to feel in his pocket for matches. There was a box in his blazer pocket, but it felt uncommonly light. He opened it gingerly and found two matches. Perhaps his hand shook; perhaps the first match was rotten. It left a luminous streak upon the roughened side of the box, jigged off with a hiss and a spirit of blue flame, and went out. He had seen his own knuckles with green smears on them, and the corner of the match-box yellow and black.

There was one match left.

He wetted his finger and held it up to see if there was a draught, but could discern none. He struck the match quickly, and it caught, the soft damp wood sizzling as the yellow flame took hold. He held it up. There was an immense static blackness for it to contend with—an old tyranny of the dark, and one little point of light to fight it with.

He held it up. He could see his own hand, and the flame dropping suddenly from a yellow tongue to a blue flare. He reversed the match, saw the glimmer fade and then suddenly sprang up again into flame. He looked away from his hand and saw wet black rock—a drop to what he thought was water—and bars. The match burnt his fingers, and he dropped it. It fell with a splutter on the wet stone and went out. A red spark was there for a moment, then it was gone.

Jervis came with a tremendous mental shock to the realization of where he was. It was the bars that did the trick. There was only one place with a barred exit to the sea, and that was Old Foxy Fixon's Cellar. It took him a minute or two to pull round from the shock. How in the world had he got into Old Foxy Fixon's Cellar? Why, there weren't half a dozen people who knew of its existence— Basher—possibly Mabel Tetterley. But Basher wasn't the sort who told his wife things, so Mabel was doubtful. Who else?

Himself, of course—and Rosamund. The rock moved beneath him giddily. His head swam. He put down a hand on either side of him and waited for it to clear. The dark cave filled with pictures. Rosamund on a visit at fourteen— the first time he had seen her. They had got on like a house on fire then. She had stayed for a month and then gone back to her mother. Five years before they met again. And then a different Rosamund—a grown-up Rosamund with a hardish streak in her. He went back to Rosamund's visit, and the very low tide which had sent them exploring along the foot of the cliffs. That was when they had found Old Foxy's Cellar. At first it looked like any other little cave; but it went on, got larger, and after a succession of break-neck boulders and dangerous pools ended, for them, in a sort of iron portcullis with a gate in the middle of it, a gate that could not be opened. They explored precariously with candle-ends stuck on splinters of wood and as many boxes of matches as they could gather from the King's Weare bedrooms. For two days the tide left the entrance bare. On the third they were very nearly drowned, and Basher had come to their rescue and made them promise to hold their tongues about the cave. He said he didn't want a lot of silly asses messing round and getting themselves drowned. When they had both promised, he showed them the landward entrance from Old Foxy's house and told them all about it. Old Foxy Fixon used to use the place to store the French brandy which he smuggled. In his time the entrance was practicable for a day or two round about spring tides. He put up the bars to keep his kegs safe from his rivals and from the Preventive men. The iron gate had never been opened since Old Foxy died, and no one knew what had happened to the key.

Jervis sat with his palms cold on the wet stone and saw these things. They were like pictures seen by flash-light, unnaturally clear, but a long way off. Himself—Rosamund, with a heavy yellow plait—Basher—the rusty portcullis— Basher telling them how Old Foxy Fixon diddled the Preventive men—Basher taking them into Old Foxy's house, where the wall-papers hung in mouldering strips and a smell of damp and must and rotting wood lurked in the empty rooms—Basher taking them into the kitchen, and from there down brick steps to a cellar which was surprisingly dry and warm—Basher shifting a barrel and lifting up a tremendous trap-door with an iron ring in it—himself and Rosamund kneeling and peering into the black uncertainties below. There was a passage that led to the cave, but Basher wouldn't take them down into it, and they had to promise on their most sacred words of honour never to go there alone. Jervis could see Rosamund, with her head tipped back, thanking Basher. She had torn her dress, and she was covered with wet green slime, but she thanked him very composedly. Jervis had not thanked him at all. It was the most wonderful moment of his life. He dreamed of it for months, recurred to it with a secret thrill for years, and had never passed Old Foxy's house without a thought of its hidden secret.

Well, he was in Old Foxy's Cellar—and what about it? Someone had put him there. It became blindingly obvious that it was Robert Leonard who had put him there, and that Rosamund had shown him the way. A cold rage stiffened Jervis from head to foot. Rosamund had come to him with a cock-and-bull story which he had been fool enough to believe, and Leonard had knocked him on the head and dumped him in Foxy's Cellar. It was so obvious, that there was nothing more to be said. The question was, what did they want? And the answer came pat in Ferdinand's words—Nan's words. "Who gets King's Weare and the money if anything happens to you?" Rosamund got it. And Rosamund knew about the cellar. And Rosamund had thrown a stone up at his window and brought him down to a convenient dark place where Leonard could lay him out without any risk.

That cold anger gripped him hard. It turned in on himself. He'd had warnings enough, and he had refused to take them. This wasn't Leonard's first shot at him, not by a long chalk. The accident that hadn't been an accident in Carrington Square. The conveniently rotten bridge over the ravine. The wheel that had come off his car on the very hill that was over him now. Even that old business of ten years ago on Croyston rocks. He believed now that on each of these occasions Leonard had tried to do him in.

He made an abrupt movement that brought him half round towards the barred entrance to the cave. Leonard and the past were pushed violently out of his mind. He bent his head and listened intently. That sound of the sea, which had been faint when first he heard it, was faint no longer. He could hear it quite plainly. Water was lapping over the sill. He could hear the smooth, glassy sound of it. Then a pause and a silence. And after the pause and the silence again that flowing glassy sound. And after each silence the sound was more. He heard a wave break against rock and fall to an unseen pool. And then another, and another. And then a booming, gurgling sound, and the rush of the sea. With ton upon ton of weight behind it, the tide was coming in.

XXXVI

JERVIS DID NOT KNOW HOW LONG HE HAD BEEN LISTENING to the tide. He was still dizzy. The sound of the water seemed to be inside his head, and the darkness pressed upon him from every side. It was a giddiness, and it passed. He set himself to order his thoughts. There had been a moment of horrid panic when he knew that the tide was coming in. It had been high tide last night—Tuesday night—at nine o'clock. It would be high tide, and spring tide, at ten minutes past eight on Wednesday morning. That made low tide just after two. It must have been somewhere about three o'clock when he was knocked out. Say that was an hour ago. . . . It was very difficult to gauge time, and he had no watch. He regretted his watch, with its luminous dial, a good deal. Well, if it was four o'clock or thereabouts, the tide had turned two hours before, and had another three hours to go. The question was—how far up was it going to come? He

was on the landward side of the portcullis in the inner cave.
Well, where did Foxy store his kegs? He didn't just leave
them banging about in the tide-water, with the chance of
being stove in and a total loss of his fine French brandy.
Basher, talking a long way off:

"You couldn't get through to the house from the sea even
if you had the key of the gate."

Rosamund, a long way off,

"Why couldn't we?"

And then Basher again,

"The passage comes out fifteen feet above the cave."

Jervis, sixteen years away:

"Then how did they get the kegs up?"

And Basher,

"Floated 'em up. Leary devil—wasn't he? Floated 'em
up on the tide and hauled 'em in like herring."

Fifteen feet. . . . . Floated 'em up. . . . . Fifteen feet of water
over where he was sitting. . . . . *Floated 'em up and pulled
'em in like herring. . . . .* Fifteen feet of solid green water.

He went giddy again.

When the giddiness had passed, he heard the sea nearer,
and the sound of it more restless. He strained back across
sixteen years to remember just what he had seen by the light
of those pilfered candle-ends. They had reached the portcullis, and thrusting their improvised torches between the bars,
had strained, as he was straining, to see what might be life
or death to him now. A candle on a stick makes quite a good
torch, but it doesn't last very long. He could see the little
wavering flames. He could see the wax melting and running
down. What else could he see? Very little. Or was it that he
couldn't remember? There was an impression of a deep
pool—a pool that looked like ink; and a wall—a black wall
rising beyond it. The little flickering candle flames dazzled
him. This rock on which he was sitting must have been
there to be seen, but he couldn't remember that he had seen
it. He could only remember the pool and the wall—the
black wall, and the black pool. He would have given half of
all that he possessed for one of those guttering candle-ends.

No good thinking of what he would do with something
which he couldn't possibly come by. If his head were a bit

clearer, he might be able to think of something. He turned over and, lying flat on his stomach, edged in the direction in which he thought the pool lay. Presently there was going to be too much water (presently would be too late). What he wanted, and wanted badly, was something to bathe his head with now. His hand found the edge and went over it. He crawled forward, lying flat and gripping a rocky projection with his left hand, whilst with his right he reached down towards the water. It was no good. There was rock, and slime, and dark empty air, but no water. If he leaned any further, he would be over. He drew back, had a giddy moment when he felt himself slipping, jerked sideways, and was flat on the rock again. After a moment he started to crawl in another direction. This time he came up against a big sprawling boulder. His third attempt brought him to a little pool a bare foot across; his hand went into it up to the wrist. He washed his face and head, and then went on exploring.

He was on a raised ledge about six feet by eight. On one side it was bounded by a slippery tilted boulder of unknown height, and on the other three sides by an equally unknown drop. He couldn't climb the boulder; it was water-worn and as slippery as glass. *Water-worn*—and that damned tide was coming in. He could hear it moving stealthily. There were no more noisy rushes. The entrance had been long ago submerged. The pools in the outer cave had filled and overflowed. The water rose quietly. When it had reached its next level, it would flood the pools immediately below him. He remembered a rise like a step on the seaward side of the portcullis. The water was lapping it now, softly, pleasantly, with here and there a little eddying gurgle.

Jervis sat up and went over his pockets again. There might be a spilled match somewhere. If he could see—if he could get behind the curtain of this darkness for a minute—a half minute—a bare second. . . . . There must be some ledge to which he could climb. . . . . The thought of the passage came into his mind. It opened into the cave fifteen feet up. Leonard must have brought him here by the passage. Then there must be a way down into the cave—and not too hard a way, because Leonard couldn't have carried him down anything of a climb. He wondered if there were steps cut in the wall. If there were, there must be something to hold to. Leonard couldn't have got him down slippery steps without some pretty good hand-purchase.

He gave up his pockets as a bad job. He hadn't really thought there would be a match. Well—what he had to do would have to be done in the dark. He must wait until there was enough water to float him, and then swim round the cave feeling for a foot-hold. His head was better now, but he felt terribly thirsty. The lapping of the water suggested a long cool drink. His thirst became intense. Thirst, and the lapping of the tide . . . Thirst—and darkness—and the tide coming in . . . The tide coming up in the dark . . . If he could see . . . "I should hate that death bandaged my eyes, and forbore, and crept past." Where did that come from? He didn't know. He must have read it. And there was something farther on about the "black minute." Black minute—black eternity—the lapping, rising water. If he could only see . . .

With the word in his mind, he saw.

A harsh dragging, grating sound made a confusion amongst the echoes of the cave, and, cutting through the black darkness and the confusion, came a white and brilliant shaft of light. Jervis looked up at it, tingling with a sense of shock. Light—a level ray of it overhead. It cut the darkness and made a shining circle on the wet black wall of the cave. Jervis saw the circle before he saw the beam. It sprang out of the darkness into which he was staring, and he saw black scarred rock all wet and shining, with fissures that ran moisture. Then he looked up and saw the beam, and turned himself about to follow it to its source.

It sprang from the wall above his head. Someone had come down the passage from Old Foxy's house and was standing in the mouth of it with a powerful electric torch in his hand; but Jervis could see nothing but the brilliant star of light and the beam that sprang from it. Then suddenly the beam swung down and hit him in the face. He threw up his arm involuntarily, as if to ward a blow; and from the black mouth of the passage Robert Leonard laughed.

"So you've come to, have you?"

"Take that damned light off me!" said Jervis furiously.

He felt it go, and then flick back and catch him blinking.

Robert Leonard laughed again.

"Not looking quite your best—are you? Like a wash and brush up? Oh, I see you've had the wash. What about a drink? You've got a bit of a head, haven't you?" As he spoke, he swung the light to and fro.

Jervis steadied himself against the intermittent dazzle, and got what he could from it. Only a four-foot drop from where he was to pool level. There were two pools, one running right back to the wall of the cave, and another between him and the iron bars. The tide was right up to the bars now, and the step was hidden. The passage from Foxy's house had been behind him. The beam cut down from it at an angle and swung to and fro. There must be a fairly foot-worthy path between the edge of the pool and the tilted boulder, because Leonard must have brought him that way. The cave was about twenty feet across, and his rock a little on one side of the middle—say eight feet from the wall where the passage came out.

The light swung in. He saw that there was just such a narrow path as he had guessed at. The ray poured down almost vertically for a moment, and then cut right across the cave and made a steady circle on the dropping wall. Jervis guessed that the torch had been set down.

"I've come to talk business," said Robert Leonard.

Jervis spoke to him for the first time. He said,

"You damned swab!"

"And I don't want any of your back-chat," said Leonard. His voice was the voice of a man who stands in a lounging attitude with his hands in his pockets. "I've got you cold—and if you haven't got enough sense to see it, and to keep a civil tongue in your head, you can stay here and drown—it would suit me better. D'you get that? I'd sooner you were drowned—dead men tell no tales, and all the rest of it. It would suit me a whole heap better to let you drown. You get that by heart and keep it in mind!"

Jervis could just see him now that the light was still. He had set it down, not at his feet, but on some sort of ledge on a level with his hand. His hands showed, and his face, and a light patch that was collar and shirt. They looked like pale funguses in the dark. The rest was shadow.

"Well?" said the easy voice. "Going to be sensible and talk? You're up against it, you know."

Jervis got up and stood against the tilted boulder. He set an elbow on it and leaned his head on his hand. Moving made him giddy for a moment. He said,

"What do you want?"

The thing seemed still so inconceivable. His thoughts felt stiff; he couldn't really bend them to deal with it. There was a blind rage waiting to sweep him off his feet, but he'd got to keep that back. A blind rage—a blind tide—rising tide— spring tide—storm tide—waiting to carry him away, to sweep him against the rocks, to dash him senseless, to drown the cave—and him.

He leaned heavily upon his hand. He heard Leonard speaking, but the words went by him. It was like a wrong tuning on the wireless—a blare of sound without words or sense. Then, all at once, his name sharp and clear, and the confusion gone.

"Jervis!" and, "What about it?"

He looked up stupidly, blinking at the ray.

"I didn't hear what you said."

Robert Leonard swore with an obvious anger which Jervis found heartening. Come to think of it, it was annoying to breathe fire and slaughter, and find that the victim hadn't been attending. Jervis laughed inwardly.

"Perhaps you wouldn't mind saying it again," he said politely.

Once more Robert Leonard swore. He had quite an extensive vocabulary and appeared to be in good form.

"Look here, I've come here to talk business, not to waste my time!"

"It's valuable of course!" said Jervis.

Leonard's voice took on a nasty rasp.

"Yours is, if mine isn't. D'you like being here? You're thirsty, aren't you? You'll be thirstier soon, unless you're dead. Perhaps you've noticed that the tide's coming in. Well, either we're going to talk business, or I go away and leave you—and if you've any idea of getting out this way yourself, you can put it out of your head. In the first place, you can't get up without a ladder, and in the next, there's a pretty tough gate, and when I go away I lock it behind me. See?''

He snatched up the torch and turned its circle of light straight downwards. Then with a crook of the wrist he brought it slowly up the face of the wall.

Jervis had argued that there must be steps cut in the rock. There were no steps. The rocky face hung over a little. It was sheerly unclimbable. The light came up to the ledge where Leonard stood. It was a mere sill like a wide door-step, with the mouth of the passage rising in an irregular arch above it.

Leonard swung the light round past his shoulder and let the beam play on a half open iron gate, heavy, rusty, and strong. Closed, it would fill the arch. A new chain and padlock dangled at its edge; the light picked out the bright steel links. Then the torch was set down again.

''Got that?'' said Leonard. ''No getting up without a ladder. The ladder's up here, and it'll stay here until we come to terms. Now—what about business?''

''What do you want?'' said Jervis.

''Now you're talking! It's not so much a question of what I want—because I've already told you that you'd suit me best dead—it's a case of what sort of compromise I'm willing to make. You ought to be damned glad I'm willing to compromise at all.''

Jervis kept his mouth shut. If he could have laid his hand on a loose bit of rock, he would have chanced it and had a shot at the pale blur that was Leonard's face. But there weren't any loose bits of rock; the drag of the tide saw to that.

Leonard went on speaking.

''I prefer you dead—but you can buy yourself off if you like.''

''Look here, Leonard—''

''I don't *want* you to,'' said Robert Leonard. ''I keep telling you so. I want you dead. You'd be a lot safer dead. *You*'d be a lot safer, and I'd be a lot richer. It's money in my pocket if you like to be a damn fool and drown.''

There was a hard, bitter silence. Jervis held his tongue,

and, like David, it was pain and grief to him. The things that he would have liked to say to Robert Leonard blared in him. His head felt red-hot. His hand gripped a rib of rock, and it was not until afterwards he knew that he had cut it deeply across the palm.

"Aren't you going to ask me why?" Leonard's voice was careless again. "No? Beast of a temper you've got—haven't you? Nasty, sulky brute of a temper! It'll get you into trouble if you don't look out—bad trouble. Well, if you're not going to ask me why it would be money in my pocket if you insist on drowning, I'll tell you all the same, because I'd sooner have all the cards on the table. Mine are all aces, so I don't mind showing them. If you're dead, Rosamund gets King's Weare and the cash—and what Rosamund gets I get. You see, she couldn't marry you the other day, because she was married already. We've been married eleven years."

"Is that true?" said Jervis sharply.

"You've got a nasty unbelieving nature as well as the devil of a temper! I don't think you'll be missed if the tide gets you. True? Of course it's true! I married Rosamund the day she was twenty-one. So you see you've kept us out of King's Weare a good long time. You know, I shouldn't have been heart-broken if you'd been drowned when you came to grief on the rocks at Croyston ten years ago."

"You were married to Rosamund then?"

"We'd been married a year. It would have been very convenient if you'd been drowned. I merely mention this to show you that I've waited quite long enough, and I'm getting a bit impatient."

"What do you want?" said Jervis.

"Thirty thousand pounds," said Robert Leonard.

"Talk sense!" said Jervis contemptuously. The sum staggered him.

"Sense?" said Leonard. "I'm giving you your life, aren't I? If I lock that gate behind me and leave you here, I get King's Weare and eighty thousand—don't I? I'm asking you a bare third—I might take the whole. I've only got to leave you here."

"Then why don't you?" said Jervis.

He really wanted to know. If Leonard was married to

Rosamund, it was quite obvious that Jervis Weare was worth a good deal more to him dead than alive. Leonard had put the matter in a nutshell. Only why didn't he crack the cut—why any hesitation about leaving Jervis to drown? He felt quite unable to credit Leonard with a qualm of conscience.

He waited for an answer to his "Why don't you?"

"Rosamund has an objection," said Leonard regretfully.

Jervis threw up his head and laughed.

"Not really! May I ask why?"

"Sentiment," said Leonard.

"Rosamund!"

"You wouldn't suspect her of it. But that's how it is with women—you never know where you are—and it's lucky for you. If you ask me, I should say thirty thousand is letting you off dirt cheap. You'd better close before I raise it."

There was a pause. Then Jervis laughed again.

"In case you're forgetting it, this *is* the twentieth century. One doesn't just disappear, and no notice taken."

"Who's going to disappear?" said Leonard. "You either pay up, and explain your absence any way you like, or else—"

"Yes?"

"Or else you're washed ashore somewhere along the coast—the current sets round Croyde Head, doesn't it? —and there has been another unfortunate bathing fatality. Rosamund will remember your having cramp once or twice this summer when you were bathing together."

Jervis said things. They may or may not have got through Robert Leonard's skin; they certainly relieved Jervis. Leonard's voice did not sound as if he had been touched. He said,

"None of that's business! We're supposed to be talking business."

"Do you think I carry thirty thousand pounds in my pockets?"

"No—and I don't expect to cash a cheque for thirty thousand across the counter either. You can stand ready for bouquets. We're prepared to take your word—and I call that a really handsome compliment. Rosamund says she's never known you go back on your word in your life, and she's prepared to go bail that you'll ante up and hold your tongue. So you see, that makes the whole thing perfectly simple.

You give your word—I drive you over to the junction—you put up any story you like to account for your absence—and not later than tomorrow you buzz up to town and tell old Page you've decided to settle thirty thousand on Rosamund. It's as easy as falling off a log.''

Jervis leaned against the rock. He was thinking hard. It had been in his mind that when the tide rose he could hold on to the iron bars of the portcullis which divided the inner and outer caves. If the portcullis didn't reach to the roof, he might get over it when the water was high enough; and, once in the outer cave, he would have a pretty good chance of getting away when the tide went down. He could float for hours in this warm water with the bars to hold on to. He reckoned that the water would be up to his waist in half hour or so. He might have to hold on for five or six hours. Well, he ought to be able to do that.

"Thinking it over?" said Robert Leonard. "You've not got too much time. Better speed up the thinking machine!"

He picked up the torch again and sent the beam glittering down upon the pool. There wasn't a pool any longer; there was one smooth blackness of water—and the edge of it was level with the rock on which Jervis stood. The light shifted and showed that smooth blackness everywhere. It came back again and rested upon the edge of the rock a yard away from his feet. It showed the water and the rock in a silver ring; and as Jervis looked at the ring, the water lifted very gently and flowed over the rock. The beam swung upwards, and the torch was set down again.

The light had never touched the portcullis. Did those bars go up to the roof—or didn't they?

"Well, are you going to come to terms?" said Robert Leonard.

Jervis said. "No," almost absently. His mind was on the portcullis and the question of whether it would be possible to get over it and into the outer cave. He could do it if there was a space. But was there a space? He became aware that Leonard was swearing at him.

"Do you *mean* that 'No,' you fool?"

"Oh yes."

If being absent and a bit dreamy was the way to annoy

Leonard, then Jervis was prepared to go on being dreamy till all was blue. It was less of a fag than letting oneself go—easier—easier—too easy. . . . . He found himself on his hands and knees in an inch or two of water. He must have turned giddy. Leonard's voice echoed above him in the dark.

"All right—you've had your chance. If you won't take it, that lets me out. You've only to stay obstinate, and I scoop the lot. Drown, and be damned to you!"

The gate at the mouth of the passage banged with a violent metallic sound that filled the cave with clanging echoes.

Jervis sat in two inches of water, and waited for the noise to stop.

XXXVII

THE WATER WAS UP TO HIS WAIST. HE WASN'T GIDDY now. He made his way to the portcullis. It would be quite easy to hold on to the bars. As a matter of fact, he would not need to be in the water for as long as he had reckoned. The tilted boulder which he had not been able to climb would be accessible now; only he must be careful not to lose himself—he must be able to get back to the portcullis again.

He floated himself off in the direction of where he thought the boulder must be, but did not succeed in getting on to it. When the water was up to his shoulder, he tried again, got a foothold, and was able to climb right out of the water on to a ledge with a back to it. He remembered that the boulder met the wall of the cave. He leaned against the rock, and began to wonder what happened to the air when the sea came into a cave like this. It seemed as if one of three things must happen.

Either the water must drive the air out—but could it, with the mouth of the cave submerged, and the air higher than the water?

Or,

The air would keep the water out.

Or,

The air would become frightfully compressed.

None of these things seemed to be happening. The air felt quite normal. Of course there were probably fissures in the roof, and the passage would help. There were odd holes and fissures all along these cliffs; it made them dangerous at night. He decided that he was in no danger of asphyxiating.

He fell into a curious fitful sleep, and dreamt that he was fishing in the black pool; and first his line brought up a keg of brandy, and then a huge and heavy sack which was full of ingots of gold. He couldn't get it off the hook, and Basher lifted it off with one hand, threw it over his shoulder, and began to climb up the front of Westminster Abbey with the sack and the keg hanging from his shoulders like milk-pails on a yoke. He cast into the water again, and up came Rosamund, drowned, with a long yellow plait. He laid her down on the rock, and she opened her eyes and said, "Thirty thousand pounds." Then he cast again, and brought up Nan, in her night-gown, with the tears running down her face. And when he saw Nan cry, something hurt him terribly. It was past all bearing, and he took her in his arms and tried to kiss the tears away; but when he touched her she was cold as ice, cold as water; and like water she slipped" from his arms and was gone.

He woke to the touch of water at his breast. The tide was up to his armpits and rising still. He let himself down into it and swam back to the portcullis.

He was feeling much better; the dreamy drowsiness had passed, and his head was clear. He was horribly thirsty, but he felt pretty sure of being able to stick it out till the tide went down—only he must get over the portcullis and into the outer cave.

After a bit he pulled himself along the bars to the side of the cave. His wet clothes impeded him, and he called himself a fool for not having stripped. He might have been able to make a bundle of his things and wedge them between the bars of the portcullis above high water level. However, it was too late now. He managed to scramble up the face of the rock with the help of the nearest bar. No way over here, or for as far as he could reach outwards. The bars ran slap up to the roof of the cave. He pulled himself across and tried the other side with no better luck; but he came on quite a decent foothold, and stayed there leaning against the bars for what seemed like a long time.

There was just a chance that whilst the bars ran straight across, the roof might rise in the middle. When the water was high enough, he crossed again, reaching upwards. There was not very far to reach now. He could touch the roof all the way across. The bars met it inexorably. Old Foxy Fixon had set his portcullis cunningly enough, at a point where the roof came down to meet it. There was no way out on the seaward side.

A cold, dogged courage came up in Jervis. He hadn't really hoped that he would be able to get over the bars into the outer cave. He put the whole thing away, and decided to make for the ledge on to which the passage opened. He ought to be able to make it pretty soon now, and it would certainly be above high water mark. As to what would happen next, it was always on the cards that Leonard might come along the passage and open the gate carelessly, in which case he would find himself floored. Jervis' fancy dwelt fondly on the thought of getting a grip of Leonard's ankles. The passage would make hard falling.

Well, he had to find the ledge first, and it wasn't going to be any too easy. The water must be still three or four feet below it. On the other hand, he thought he could find the tilted boulder. Most of it would be under water by now; but if he could identify it, it would give him the direction of the ledge. As it turned out, he found the ledge without difficulty. But it was another matter to haul himself up on it. The sill of rock was a couple of feet above water level, and beneath it, and upon either side, the wall was as smooth and as slippery as ice. He could never have climbed to the ledge if he had not chanced on the ring. It was away to one side of the sill. He had pulled himself up a dozen times, only to be dragged back by the weight of his drenched clothes and his own tired limbs, when his desperate fingers closed upon it. It was of iron, heavily rusted, and had doubtless served to secure the rope used for hauling in Old Foxy's kegs. It was a god-send to Jervis.

Straining and panting, he got a knee on the sill and fell forward.

XXXVIII

ROSAMUND CAREW WALKED INTO OLD FOXY FIXON'S HOUSE and called, "Robert!" She left the hall door open behind her and stood in the narrow hall.

"Robert!"

Robert Leonard opened the door on the right and frowned at her.

"Why have you come here?" he said.

"What an affectionate cousin you are!"

"*Cousin?*"

"Cousin," said Rosamund firmly. "And, *officially*, I'm here to fetch eggs. Mabel's hens are on strike, so I've got a perfectly good excuse for coming."

She walked past him into the ugly square room, shut the door on them both, and asked quickly,

"Has that old woman of yours gone?"

"Yes—she goes at three, when she's washed up."

"Sure she's gone?"

"Yes."

"Well?"

"Well what?"

"Robert, where is he? What has happened?"

"Nothing's happened," said Robert Leonard.

"D'you mean he *won't*?"

"He's a damned obstinate fool."

"You must give him time. You didn't imagine he'd give away at once, did you?"

Robert Leonard set his jaw and made no answer.

"I could have told you he wouldn't," said Rosamund. "And I never thought he'd do it for you either. That's why I've come. I want to see him."

"Well, you can't."

"Oh, I'm going to. I can do a lot more with Jervis than you've the least chance of doing."

"No names!" said Leonard quickly.

Rosamund regarded him with a touch of scorn.

"I thought your old woman had gone."

"So she has."

"Then who is there to listen?"

He gave a short laugh.

"No one, I hope."

"Old Foxy Fixon?" said Rosamund. "Now look here, Bob—I've got to see him. I bet you anything you like you've got him on the high horse, and he's ready to see you somewhere before he gives you a penny. You've probably been blowing hot air at each other—and we shan't get our thirty thousand that way. Now, I shall play up the horrible scandal, and isn't it better to pay than to wash all the family linen in public. Jervis mayn't be in love with me, but you can bank on it that he won't send me to jail."

"Oh, hold your tongue!" said Robert Leonard angrily.

"A bit nervous this morning, aren't you?" said Rosamund. "Well anyway, that's my line, and I want a chance of trying it. Thirty thousand's worth having."

"Eighty thousand's better—to say nothing of King's Weare."

"What d'you mean by that?" said Rosamund sharply.

The room was bare and hideous. It contained a battered office table and a couple of dilapidated chairs. Leonard stood by the table, his head thrust forward, his overhanging brow seeming to weight it. His eyes, small, hard, and deeply set, were on Rosamund's face. She did not change colour, but she looked startled as she repeated her

"What d'you mean by that?"

"What should I mean?"

"I don't know. Where is he?"

"Where do you suppose?"

"I'm not supposing. I want to see him. You're to take me to him. Is he in the passage?"

Leonard watched her face.

"No—he's in the cave."

"The cave?" said Rosamund. She looked incredulous for a moment, and then horrified. "But the tide—doesn't the tide come up into the cave?"

"It does."

"Robert! What have you done?"

"I? Absolutely nothing."

Rosamund took a step backwards.

"Does the tide—come right up?"

"I believe so."

She took another step backwards and touched the door.

"What have you done?"

Leonard jerked his head back.

"I've done what I promised. I gave him the chance of paying up, and he wouldn't take it. I can't say I'm sorry. King's Weare and eighty thousand is better than thirty thousand and the Argentine, with the off chance of Jervis doing the dirty on us."

Rosamund leaned hard upon the door.

"If he's dead, you'll never touch a penny! I told you so! Not one penny, Robert!" She made a sudden movement forward. "When is it high tide?"

"You mean when *was* it high tide, I suppose. It was high tide at ten minutes past eight this morning, and will be again at about a quarter past seven this evening."

"You left him in the cave?"

He nodded casually.

"Have you been down since?"

"No."

"Well, I'm going down now."

Robert Leonard shrugged his shoulders. There would be a scene, and then she would come round. The sooner they got it over, the better. He followed her into the kitchen and down the cellar stairs, shifted the barrel from the trap-door, and raised the trap, all by the light of a candle stuck in a grease-stained kitchen candlestick.

Rosamund looked at the damp brick steps.

"I'm not going down there with that candle."

"I'm not really asking you to go down there at all," said Robert Leonard as one who states a fact.

"I'm going—but I want a good torch."

When she had it, she went down two or three steps, and then turned round.

"Want me to come too?" said Leonard.

"No. How much passage is there?"

"From here to the cliff—and it slants."

She went down the remaining steps. He heard her stop for a moment at the foot and then walk away from him. The echoes of the place made a strange sound of her footfall.

Jervis had been asleep. He could lie full length on the sill. He had taken his blazer off, passed the sleeves round one of the bars, and knotted them about the thick of his arm, so that if he turned in his sleep, he would not roll off the ledge. He slept, and woke to the sound of Rosamund's footsteps. His throat and mouth were so dry that the waking was a cruel one. He listened for the sound that had waked him, and heard it come nearer. He scrambled up, unknotting the sleeves of his coat. If he could get his hands on Leonard, even through these bars . . .

There was a light coming. The passage made a sharp turn immediately; in a brightening dusk he could see where it bent away to the left. He clenched and unclenched his hands to get the stiffness out of them, and saw Rosamund come round the turn, with the torch making a lighted pathway for her. She walked slowly. He could see the rosy linen of her dress. The beam made a bright panel on it. He drew away to the side of the sill and waited to see if she would open the gate; but she only flashed the light through it and called,

"Jervis!"

Jervis watched the beam go down into the dark. It showed the cave as he had seen it when Leonard spoke to him. The tide was down. The rocks ran moisture. The two dark pools caught the light. He shot out a hand and caught Rosamund by the wrist as she leaned forward and called his name a second time. The name broke, only half said. He felt her stiffen and fall back. His grip tightened. She began to try to wrench herself free. He got her other wrist with his left hand and pulled her down on her knees. She kept her hold of the torch. She ceased to struggle. They were kneeling face to face with the bars of the gate between them.

After a moment Rosamund laughed.

"You needn't hold me so fiercely! I've come on purpose to see you—I don't want to get away. You're thinking what a pity I'm not Robert."

Jervis' grasp relaxed. He drew his hands back through the bars, and was humiliated to find that they were shaking. He wondered whether he would have been able to hold Robert Leonard for very long.

Rosamund flashed the light on his face and exclaimed, "Are you all right?"

"That—comes well—from you," said Jervis. He spoke with difficulty, his voice hoarse and toneless.

"What's the matter?"

"Nothing. I'm thirsty."

"Damn!" said Rosamund.

The torch swung round in an erratic circle as she jumped up. Next moment she was round the bend. He could hear her running. The dusk went black.

Robert Leonard heard sounds in the kitchen, and went in, to find Rosamund coming out of the larder with eggs in one hand and a jug of milk in the other. She had set a kettle boiling on the oil stove. She turned on him in a cold fury.

"I didn't say you were to starve him!"

"Dead men don't eat."

"He's not dead."

"That's bad luck. Won't he drown?"

"Look here, Robert, for two pence I'd ring up the police! You needn't laugh—I mean it this time!"

"May I ask what you're doing?" said Leonard.

"I'm going to feed him. Go upstairs and get me a blanket! He's chilled to the bone. I suppose his clothes are soaked. I'm going to dry them, and I'm going to feed him—and if you try and stop me, I shall just ring up the police. I don't mind taking the money, but you're not going to torture him.''

"Don't be a fool!" said Leonard.

"Don't push me too far!" said Rosamund. "I got him out of the house for you, and you went back on me by hitting him over the head. You swore you wouldn't interfere. I'd got my story all ready. I could have brought him here, and you could have drugged him—but, no, you must behave like a savage and risk killing him! I won't have it! And I swear to you most solemnly that if you do him any harm, I'll give you away!"

"You're making a lot of noise," said Leonard—"and a wife can't give evidence against her husband."

"She can't be *made* to give evidence against her husband. But I shan't want any making."

"Have it your own way," said Leonard.

He shrugged his shoulders and went back to the front of the house. If he let Rosamund have her head now, he could pull on the curb later on. He wasn't really afraid of her going to the police. He was sure that when the time came, she would prefer King's Weare to being tried as an accessory in a murder case.

Jervis remained staring into the blackness. He was sure that he had seen Rosamund—or was he sure? His head swam, and his tongue, and gums, and the roof of his mouth felt like the slag of a furnace. Why hadn't Leonard come? He experienced an extraordinary narrowed-down determination to come to grips with Leonard. And then he became aware that he was shaking from head to foot, and that he was deadly cold. Could he hold Leonard with such shaking hands? He thought he could. If Leonard came up close to the bars as Rosamund had done, he thought that he could hold him. He wasn't sure if he had dreamed the part about Rosamund; but he was sure, if he once got his hands on Robert Leonard, that he would never let him go.

He thought these things. And then the black turned grey, and he saw the bars of the gate running up and down, and behind the black pattern that they made, Rosamund coming round the bend of the passage. She had a blanket over her arm, and she was carrying a tray in her two hands. She held it a little in front of her; and on the tray there was a candle in a guttered candlestick, and by the light of it he saw a teapot, milk and sugar, half a brown loaf, a rough chunk of butter, and a couple of eggs with one chipped egg-cup between them.

Rosamund set down the tray close to the bars and stuck the candle on a ledge about three feet above the floor.

"I've been as quick as I could," she said in a perfectly matter-of-fact voice. She might have been apologizing to any visitor for some casual delay.

She knelt down and took up the teapot.

"You'd better start with a drink. I'll put heaps of milk in. I thought tea would be the best thing on the whole—it's very quenching, and it's hot."

She pushed the cup through the bars. Jervis' hands closed on it hard. He had wanted to snatch like a starving animal. He controlled his hands to take it, but a third of the tea jerked from the cup before he got it to his lips and drank.

"You'd better go slow," said Rosamund on the other side of the bars.

He could have killed her when she said that. Whether it was the release from his torture of thirst, or something in her voice, he couldn't tell, but a gust of rage came over him and was within an ace of carrying him away. She was feeding him, she had given him drink, and it was only one last effort of self-control which kept him from dashing the empty cup in her face. What? You trepan a man, have him knocked on the head, demand money from him by threats, leave him to drown—and then pour out tea for him with the most perfect social calm!

"Better have an egg next," said Rosamund. "They're very soft-boiled—I knew you'd hate them raw." She was cutting and buttering a piece of brown bread. "Give me back that cup when you've finished, and I'll pour you out some more."

Jervis eyed the knife. It was a small carver, and it looked sharp, but he couldn't reach it. She had taken the bread off the tray and had turned away from him to cut it.

"Why doesn't Leonard come himself?" he said.

"Conscientious objections to feeding prisoners."

"Are you really married to the swine?"

"I am. Here's your second cup. So you see I had to jilt you."

"Why did you ever get engaged to me? You were married then, weren't you?"

She nodded.

"Stupid affair—wasn't it? Go a bit slower with that egg."

"What was the point of getting engaged to me?"

Rosamund produced her cigarette-case and lit a cigarette. She had matches. Matches meant light. If she would put them down where he could reach them.—He didn't really care why she had got engaged to him; he wanted those matches. But she was answering his question.

"I don't mind telling you the whole truth." She paused and blew out a pale cloud of smoke. "I've been married to Robert for ages—one of the fool things one does. I was twenty-one. It was just before I came to King's Weare. The great idea was that I should do the angel niece at Uncle Ambrose, confess all, and get him to provide handsomely for us." She shrugged her shoulders. "Well, of course I was a fool. Robert came to stay, and Uncle Ambrose simply loathed him—you remember, it was just before you had that accident on Croyston rocks."

"Accident?" said Jervis.

"Wasn't it one?"

"Leonard tried to do me in."

"Who told you?" said Rosamund.

"Nan. She saw him. I didn't believe her."

"No—you wouldn't!" said Rosamund. There was a bitterness in her voice. "Well, Robert was in the soup. He had to have money, or get out of the country. We had a most awful row. I guessed what he'd done, and he cleared out. He went to South America, and I didn't know whether he was dead or alive for eight years. Then he wrote to me, and last year he came back."

"None of this explains why you should have gone out of your way to get engaged to me, when you knew you couldn't marry."

"Here's your second egg," said Rosamund. "I'll cut you some more bread and butter."

She turned away, spread the loaf with butter, and cut a thick slice. She went on talking all the time, slowly and without any emotion.

"It was Robert's idea. Uncle Ambrose was dying, and Robert thought he'd settle a goodish bit on me if he thought I was going to marry you. And then when he left me practically nothing, I must say I saw red. You can't really blame me for taking advantage of the clause about your forfeiting the lot if you weren't married within three months." She threw back her head and blew a smoke-ring. "Especially as you did me down over it," she added. "Like another cup of tea? And then you'd better get those wet clothes off. They'll dry in no time in the sun. I've got a blanket for you to put on."

That anger came up in Jervis again. In what sort of nightmare did you combine cousinly affection and attempted murder—or if not murder, at the very least the risk of it, and blackmail?

"My clothes are nearly dry."

She put a hand through the bars to feel his coat. There was something horrible about the whole thing. He jerked away, and was nearly over the edge of the sill. The thought of the rocks below sobered him.

Rosamund, on her side, drew back from the bars. She was kneeling. The floor of the passage had stained her dress. The candle-light cast dark shadows on her temples. It made her ghastly pale. Or was it something more than the candle-light? She had let fall her cigarette; the fingers that had held it were clenched against her palm. There was a strained pause.

"I'm not to—touch you?" she said at last.

Jervis did not speak.

After a moment she lifted her head and laughed.

"Stay wet if you like! It doesn't matter to me! Now look here—are you going to be sensible and pay up?"

"No," said Jervis.

"Not very grateful—are you? I've really been rather nice to you—much nicer than Robert—and the least you can do is to be friendly. You see, we've got to have the money. I told you all along that I couldn't get on without a decent allowance. If you'd settled twenty-five thousand on me as I suggested, we shouldn't have had any of this bother. I could have choked Robert off with twenty-five thousand down and no risk. What's he asking you now?''

"Thirty thousand."

"Well, it'll be thirty-five thousand tomorrow, and forty the day after. You see, if you go west, I get the lot—and naturally Robert can't help thinking of that. Seriously, Jervis, you're being a fool. I'm holding Robert back, but I can't go on holding him back. We've been pretty good pals, and why shouldn't you settle thirty thousand on me? We'll go off to Peru, and you'll be rid of us. Come—is it a deal?''

"No," said Jervis.

If she hadn't said that about their having been pals, he might conceivably have thought of making terms. Life was sweet, and Nan was sweet—and Robert Leonard wasn't bluffing. But that appeal to a friendship so grossly betrayed sent the hot blood to his head.

"I'll see you both a good deal farther than Peru before I give you a penny!'' he said.

XXXIX

NAN SLEPT. IT WAS AS IF SHE HAD PLUNGED DOWN INTO unimaginable depths and then after a long time begun slowly, very slowly, to come up again. At first she might have been dead; she neither stirred nor was visited by any glimmer of consciousness. Then, when hours had passed, she moved, half woke, and was aware of an immense fatigue.

She slept again; but now she had a consciousness of trouble which took the form of one fitful dream after another. She was walking over a pebble beach, and the stones cut her feet. Her feet were bare, and the stones cut them. She could see her footprints like bloodstains stretching away on a vast unending shore.

She was looking for something, and she couldn't find it. She didn't know what she was looking for. She wasn't on the sea-shore any more. She was in London, but she was still barefoot and with only a chemise to cover her. She ran up Dover Street and down Hay Hill, and all round Piccadilly Circus, but she couldn't find what she wanted. And then all of a sudden she was on an endless moving staircase which went down and down and down, and carried her farther and farther away from the thing that she was straining to find. The stair went faster and faster. She was wet with her own tears, and Mr Page said in a loud, unfriendly voice, "You can't find him, because he's drowned." Then she knew that she was looking for Jervis, and the dream broke.

Nan didn't wake with the breaking of the dream. She gave a sobbing cry that brought Bran to his feet: then she turned over and dreamed again.

She was in a dark place, and she was weeping bitterly. She covered her eyes to shut out the darkness, and she pressed her eyelids down to stop the tears, but they went on falling. Then there was light. It shone through her hands, and through her closed lids, and through her tears, and she looked and saw what she had seen once before in a dream. She saw wet stones, and Jervis lying on them, his head back and his eyes open as if he were dead. A wave of agony broke against her heart. She cried out in her sleep and woke, shuddering from head to foot.

She thought at first that the morning had come, because the room was full of light. She could see the door into Jervis' empty room, and she could see Bran reared up beside the bed, and the curtains drawn back at all the windows to let in as much air as possible. Everything was bright, and sharp, and clear for just that waking instant, and then the darkness and the thunder fell together in one appalling crash. Bran thrust against her. She flung her arms about him, and felt the deep rumble in his throat. There was a breathing-space before the next flash came, and then a long pause filled by a curious distant droning. The thunder was farther away.

Nan got out of bed. She had dreamed that dream twice; and the first time Jervis had come to her. Now she must go to him. She was quite sure of this. Her fatigue was gone, and the trouble in her mind was gone. She had gone to bed crushed down by the thought that Jervis and Rosamund were together. This had gone too. She only knew that she had to find Jervis. She dressed herself, putting on a thin dress and a waterproof over it. She shut Bran in the room and went down to the study.

She had unlatched the window, when a sudden thought turned her back to the writing-table. She found a block and pencil, and wrote, "I'm going to look for Jervis. I'm going to Mr Leonard's house first. I am quite sure he knows where Jervis is." She folded the sheet, put it in an envelope, and addressed it to Ferdinand Fazackerley. Then she picked up an electric torch that was lying at the back of the table and went out of the long window, closing it behind her.

All this time she had been so intent that she could not have said whether the lightning and the thunder continued, but she stepped out into a sudden violet glare in which everything looked huge, and black, and blank. The trees were like forests of sea-weed under the ash of a phosphorescent sea. In the blackness that followed the flash she felt surrounded by strange things which she had never known before.

The thunder set her running. It was like a door banging behind her. She ran, and the wind that was blowing off the sea came up and carried her along. She had pushed the torch into the pocket of her rain-coat. Its little spark would be a glow-worm in the immense illumination which lit the sky and lit her path. It came and went, and came again, with a crash of enormous drums to hurry her on, and, between the drums, that strange droning note of the wind. It was all like a dream. There was the same certainty, the same consciousness of something with which reason had nothing to do. Nan had not thought of where she was going. She had known.

When she came into the deep lanes, the wind failed her, and the lightning showed it far overhead, twisting the tall branches of black trees a long way up in the air. The sound of it between the thunder claps was like the sound of an express train. She came out of the lanes and began to climb the road along the cliff, and here the storm caught her like a leaf. One veering gust seemed to lift her as if with wings, and another flung her against the bank and held her there bruised and impotent, until the breath was beaten out of her. Spray drenched her. She fell twenty times. She was near the sheer drop over the cliff, again and yet again; and then, just as she could fight no more, the wind would lift and carry her along.

She came to Robert Leonard's gate just as the rain broke, and the last flash of lightning showed her the house with its square ugliness and all its blank windows staring.

Nan held the gate with her hands and leaned against it. She was out of breath, and the wind had beaten her until it was all that she could do to stand. There was no more lightning. The thunder rumbled a long way off. Through a lull in the wind she could hear another sound, the roar of the storm-driven sea. She heard the crash of waves that broke against the cliff. She leaned on the gate, and the rain came down, straight and heavy and cold. Perhaps nothing else would have roused her. After a minute or two she straightened up and began to feel for the latch; and as she struggled with it, the wind caught her and the gate together, and, the latch slipping, she was swung half across the path and flung down. She picked herself up slowly and began to walk in the direction of the house.

The path ran straight, but she could see nothing, though when she looked up the sky was grey, not black, and full of movement of great hurrying clouds. She did not know at all what time it was. She came to the front door, and guessed where she was by the feel of the worn paint under her groping hands. There was a step, and she stumbled at it and struck her forehead against the iron knocker, but without sounding it. She felt for the handle, turned it, and knew at once that the door was fast. She could not have expected anything else, but it was like a blow over the heart. She stood there struggling for breath and gathering her strength; then slowly, keeping her hand on the wall, she made her way about the house. It stood bare on the cliff with its face to the sea. She turned the second corner and came, her feet on cobbles, to the back door, and the latch of the back door lifted to her touch.

She stayed like that, with the rain drenching her short hair and running off her rain-coat. Then she pushed the door in and stood on the flagged step. There wasn't any sound. The house was dead, not dreaming as a house should be in the middle of the night with everyone in bed and asleep. There was no one asleep in this house; Nan knew that as soon as she came inside the door. But there was no one awake either. The house was stark empty.

Nan stood in the middle of the kitchen and felt the dead emptiness of the house come in on her. It gave her an odd numb feeling as if she had come to the end of thought and action. And then all of a sudden the telephone bell rang stridently. It sounded as loud as if it was in the room. No one had a telephone in their kitchen. The door must be open.

She moved toward the sound with her hands out, and the bell rang again, and kept on ringing. She was in a narrow passage, and the bell was ringing in front of her and to the left. The door of that room must be open too. And all at once, very faintly, she could see it—the two jambs and the sill, and a dark oblong that was the empty doorway. On an instinct quicker than thought she looked over her shoulder and saw the kitchen door, and the kitchen in a yellow twilight. The light moved and brightened. Where it was coming from she had no idea. She ran from it into the room on the right of the passage. And all the while the telephone bell kept calling from the other room across the way.

Nan stood behind her door and waited. The light was coming towards her, and footsteps with it. She left a crack to look through, and saw Robert Leonard go into the left-hand room with an unshaded paraffin lamp in his hand. It was a wall-lamp with a tin reflector. There was a smell of warm oil and soot. She saw him set the lamp on a table and turn it down a shade. Then he passed out of sight, and the bell stopped as he took the receiver off the hook.

Nan opened the door a little wider and listened breathlessly. Who could be ringing up at such an hour? it must be long past midnight. From the sound of the sea, the tide must be nearly full—and high tide would be somewhere about five o'clock. At the very least the night was far gone, and the dawn not far away.

"What are you ringing up for?" said Robert Leonard in a low, furious voice.

Nan could hear the sound of the answer; it rustled and whispered against the microphone. If she had been in the room, she might have caught the words.

Robert Leonard said, "Don't be a fool!"

Nan opened her door and slipped into the passage. Try and strain as she would, she could hear no more than that ghostly whispering. She had no picture of Rosamund sitting up in bed with her lips at the mouthpiece of her bedside telephone and her voice hard with alarm.

"The storm waked me."

"Go to sleep again."

"I can't. I'm thinking of the tide—spring tide, with this wind behind it."

Robert Leonard said, "Don't be a fool!"

"Take him up into the cellar, Robert."

"Anything else?"

"You must! I shall dress and come down unless you promise."

Nan made nothing of this—"Don't be a fool!".... "Go to sleep again." .... "Anything else?" She turned her head, and became aware that light was still coming from the kitchen. At once she passed down the passage and stood at the door looking in. The light was not in the kitchen. It came from an open door in the corner by the dresser, and it struck upwards with a faint, uncertain glow.

Nan came nearer, and saw the brick steps that went down into the cellar. She knew now why she had come to this house. She stopped being tired, and she stopped being afraid. She went down the steps, and saw a brick cellar, and in the middle of it a barrel standing on end with a candle on it in a greasy candlestick; and in the corner, propped back against the wall, the lid of a trap-door, with the trap very black below it. Robert Leonard had come up from here with the lamp in his hand.

She took her torch out of her pocket and sent its beam to search that black opening. It showed more steps, and she went down them, and so into a long low passage which was cold and very silent. She walked in the shining path which was made for her by the beam of her torch. Only once in a way when her hand shook did she see anything but that straight, shining path. Her hand did not shake because she was afraid, but because she had herself been so buffeted and shaken by the wind that from time to time an involuntary tremor passed over her. When this happened, she saw the roof, or a bit of the wall, most terrifingly black and near. The path had a very slight downward slope. It ran straight for about a dozen yards, and then there were more steps, and after that a steeper and more irregular slope. Somewhere at the back of Nan's mind was the knowledge that she was going down towards the sea; but her thoughts were not concerned with this knowledge, they were concerned only with Jervis.

The path became rougher. At first it had been paved with brick; now it was stony, and the walls, when she caught a glimpse of them, were not built any more. The passage was ceasing to be a passage and becoming a fissure. It bent sharply once or twice.

All at once the circle of light from her torch dazzled on a huge jutting rock which blocked the way. Nan stood still and swung the light first to the right, and then to the left. On the right a narrow fissure ran up to the roof and split it. On the left the path went on, curving round the great boulder.

Nan came round the bend, and saw, about five yards away, Jervis lying as she had seen him lie in her dream. The light fell on his upturned face and on the wet stone that made his bed. He was wrapped in a blanket, but one arm lay outside and the hand was clenched on the bar of an iron gate which rose from floor to roof between them.

Nan stood quite still. Her eyes were shut. In her dream they had been open. She moved the light from his face, and saw how the bars ran up and were fastened into the stone. She moved it again, and saw the light flicker over a wide darkness of water. At once she ran forward. What she had at first thought to be a continuation of the passage was a mere ledge like a doorstep, thrust out from the gate over who could say what threatening depths.

She came to the gate and shook it, and as she did so, the water lifted with a huge gurgling swell, stood level with the ledge, and then dropped back again with a sucking sound.

At the same moment Jervis opened his eyes and, pulling on the bar, sat up.

XL

JERVIS HAD BEEN IN THE CAVE FOR FORTY-EIGHT HOURS. Rosamund Carew had visited him twice. He had had enough food to keep him going, and she had left him the blankets, but he had never been within reach of a candle, matches, or the much coveted bread-knife. Robert Leonard had been once again. But all that was many hours ago. There had been moments when he was ready to sign away, not a part, but the whole of his birthright. These were not, however, the moments when Rosamund or Leonard were making their demands. To give way under threat, to knuckle down to Leonard's increasing insolence, to fall in with Rosamund's calm assumption that because she wanted money it was for him to provide it, was beyond him. When the dark closed down, and each successive tide reached higher, he might contemplate surrender; but at the first glimmer of returning light, the first sound of Rosamund's calm or Leonard's brutal voice his resistance stiffened.

He woke with the light on his face, gripped the bar, sat

up, and saw, not Rosamund—it wasn't tall enough for Rosamund—not Rosamund, but one of those dreams which come out of the darkness and the silence. His wrist was bound to the bar with a handkerchief. He fumbled at the knot, and Nan went down on her knees and put her hands on his and held them fast. The torch rolled over on its side and sent a shaft of light between them. Her hands came into it—little brown hands that he knew; not Rosamund's hands. The knot parted, the handkerchief dropped down. He waited for the dream to go away. But it stayed. The little brown hands were warm on his, and one of them wore his ring. He said, "Nan!" and she said, "Jervis!" and all at once it wasn't a dream any longer.

He rose on his knees and caught her by the shoulders with his hands thrust through the bars.

"Nan!" he said. "Nan!" And Nan put up her face, and he kissed her with a desperate straining towards life, and love, and happiness, and all those other everyday things which were in jeopardy.

Nan kissed him back. He had been lost, and she had found him. And in her dream he had been dead, but he was holding her with living arms and kissing her with living lips. How could she do anything but hold him with all her strength and kiss him with all her love? Her happiness was almost more than she could bear. They clung together, and scarcely knew that the bars were there.

Then the black swell lifted again and washed right over the sill. Jervis got on to his feet and pulled her up. She stooped for the torch, and found it lying in water. The tide was about their ankles, and even as she straightened herself, it lifted again without any sound. Nan caught at the padlock with both hands.

"It's no use," said Jervis—"he's taken the key." Then, quickly, "How did you come here?"

"I don't know," said Nan. "I came. I saw you in a dream." She added after a moment, "There's a storm."

"It's driving the tide. What is it—thunder, or wind?"

"Both."

"Wind off the sea?"

"Yes—yes, it is."

The water rose again with a gentle swirl but no sound. It had never come higher than a good hand's-breadth below the ledge. At this rate it would be up to their knees before he could so much as think what to do.

He said, "Does anyone know you're here?"

"No. F.F.'s away. I left a note for him."

"We must get out of here," said Jervis. "You must get out and get help. You're not shut in?"

"No."

"You'd better get hold of Basher—there's no time to do anything about the police."

"He's away."

"Then you must knock up Martin at the lodge. He'd better get hold of the chauffeur. Leonard's armed. Is he in the house?"

"Yes—telephoning. The bell rang—he came up out of the passage and left it open."

"Then he'll be coming back. You must go."

She leaned towards him, and they kissed again.

He said, "I'll be all right—I can hold on to the bars."

He felt her quiver; he felt her cheek cold against his. And then without a word she ran from him round the bend.

From the moment of her waking until this very moment Nan had been in some strange prolongation of the dream in which she was looking for Jervis and had no room in her thought for fear. She had to find Jervis, and nothing else mattered. All the ordinary movements of thought were benumbed. Now, as she ran from Jervis, the dream went, and the numb thoughts quickened into painful life. She had left Leonard telephoning. If he had finished, he would come back and shut the trap. Perhaps he had already shut it, and she and Jervis were closed down here together in the dark. Perhaps he was coming down again, and she would meet him suddenly.

She turned the last bend, and as she came to the steps which led to the straight paved end of the passage, she switched out her torch and caught her breath in a gasp of relief. There was an uncertain glow ahead of her. The trap was still open, and a faint candle-light showed the worn edges of the brick steps going up into the cellar.

And then all at once there was something wrong. The light was brighter—it was too bright for candle-light. Nan stood stock still and stared at the open trap. It was about a dozen yards away. A broad yellow beam was coming through it, and suddenly there was a man's foot in a heavy boot on the topmost step. Robert Leonard was coming down.

Nan turned and ran wildly down the steps and along the black passage with her hands stretched out in front of her as if to ward the darkness from her face. It was sheer panic, and it might have ruined them both if she had not run into the rock at one of the turns and so brought her up short. She had cut her hand, but she did not feel it. She could see a yellow glow behind her, and she could hear Leonard's footsteps as she turned the bend. He couldn't see her now. She switched on her torch, turned another corner, and clutched at her courage with all her might. If she could find anywhere to hide, if she could let him pass her, then she could run back and get help for Jervis. She remembered the boulder at the last bend—the path went round to the left of it, but on the right there was a fissure that went right up to the roof. She ran on, fighting the thought that it was too narrow to be of any use. She came to the place, and her heart sank. The cleft was not a foot wide. She ran on down the path, and saw Jervis nearly up to his knees in water holding on to the bars of the gate. Her feet splashed in a ripple that ran to meet her.

She came to him panting.

"He's coming!"

Jervis reached through the bars and turned the torch in her hand. She looked along the beam. The cleft on this side of the boulder was a much wider one. The action of water had so far hollowed it out that it was just conceivable she might escape notice there.

He said, "Quick!" and pushed her, at the same time turning out the torch; and as he did so, the light of Robert Leonard's lamp threw the boulder into black relief. It was horrible to have to run towards it, but she ran, reached the cleft, and crouched down in it, squeezing herself back and back and back until she felt as if the solid rock had been built up round her and would never let her go.

Robert Leonard came round the bend with the paraffin lamp in his hand, and stopped three yards from the mouth of the cleft because the rest of the passage was under water. He held the lamp above his head and laughed.

"Getting a bit wet?" he said.

"A bit," said Jervis.

"I've come for the blanket Rosamund was fool enough to leave you. It's a good blanket, and you won't be wanting it any more."

"Awkward for you if by any chance it got washed out to sea."

"Bull's-eye!" said Robert Leonard. "It's not very likely, but accidents do happen—so you can hand it over."

Jervis looked down at the sodden mass. It wouldn't be long before it floated off on the rising swell; half of it was afloat, and if he shifted his foot—

"Come and take it," he said.

Nan moved in the grip of the rock. Robert Leonard's square bulk was between her and Jervis. She must see Jervis—she must look at him. Perhaps she would never look at him again. If she could get out, she could get round the bend. If Leonard would go a little farther away—if he would go forward to take the blanket . . . He wasn't going to. He laughed and said.

"Too wet for me! I can always get it when the tide goes down."

Nan could see Jervis now. He was drenched and haggard, but he still had that look of having bought the earth; it was even a little intensified, and Nan's heart leapt to it.

"You're spoiling my night's rest, you know," said Leonard. "Rosamund's quite anxious about you. She's just dragged me to the telephone to ask me whether I've noticed that there's a storm, and that being the case, there's likely to be a particularly high tide. She's quite fussed about it."

"Damned good for her!" said Jervis.

"*Isn't* it? And do you know, it strikes me that she's right about the tide. She says last time you'd a gale off the sea and a spring tide together the waves broke right over the cliff road. She seems to think you won't be very comfortable where you are, and she wants me to unlock the gate."

He held out his wrist and turned it to get the light on the dial of his watch. "It's getting on for a quarter to four. It's not high tide till five, and as far as I could judge when I stepped outside a little while ago, the gale is still rising. Rosamund's wishes are, of course, my law, so I've come to give you your last chance. The price, by the way, is up to fifty thousand."

Nan moved again. She had got to do something. If she could get away, she could save Jervis. If she couldn't get away, he wouldn't be any worse off.

"Ask a little more!" said Jervis.

Robert Leonard swore with a sudden savage violence.

"And so I will for that!" He pulled out a key on a steel chain and swung it to and fro. "Here's the key. D'you see it? You can buy it for sixty thousand pounds—and before you're dead you'll think it's cheap! *Sixty thousand!*"

Nan stood up in the mouth of the cleft. She was cold, and her heart shook her with its beating.

"Suppose I say yes?" Jervis had seen her and was making time.

She passed like a shadow along the boulder, touching it with her hand, keeping her face towards Leonard. The dreadful moment would come when she must turn her back on him and run for it. She had reached the boulder's edge, when he looked over his shoulder and saw her. For an instant the lamp-light dazzled in her eyes. She saw Jervis, the barred gate, the glistening walls, and a sudden surge of water. She saw Leonard against the light, and his shadow, black and formless, reaching towards her. Then, with the water about his ankles, he swung round, slipped, and came down with a splash. The paraffin lamp jerked out of his hand and smashed against the rock. There was a moment's wild flare of blazing oil.

Nan ran from it desperately, her fear choking her.

XLI

NAN RAN FOR HER LIFE. NO, NOT FOR HER LIFE—JERVIS'
life. If she could reach the cellar and slam down the trap, if
she could get out again into the wild wind and the rain, she
would be able to save Jervis. She had started to run with
that thought in her mind; but as she ran, she knew nothing
but terror—the acute nightmare terror of feet that follow in
the dark. For a moment there was a flare of fire behind her,
the glow of it filtered round the bend. It came with the
sound of Leonard's furious cursing, and it died as he
stumbled round the boulder and gave chase. She had about a
dozen yards' start, but the sound of him and the sense of his
pursuing rage had overtaken her already; yet she reached the
first of the brick steps and saw the straight end of the
passage, and the light from the cellar coming through the
trap. For the first time, a real hope touched her. And then
she too slipped and came down, falling hard, her hands
stretched out on the brick paving, and her face all but
touching it. For a moment a wild spasm of terror stopped
her heart.

Robert Leonard passed her, running heavily; his wet foot
brushed her arm. If he had trodden on her, she would hardly
have felt it. He stood on the brick steps cursing her, but his
words were just noise in her ears. She was so nearly fainting
that she felt nothing when he slammed down the trap. The
sharp sound of its fall came to her from far away, and after
that a rumbling. He was rolling the barrel back into its place
upon the trap door. Then there were no more sounds. It was
very quiet, and very dark.

Nan lay where she was and let her forehead fall upon her hands. She had failed Jervis. There wasn't anything else that she could do. She wanted the tide to come up and drown her quickly.

Presently she remembered that it wouldn't reach her here. She got up very slowly and stiffly. She must go back to Jervis. But first she would see if she could raise the trap. She hadn't any hope, but she wouldn't go back to Jervis without trying. She felt her way to the steps, went up them as high as she could, and pushed with all her remaining strength. She might as well have pushed against one of the walls. She came down again, remembered that she had put her torch in the pocket of her rain-coat before she came out of the cleft, and felt for it.

She came at last to the boulder, and stood still in a new terror. The water ran to meet her in a low, dark wave with a tiny edge of foam where the rough rock path fretted it. She called, "Jervis!" and ran into the water. On the other side of the boulder it was up to her knees.

Jervis stood as he had stood before, with an arm round one of the bars. Even as she caught sight of him, the water lifted to his waist, fell a little, and lifted again.

He said, "Nan!" and all at once her terror was gone. It didn't really matter if they were together.

She came to him through the water, and found a place to set her torch, all very quietly. Then he was holding her, and nothing mattered.

Jervis said, "He caught you?"

"Yes—I fell."

"He hasn't hurt you?"

"No. He's shut me in."

He held her close and kissed her. Nothing mattered. The water rose, and would have lifted them if they had not held to the bars. Strange and cold, to have bars between them.

"Why did you marry me, Nan?" said Jervis.

"Didn't you know?"

"No. I thought. . . . . . Why did you?"

Nan trembled. His arm was cold and stiff, but it held her close.

"I loved you so much."

"*Then?* You loved me *then*?"

"Of course!"

"Why?"

"I loved you when I was a little girl. I loved you so much that it used to hurt. And I never forgot. I used to dream about you. I never thought I should see you again. And the first time you came into Mr Page's office I thought I was asleep, and that I should wake up and find that you weren't there at all." Her voice was sweetly shaken with laughter.

"Oh, Nan!"

"*Yes*. And then when you came in that day and said that Rosamund had thrown you over, the door was a little bit open into Mr Page's room, and I listened. You said dreadful things, and I didn't think I could bear it if you went away and married just anyone whom you could pick up like that—I *couldn't* bear it."

"Nan—Nan! I'm not worth it. I've been a beast to you. But I do love you now."

"Better than Rosamund?" said Nan in a whisper.

"I never loved Rosamund."

"Are you *sure*? She's so beautiful."

"What's that got to do with it? Of course I'm sure! I love you."

The cold wash of the water shook them.

"Nan—" said Jervis. "You mustn't stay here."

Nan pressed closer.

"Nan—darling—you mustn't. Go back up the passage. I may have to swim for it."

"I'm not going."

"Darling, you must! You see, I shall be able to keep afloat all right, and then when the tide has turned—"

"How high will it come?" said Nan.

"Oh, not much higher."

"He said—there was more than an hour to high tide."

A sudden movement of the whole dark flood thrust Jervis hard against the bars and almost took Nan out of his arms. It dragged back and he was put to it to keep his feet.

"You must go now," he said. "Nan—*if you love me*."

"I can't," said Nan. "I'm not afraid if you hold me."

That surging lift of the tide came again. They clung

together, and felt the bars between them strain with the force of the water. And then with the backward pull something hard whipped about Nan's left ankle and clung there. She felt the sting of it, and in a flash of trembling hope she pulled herself free of Jervis and stooped down into the water, holding the bar with one hand. She had to go right under, to feel the cold weight of the sea upon her back, and the rushing saltiness against her lips, her ears, her eyes. The whole tide moved with her, and she had only her tired grasp of the bar to hold by.

And then she felt the chain. Her fingers closed on it, and she came up laughing and crying, and thrust it into the beam of the torch for Jervis to see. Eighteen inches of bright chain, and a small bright key with the water dripping from it in bright drops like diamonds. As far as they were concerned, it was the key of the world.

"He dropped it when he fell!" said Jervis. The words started with a shout, and ended in a gasp, because the water swirled up again, and the cold of it took his breath. He said, "Quick—quick!"—but they had both to hold on to the bars until the upward surge had spent itself.

He held her then, and she found the padlock and felt for the keyhole. Her hands shook and were cold, and the key jammed. And then the water rose again. It came right up to her neck, and over her chin and against her mouth; but she held on to the padlock and the key, and Jervis held on to her. The bars of the gate cut into her as he strained her against them. Then, as the water lapsed again, the key turned and the padlock fell.

At once the gate swung in with them, and so suddenly that they lost their footing. Nan was flung against the rock. Then Jervis had her by the arm and was striking out for the boulder. The forward rush of the water helped them. The passage rose to meet their stumbling feet. Drenched, panting, and exhausted, they came into water that was knee deep, ankle deep; and so, through splashing shallows, to the other side of the boulder, and a place where they could stand dry-shod and look back upon the danger out of which they had come. The faint glow of Nan's abandoned torch just made the darkness visible. The beam would go on shining across the black lifting water until it drowned, or until the battery failed.

They stood for what seemed like a long time, holding one another, looking back. Then Jervis said,

"We've left the torch. What mugs! I believe I could get it."

Nan flung her arms round his neck and burst into tears. "No—no! I'll never speak to you again if you do!"

They went back up the passage with the light fainter and fainter behind them. There was no glow from the trap to guide them now. It seemed a long time before they came groping to the steps. Jervis pushed and strained at the trap, but he could not move it.

He came down again.

"We'll have to wait till someone comes."

He felt Nan tremble against him.

"Will anyone come?"

"Bound to." But in his heart he wondered.

"Who?"

"Oh—Rosamund—or Leonard. They've both been coming. I expect Leonard will want to make sure that I'm safely drowned."

Nan shivered. All at once she felt as if she didn't care. She was too tired to care. They sat down on the steps. She shut her eyes and leaned against Jervis. Perhaps someone would come—perhaps no one would come—it didn't really matter—

XLII

ROSAMUND CAREW PUT THE TELEPHONE BACK UPON THE table by the bed. She was surrounded by the soft pastel shades beloved of Mabel Tetterley. There was an old-rose canopy over her head, and an eiderdown of shot lavender and blue folded back from her feet; a pale blue blanket and a pale pink blanket showed beneath it. Rose and lavender curtains fell from the silver cornice to the pale grey floor. A pink veiled light filled the room with a rosy glow.

Rosamund sat up straight against her pale blue pillows. She threw an oddly contemptuous glance about the room. Her own taste ran to something stronger. She pushed back the pink linen sheet, got out of bed, and went to the window that looked towards the sea. Hot as the night was, it had not been possible to keep it open. She stood and watched the wind shake it with gusts so strong that the whole room shook too, and even through the sound of the wind she could hear the roaring of the sea. She looked at the pink enamel clock on the mantel-piece. It was half past three. And it would be high tide at five. She turned away from the window with abrupt decision and dressed, putting on country shoes—a tweed skirt—a mackintosh. She covered her hair with a close tweed cap and got out of one of the dining-room windows.

As far as the lodge, she had the shelter of a high bank of evergreens. She could hear the wind overhead with a sound like the flight of great airplanes passing. The noise deafened her. When she had passed the lodge, the full force of the storm caught her. Rosamund was a strong woman, but she could not keep her feet. There was a quarter of a mile of exposed road between the lodge and Old Foxy Fixon's house, and for the most part of the way she was crawling on hands and knees.

It was four o'clock before she made the house, and all the breath was out of her. She stood in the porch, a bare, half hollowed arch, and beat upon the door. The wind flung her into the passage, and flung the door back against the wall as Robert Leonard lifted the latch. It took both of them to get the door to again. There was a light in the office, a paraffin lamp with a white china shade. The steady yellow glow gave a curious impression of stillness. There is no light so still as lamp-light. It seemed to Rosamund as if the room was holding its breath. She struggled for her own. She needed all her composure for this interview with Robert.

She stood just inside the door waiting. She had wondered whether he would be up, or whether her telephone call had roused him from sleep. She thought not; he was dressed in his usual rather loose tweeds. Her eyes went beyond him, and saw a suit-case, half packed, standing on a chair. Then she struck through the angry expostulation which had been flowing past her.

"Are you going away?"

"If I choose," said Robert Leonard.

Rosamund straightened herself.

"Why?"

"That's my business."

"Where's Jervis?"

Leonard went over to the suit-case and closed it.

"Not much of a night to travel."

"Why are you going?"

"Best for you, and best for me. You'll finish us both if I stay. It's damnfool madness your coming here like this! The thing was as safe as houses if you'd kept out of it. As it is—" he shrugged his shoulders—"I'm off before you fit a rope round my neck."

"I said, where's Jervis?" said Rosamund.

"Where should he be?"

"I'm going down to see."

"No, you're not!"

She put out her hand.

"I want the key of the gate."

Robert Leonard laughed.

"You're a day after the fair!"

"What do you mean?"

"Well, I fancy you'd have to dive to find the padlock."

She stood quite still for a moment, and then turned to the door, but before she could reach it she was flung on one side.

"Robert! How dare you?"

Robert Leonard put his shoulders against the door and laughed.

"*Finito!*" he said.

"Robert!"

"My dear Rosamund, you're making a fool of yourself.

The water's well up to the roof of the cave by now, and all the King's horses and all the King's men couldn't get Jervis out of it."

"I'm going down."

"You're not!"

Rosamund walked to the telephone and took off the receiver.

"Give me Croyston police station." Then she covered the mouthpiece with her hand. "Am I going down?"

She looked into the mouth of Robert Leonard's automatic only half a yard away.

"Going to shoot me, Bob?" she said.

"Not unless I'm obliged to."

Her eyes held his.

"I'm worth something alive. I wonder how long I'd have to live if I weren't."

"Come off it!" said Robert Leonard. "And come off trying to bluff me! That was bluff just now—you don't get a Croyston operator as quick as all that in the middle of the night."

A faint thrumming came from the instrument. It throbbed against the palm of her hand. She pressed the palm closer.

"Yes, that was bluff—but it won't be this time. Am I going down? The operator's there now all right, and he'll hear if there's any shooting."

Robert Leonard flung his pistol down on the table.

"Hang up that damned receiver!" he said.

Rosamund hung it up.

"Now look here—I'll tell you the whole bed-rock truth. I never thought of the high tide any more than you did. I was out to scare him. I thought he was just about ready to come across, and we wanted the money—didn't we? Then you rang up and said your piece about the tide. Well, I wasn't to know you were liable to get a crazy tide when there was a storm—was I? I did my best. I went down into that damn passage and found the whole place under water. I tried to get to the gate and unlock it. If you don't believe me, go into the bedroom and look at the clothes I've just taken off—I've had to pitch them into the bath, or the water would be coming through the ceiling. I went in up to my neck—I couldn't do more than that. I suppose you didn't expect me to drown myself?''

"No," said Rosamund—just the one word, hard and cold. Then she put out her hand. "Give the key—I'm going down."

"I'm damned if you are!"

She walked to the door, and met his outstretched arm.

"Let me pass, Bob!"

"Not much!"

She struck him a stinging blow in the face, and at the same moment there came the sound of loud and heavy knocking upon the back door.

Robert Leonard's clenched fist was stayed in its descent.

Rosamund set the hand with which she had struck him against his breast, holding him off.

"Let me pass, or I'll scream!"

The knocking continued—hard, heavy knocking.

"Who is it?" said Rosamund suddenly. The fight had gone out of her. Instead of holding him off she pressed against him.

"I don't know. They mustn't see you."

And with that the knocking ceased.

Leonard opened the door and stepped out into the passage; and as he did so, the wind blew in through the kitchen, and along with it came Bran, and separated from him by a short length of chain, Mr Ferdinand Fazackerley. They seemed to be in a hurry.

Robert Leonard shut the door sharply behind him. He thought regretfully of the automatic on the office table.

Bran pulled on his chain, growling, and Ferdinand said,

"I guess I've no time to apologize. Your folk aren't slick at answering doors, so we walked right in. We're calling for Mrs Weare."

"For Mrs Weare?" said Leonard.

"For Mrs Jervis Weare."

"I don't understand. It's Mr Fazackerley, isn't it?"

"Where is she?" said Ferdinand sharply.

Robert Leonard made a gesture.

"I haven't the slightest idea what you're talking about."

"You'd better have! I'm putting all my cards on the table.

I got back from a wild goose chase an hour ago, and I found a note from Nan to say she was coming here to find Jervis. Well, I've come here to find both of 'em, and Bran's come along to help me—so you can get a move on—I'm liable to get tired holding him.''

"I really don't know what you're talking about, Mr Fazackerley.''

Ferdinand lengthened the chain, and as Leonard jumped back, the great door ran snuffing up the passage. He passed the door through which Leonard had come, and pushed whining against the one opposite. Nan had stood behind it listening, but the room was empty now. Ferdinand with a quick movement flung open the other door, and was taken completely aback. Rosamund Carew was leaning on the study table with her hands behind her, half sitting, half standing in an attitude of careless indifference. Ferdinand dropped Bran's chain in his surprise.

"Isn't this a very early visit?'' said Rosamund. "Hullo, Bran!''

The dog wrinkled his brows, snuffed the air, and backed away from her outstretched hand.

"Where's Nan?'' said Ferdinand.

"Well—not here.''

"She said she was coming here,'' Ferdinand began; and then he saw Leonard's pistol lying where he had thrown it across the dingy blotting-paper. He walked past Rosamund and pocketed it, then turned to see Bran with his nose to the ground.

"Seek her, boy—seek her!'' he said, and followed back to the kitchen, and across the kitchen to a door behind the dresser where Bran scratched and whined. All the light there was came from a guttering candle set down at random on one of the shelves.

As they went down the steps into the cellar, Robert Leonard let himself out of the front door, and was at once beaten to his knees by the wind. He had to crawl thirty yards to reach the shelter of the garage. His suitcase lay forgotten in the office.

Rosamund came down into the cellar with Fazackerley and Bran. If Jervis was dead, she had done with Robert— but he should have his chance to get clear.

The cellar was full of strange shadows; they rushed downwards when Fazackerley lifted the candle and looked about him. Bran was sniffing and scraping at the trap. Ferdinand Fazackerley set down the candle on an up-turned packing-case. He was soaked and grimy, his face white beneath its freckles, and his red hair wildly rumpled.

Suddenly Bran threw up his head and broke into a loud baying.

Rosamund had a moment of pure terror. As vividly as if it were happening now, she saw Basher lifting the trap, and her head and Jervis close together, craning over the dark hole. She dug her nails into the palm of her hand, and the picture was gone. The trap was closed. The barrel that masked it cast a shadow that ran up the wall and wavered there.

Ferdinand began to roll the barrel away, and as he did so, there came a knocking on the underside of the trap.

Rosamund stood where she was, and saw the barrel and the shadow of the barrel move together. She saw Ferdinand take hold of the iron ring that had been under the barrel and heave. She saw the trap rise, and Bran's great head thrust forward. He whined frantically. And then she saw Jervis coming up out of the trap, and her heart stood still and her bones turned to water. He came up out of the dark. The faint candle-light showed his drenched hair, and his ghastly pallor, and his eyes set and staring. A drowned man might look like that. Then he came up higher, and she saw Nan's face against his shoulder deathly white. Her eyes were closed, and her lips a little parted. She looked most piteously young.

Jervis took a step forward and then stopped, and there was a sudden dead silence.

Then, as Ferdinand Fazackerley reached for her wrist, Nan opened her eyes and looked all about her like a child waking in a strange place. Her gaze passed Rosamund and rested on Ferdinand.

"Did you—find us?"

"Bran found you."

Jervis set her down, and she stood leaning against him with a hand on Bran's head. Rosamund might not have been there at all.

"Where's Leonard?" said Jervis harshly.

Ferdinand exclaimed and ran up the cellar stairs. The front door stood open, and the wind blew through the house. The light of a stormy dawn came with it. As he crossed the threshold, he saw Robert Leonard's car go labouring through the gate. And with that there fell a lull. He started to run after the car with a hand on the pistol in his pocket and Jervis coming up behind him. The car, still running heavily, began to take the steep descent.

Jervis was running with a long shaky stride and heaving panting breath. They came to the top of the hill, and saw the car below them gathering speed. The wind had shifted a point and blew past them down the hill. Jervis stopped, gasping for breath, and caught at Ferdinand's arm. They might as well have hoped to catch the wind as to catch the car with the gale behind it.

And then, in a moment, the thing happened. The car lurched, skidded, and swung across the road. It struck the low stone parapet and crashed through it. There was an instant when it hung there, black against the grey emptiness beyond. Then the last huge gust of the storm struck it full, and it dropped like a stone into the sea.

Jervis stood there swaying on his feet. The great gust failed and died. They stood looking at the gap in the wall and the wet, empty road. Suddenly Jervis flung round with an arm over Ferdinand's shoulder.

"Let's get back to Nan, F.F." he said. "I want to take her home."

THE END